Praise for Christina B...

"Each scene is more s... the last." —*Publishers Weekly* (starred review)

"Riveting tale of life, loss, convenience, and heart-wrenching love! Superbly written!" —*Fresh Fiction*

"With this delightful debut Brooke demonstrates her ability for creating a charming cast of characters who are the perfect players in the first of the Ministry of Marriage series. Marriage-of-convenience fans will rejoice and take pleasure in this enchanting read." —*RT Book Reviews*

"Clever, lush, and lovely—an amazing debut!"
—Suzanne Enoch, *New York Times* bestselling author

"A delightful confection of secrets and seduction, *Heiress in Love* will have readers craving more!"
—Tracy Anne Warren

"One of the most compelling heroes I've read in years." —Anna Campbell

**Also by
Christina Brooke**

Heiress in Love

Mad About the Earl

A Duchess to Remember

CHRISTINA BROOKE

St. Martin's Paperbacks

This is a work of fiction. All of the characters, organizations, and events portrayed in this novel are either products of the author's imagination or are used fictitiously.

A DUCHESS TO REMEMBER

For information address St. Martin's Press, 175 Fifth Avenue, New York, NY 10010.

ISBN: 978-0-312-53414-1

Printed in the United States of America

St. Martin's Paperbacks edition / July 2012

St. Martin's Paperbacks are published by St. Martin's Press, 175 Fifth Avenue, New York, NY 10010.

10 9 8 7 6 5 4 3 2 1

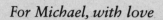
For Michael, with love

Acknowledgments

The team at St. Martin's Press never fails to amaze me with their passion and commitment to publishing. In particular I'd like to thank my editor, Monique Patterson, who understands the romance genre and continues to challenge me to write better novels. Thanks also to the fabulous Holly Blanck and to everyone who plays a part in publishing the books I write.

To Helen Breitwieser, my gratitude for your professionalism and savvy, but most of all for your unwavering belief in me. I love working with you.

To Anna Campbell and Denise Rossetti, your friendship means even more to me than your critiquing skills, which is praise of no mean order. To Kim Castillo, dear friend and assistant extraordinaire, what would I do without you and Gil?

To the Romance Bandits, I hope we're all still blogging together in the nursing home!

And of course, to my family and friends, who have to suffer through deadlines right along with me, I love you. Thank you for always being there for me.

A Duchess
to Remember

Chapter One

Lady Cecily Westruther was not often at a loss for words. In fact, it was said by her family that she had far too many of them at her disposal and was all too ready to use them at every opportunity.

But the sheer audacity of this request shocked the speech right out of her.

Lavinia pouted and her china blue eyes darted sparks. "You are so disobliging, cousin! I ought to have known how it would be."

Lavinia, Countess of Davenport, was a pretty, voluptuous blonde with a gaming habit and a penchant for dangerous men. Dangerous men who weren't her husband, that was.

Cecily exchanged an exasperated look with the small pug dog who sat drooling into a pink satin cushion on top of an ornate chaise longue. The furniture in Lavinia's boudoir was gilded and tasseled and braided to within an inch of its life. Lord, but the woman had terrible taste. It hurt the eyes to look upon all that pink and gold.

"I know what it is," said Cecily. "The décor of this room has finally turned your brain. You ought to refurnish it in blue, dear cousin. A very calming color, blue. Then you will feel much more the thing."

"Oh, come now, Cecily," said Lavinia, her voice growing sharp. "Surely it is not such a great favor to ask."

"Not a—?" Cecily found her voice and her words. Slowly, she said, "You want me to remain here after your houseguests leave so you can carry on an affair while your husband—*my cousin*—is away from home."

"*Must* you be so vulgar?" sighed Lavinia. "Really, such plain speaking will get you into trouble one of these days. Lord Percy is a *friend,* that is all. I find him amusing *company,* and with Bertram called away to Town, how *else* am I to occupy myself, pray?"

By visiting your tenants and seeing to their comfort, thought Cecily. *By reading something to improve that wasteland of a mind of yours. By taking the smallest interest in anything or anyone but your own spoiled self.*

"Don't look at me like that," snapped Lavinia. "Once you are married to your dull old duke, you will understand precisely how it is."

"He is not old." The response was automatic by now. Norland *wasn't* old—he just appeared that way. And besides, Cecily had always been accounted mature for her age.

But she refrained from voicing the argument. It was true that she harbored no romantic feelings toward Norland. On the other hand, she had better things to do with her time than to bed an end-less succession of men behind her husband's back.

She had plans for her future that did not rest upon the opinions or permission or even the par-ticipation of any man. Except as a means by which she might get her hands on part of her inheritance, of course. If she chose not to marry, she'd be obliged to wait until she was thirty to come into her for-tune, and that didn't bear thinking about. Besides, married women had so much more freedom than unmarried ones.

Of course she understood how marriages of convenience were supposed to work. Equally, she knew Norland would keep his current mistress after the knot was tied. But the sort of lifestyle pursued by countless bored aristocrats of the ton was not for her. She detested hypocrisy in any form. If she followed Lavinia's example, she'd soon grow to despise herself for such sneaking, sordid be-havior.

And now Lavinia wished Cecily to be a party to duping Bertram. Well, she would not do it, no mat-ter what threats Lavinia held over her head.

It wasn't as if she owed Lavinia any favors.

Returning to Garraway Hall since Cousin Ber-tram inherited it from Cecily's brother was always a painful experience. Ordinarily she'd inveigle her cousin Rosamund into coming with her, but Rosa-mund was busy with her new husband.

At least, thought Cecily, she might congratulate herself on suffering through this tedious house party with good grace.

The house party culminated in this evening's ball.

Everyone left tomorrow—everyone save Lord Percy, it seemed—and Cecily could at last return to the London residence of her guardian, the Duke of Montford. There, she would wash the bad taste of Bertram and Lavinia from her mouth with a good dose of her more congenial relatives' company.

"I'm afraid I could not stay even if I wanted to, Lavinia. Montford has accepted all sorts of engagements on my behalf. The season proper is about to begin, after all. Besides, if you are intent on this scheme, you need a matron to chaperone you, not a debutante."

"I suppose you are right," said Lavinia, toying with the scent bottle on her dressing table. "Could you lend me Tibby, then?"

"No." As if she could pass her companion around like a handkerchief! "Why don't you try Mrs. Arbuckle? As long as you feed her well, I'm sure she will look the other way."

"I could, I suppose." Lavinia rose and moved gracefully to stand before the looking glass. "If you will not oblige me, I fear I must." Lavinia bit her lush lower lip. "If only she will be discreet."

She tweaked the lace at her bosom, then swept delicate fingertips over her impressive décolletage. A dreamy smile flitted across her face, as if she recalled something pleasant.

She transferred her attention to Cecily. The blue eyes widened, then narrowed, homing in on the necklace Cecily wore. A double strand of exquisite pink pearls. They were among the few jewels her mother had left her that the duke thought it suitable for a girl in her first season to wear.

Cecily knew a sudden foreboding and wished she had not worn this necklace tonight.

"Ah! *I* remember what I meant to tell you, Cecily," said Lavinia. "I discovered Jonathon's diary in an old trunk in the attic the other day. Lord, it must have lain up there gathering dust these nine years or more."

Lavinia's careless words came at Cecily like a fist.

The well of grief that always lay inside her seemed to swell until it flowed into her chest, her throat, the backs of her eyes.

Jonathon . . .

It was a few moments before Cecily could speak. "His diary?"

Her voice scraped. She knew she ought to try to sound as unconcerned as Lavinia, but she couldn't smooth the rawness of longing from her tone.

Jonathon. The dearest and best brother in the world.

When Cecily had inquired years ago, Lavinia told her that she'd burned all Jonathon's papers. How like Lavinia to tell her such a spiteful lie.

With Jonathon's death, Cecily's world had been upended. Suddenly everyone she'd ever loved was gone. Everything she'd taken for granted as hers for eleven years became theirs—Bertram's and Lavinia's.

And nothing could rid Lavinia of the notion that even the jewels Cecily rightfully inherited from her mother belonged to her as the new countess.

"Yes," said Lavinia. "I thought perhaps you should have the diary." Her attention never wavered from Cecily's necklace. "Would you *like* to have it, do you think?"

Immediately, Cecily understood. Her hand stole up to her throat in a gesture that was absurdly protective. She fingered the smooth, round pearls that had grown warm against her skin.

Her heart revolted at the mere thought of Lavinia wearing them. The necklace was more than an exquisite, expensive piece, more than a mere keepsake. These pearls had absorbed the warmth of her mother's skin, just as they did Cecily's own at this very moment. Each small, lustrous globe contained a hint of her mother's essence.

A romantical notion. An uncharacteristically sentimental one. And how could she hold on to it when Jonathon's diary lay almost within her grasp?

"How kind of you, Lavinia." With an effort, Cecily kept her voice even. "Will you show me the diary now, please?" Perhaps if she ignored the clear implication of Lavinia's manner, she might negotiate a different price.

Lavinia pursed her lips. Her eyes narrowed. "I don't see why I should when you won't do the smallest thing for me."

Risking her own reputation to guard Lavinia's did not count as a small thing in Cecily's book. But it didn't take a soothsayer to predict where this conversation would lead. Cecily couldn't immediately think of anything else she might offer in lieu of the pearls. Besides, Lavinia was so capricious, she might burn the diary if Cecily didn't instantly fall in with her wishes.

Her mouth went dry. "What if . . . What if I lent you my pearls for the evening?"

Lavinia looked thoughtful. "That is tempting, but . . . *One* evening does not seem quite enough, does it?"

Cecily licked her lips. Surely Lavinia didn't intend her to give her the pearls outright. Even if she wished to do so, she couldn't. Her maid would notice their absence as soon as she took an inventory of Cecily's jewel box. Once the duke discovered the loss, there'd be hell to pay.

"All right, then," she said reluctantly. "You can have them until you return to Town." She would have to make up some tale to satisfy Saunders.

Lavinia had never concealed her emotions well. Avarice and cold calculation made her pretty features as hard as the looking glass that reflected them.

Cecily feared Lavinia would try to drive a harder bargain, but instead, the countess nodded. "Put them on for me, will you? I'll wear them tonight."

The thought of the delicate shell pink hue of those pearls against Lavinia's mint green silk bodice made Cecily shudder to the bottom of her fashionable soul. But she reached behind her own nape to unfasten the diamond clasp. She must seal the bargain quickly, before Lavinia demanded more.

It made her heartsick to lend her mother's pearls to such a woman as her cousin's wife. But for that small connection to Jonathon, she would pay the price.

The pearls felt alive in Cecily's hands as she carried them to her cousin. Standing behind Lavinia, she took several seconds to summon the will. Then she reached up to her relation's superior height and used her fingertips to brush away the bright curls that tumbled in an arranged profusion from an ornate bandeau.

Carefully, Cecily draped the pearls around that slender neck. She fastened the diamond clasp and let the necklace drop against the milky perfection of Lavinia's nape.

Lavinia preened as if Cecily had set a crown upon her head.

When she couldn't stand the sight of her cousin admiring herself in those pearls any longer, Cecily said tightly, "The diary. Now, if you please, Lavinia."

"Ah. Yes, of course." She made a twirling motion with her index finger. "Turn your back."

Cecily nearly rolled her eyes. She already knew Lavinia's hiding place. She'd discovered it as a curious child. Somehow, she doubted Lavinia would have changed it since then. She lacked the imagination.

However, Cecily did as she was told and listened while Lavinia moved around her dressing room for an inordinate amount of time.

Before Cecily's patience gave out entirely, Lavinia brought the diary. She all but tossed it at Cecily before returning to the looking glass to continue admiring her reflection.

With shaking hands, Cecily clutched the diary to her. Her fingertips tingled as she smoothed them over the tooled leather binding. If Lavinia had found this, might there be other possessions of her brother's lying discarded, unloved somewhere in this house? She'd thought Bertram and Lavinia had taken everything of value for their own use and burned or sold the rest.

Now, the notion that this was not the case sprang to her mind. Remembering the last letter she'd ever written to Jonathon, Cecily felt a cold hand clamp around her heart.

"Do you happen to know what became of the rest of my brother's papers?" she asked. "I should like to have the letters I wrote to him." She hesitated. If Lavinia knew how badly Cecily needed to retrieve that one letter in particular, she'd surely withhold it.

She tried to keep her voice light. "Did you happen to find any correspondence with the diary?"

Lavinia frowned. "No, nothing like that. What on earth do you want with letters *you* wrote?"

Cecily ignored that question. "What about his scientific notes and such?"

Surely Bertram and Lavinia had no use for those.

"Oh"—Lavinia gave a Frenchified shrug of her shoulders—"someone came looking for all Jon's papers and I said he might take them with my goodwill. But that was years ago."

Lavinia had sold them, Cecily deduced. She would never part with anything without demanding a price. What if the letter were among those papers? Dear God, the scandal if the letter were published did not bear thinking about.

"Who was it?" asked Cecily. "Was he an acquaintance of Jonathon's?"

"It was the Duke of Ashburn, if you *must* know." Lavinia's tone was careless but she didn't fool Cecily. "Such an attractive man. That dark hair. And those eyes!"

Astonished, Cecily repeated, "The Duke of Ashburn? What could he want with Jonathon's papers?"

"How should I know?" Lavinia rolled her eyes. "But when a duke makes such a request, you don't deny him. Particularly *that* duke."

Cecily could well believe it. Ashburn's was the kind of autocratic personality that brought Cecily out in a rash. Oh, she didn't know him, but she knew who he was. A power broker with a finger in every imaginable pie. His reputation for omniscience rivaled Montford's. In fact, it was said Ashburn had become quite a thorn in Montford's side when it came to politics.

"Those papers were likely to have been valuable," said Cecily coldly. "I trust His Grace paid you handsomely for them."

Lavinia glanced away, but not before Cecily detected a triumphant sparkle light the countess's eye. She concluded that a handsome sum had indeed changed hands. She also deduced that Lavinia had not seen fit to pass this information on to her husband. She'd spent the proceeds on new gowns or squandered them on the gaming tables, no doubt.

"When did this occur?" asked Cecily, frowning. "I didn't know His Grace was acquainted with Jonathon."

"Oh, yes, I believe so. It was very soon after Jonathon's passing." Lavinia picked up a strand of the pink pearls and ran them against her teeth with a *clack-clack-clack*, her lips drawn back in a slightly terrifying grimace.

"In fact," said Lavinia, "it was the Duke of Ashburn who brought us the news of Jonathon's death."

Cecily lost no time in more conversation with Lavinia. She sped back to her bedchamber, nearly tripping over the flounced skirts of her sprigged muslin gown in her rush.

She gained her room and plumped down on the bed, holding Jonathon's diary to her chest as if his spirit resided between its tooled leather covers.

She tried to calm herself. This was only a diary, after all. It could not bring her beloved brother back.

She hadn't wept when they told her Jon was dead. She'd been ten years old and Jonathon was her world. The loss seemed to swallow her whole; the pain too great for tears. So she'd buried that jagged agony deep inside herself and never exhumed it.

Until tonight.

He'd been four-and-twenty to her ten. Almost a father figure, but not forbidding or aloof the way her guardian, the Duke of Montford, was. Nor had he been absentminded like their scholarly papa, who'd died along with their mother in a carriage accident when Cecily was six. Jonathon was simply the best, most beloved brother in the world.

And then his mad intelligence, his brilliance and exuberance were gone, incinerated in a fire that tore through his laboratory one bright summer day.

Bertram and Lavinia had taken possession of Jonathon and Cecily's home immediately. Cecily needed them to look after her, they'd said.

She hadn't needed them. She'd needed Jon.

Days later, the Duke of Montford had swooped down and plucked her from this place like an eagle bearing off his prey. Only to tuck her safely in a cozy nest with his other orphaned chicks.

A trite metaphor. One could scarcely equate the

palatial Harcourt with a cozy nest, nor her confident, vibrant Westruther cousins with helpless fledglings. And she herself had been far from docile on the way to London. She'd given Montford a hellish journey, used every opportunity to ruffle his dignified feathers, made several determined attempts at escape.

But Montford had been unmoved by her antics. Looking back, she rather thought they'd amused him. Now, she enjoyed the challenge of making Montford smile at her tricks. Then, she'd found his equilibrium infuriating.

And here she was, twenty and making her debut this spring. And at the height of the season, she was to be married to the man her parents had chosen for her when she was little more than an infant.

She looked down at the journal's brown leather cover. Why hadn't Lavinia sent this to her years ago? Cecily had so little to remember Jonathon by. Bertram inherited everything that was Jonathon's, even her brother's personal belongings. She wondered exactly how many of Jonathon's writings Lavinia had cold-bloodedly sold to the Duke of Ashburn.

One thing was certain: Cecily needed to retrieve that letter.

Perhaps there was no need for concern. Perhaps the letter had been overlooked, discarded, buried under a superfluity of other documents and notes Jonathon had amassed over the years.

But she could not be sure, could she? What if the forthcoming announcement of her betrothal caused someone to make the necessary connection? If that letter became public, her chances of marriage would be ruined. *She* might be ruined into the bargain.

Running her fingertips over the diary's tarnished clasp, Cecily paused.

Ought she to open it? Diaries were private things, after all. She'd not have dreamed of reading it if Jon were alive.

But the longing for him was so strong that such scruples seemed irrelevant. She needed to read his thoughts, hear his voice, if only through his words on the page.

She muttered, "You wouldn't mind now, though, would you, old thing? I know you would not."

With a deep, unsteady breath, Cecily opened the diary. She hoped for something. She didn't know what. A connection, perhaps? A balm to the ache inside her that never went away?

The scant lines of bold, hasty handwriting did not comfort her or assuage her lingering grief. Disappointment spiked through her. The diary was little more than an appointment book. All these places and times at which her brother had been alive and present. And now, no more.

Her brow furrowed as she scanned the pages. One item repeated—she flipped back and forth—monthly. Hmm. The Promethean Club. What was that? She'd never heard of it before.

Clearly, it was not an ordinary gentlemen's club like White's or Brooks's, for its meetings were held at Ashburn House, the town residence of the Duke of Ashburn. Cecily thumbed through more pages but couldn't find any other details that would enlighten her.

Ashburn had become a recurring theme in this

particular story. What did he have to do with Jonathon? What did he want with Jonathon's papers?

She needed to find out. But most of all, she must get that letter.

Chapter Two

Rand, Duke of Ashburn, eyed his nineteen-year-old ward. Lord, male adolescents were even more tedious than the fresh-faced debutantes Lady Arden insisted on throwing at him this season.

"Of all places to accost me and demand money, surely a ball must be the worst," Rand remarked.

He'd called for his carriage, his coat, and his hat and stood in the entry hall of Lady Eversleigh's house, waiting for them to be fetched. If he had to waste much more time on this discussion, he'd be late for the meeting of the Promethean Club. As he was to host the meeting, that would be bad form. Besides, a fascinating development had made him anticipate the gathering with more than usual interest.

Rand watched the flush rise in his cousin's face with a sense of fatalism mingled with distaste. He detested public scenes. Or scenes of any variety, for that matter.

Stiffly, the young man said, "I should scarcely

accost you here were you ever at home to me when I call."

And if you ever called on me for reasons other than money, I might be at home to you more often.

Boredom crept over Rand. "Your financial woes are not of the smallest interest to me, Freddy. Last time, I warned you I'd no longer pay your debts if you continued along your present habits of extravagance. You said you'd go to the Devil your own way. Well, *bonne chance,* my dear cousin. I'm not stopping you."

His young relative forced the words out between rigid lips. "But it's a debt of honor, Your Grace—"

"Oho, Your Grace, is it?" said Rand, grimly amused. "Come off your high horse, Freddy. It doesn't suit you, believe me. If you can't stand the nonsense, don't play." Mildly interested, he added, "To whom is this debt owed?"

"The Earl of Davenport."

Now that *was* interesting. "Exalted company you keep," Rand remarked.

In Davenport's shoes, Rand or any other gentleman worthy of the name would have found a way to avoid gaming with a nineteen-year-old greenhorn. But Davenport had lately developed the habit of fleecing the young, wealthy, and inexperienced gentlemen who thought themselves far cleverer at games of chance than they were.

Rand would not go so far as to accuse Davenport of cheating, but such behavior might get him ejected from his clubs if he wasn't careful. If the earl wasn't careful, Rand might see to it himself.

"And, er, exactly how much do you owe Lord Davenport?" he asked his cousin.

Freddy's expression turned first hopeful then anxious. The lad hadn't quite grown into his Adam's apple; it bobbed with distressing prominence as he swallowed hard. "R-rather a large sum, one might say."

"Indeed?" Rand waited.

"One thousand pounds!" Freddy blurted out.

Rand had expected worse. "How unfortunate for you," he said politely. "Will the earl wait until next quarter day?"

"Of course he won't!" Freddy said, clearly amazed at Rand's obtuseness. "Everyone knows a debt of honor must be paid at once."

"Everyone but you, it seems," said Rand. "Or did you rely on me rescuing you, yet again? I meant what I said, Freddy."

"But that was over tradesmen's bills! No one cares if they go unpaid."

"I expect the tradesmen care," said Rand, but his relative took no heed of that interjection.

"Damn it, you're a cold fish, Rand. I ought to have known you wouldn't help me," Freddy said.

"If you had, you might have curbed your gaming habits," agreed Rand. "And don't think for one moment of going to moneylenders to solve your problems, because you'd only replace them with far greater ones. Besides, and far more terrifying, if you do that, I will hear of it and then you will have me to deal with."

Freddy's shoulders slumped. "So what am I to do?"

Rand flicked a piece of lint from this dark sleeve. "Sell off your horses. They ought to bring in sufficient funds, I should think. I'll even find you a buyer if you like. You may be a cloth-head when it comes to cards, but no one can fault your judgment of horseflesh."

"Obliged to sell my horses like some moth-eaten bankrupt?" Freddy demanded, outraged. "Why, I'm the heir to a dukedom!"

With that statement, his own mortality slammed into Rand like a fist. Provoked and annoyed that the silly boy had landed such a blow without even knowing it, Rand managed a short, mirthless laugh. "Don't count on stepping into my shoes, Freddy. I'll be married by the end of the season."

Ruefully amused at his own absurd vulnerability—he was only nine-and-twenty, for God's sake!—Rand watched his relative storm off.

He'd leave Freddy to stew in his resentment and growing fear for a few days. After that, he'd undoubtedly come to the boy's rescue. But he would exact his own pound of flesh in exchange for such beneficence. These days, he gave nothing away freely. Not even to his favorite relative.

That Freddy *was* his favorite relative said a lot about his family, didn't it?

"Forget the carriage," he told a hovering footman. "I'll walk."

Before he could make his escape, someone hailed him. He turned to see the Duke of Montford reach his side. The duke had already donned his coat and stood with his chapeau bras and cane in hand.

"Evening," said Rand with a slight bow. He respected Montford as a worthy adversary in the House of Lords, but he didn't altogether like him.

The man was perceptive and intelligent, but like

so many of his ilk, his thinking was hampered by the desire to arrest the march of progress. Or, at least, stall it for as long as humanly possible.

Change was coming. You could smell it in the air, but the old guard wanted to ignore it, suppress it, stamp it out before it could flourish and threaten their comfort. Rand was too curious to be afraid of innovation. He embraced it. He wanted to explore its potential, to harness it, not smother it into oblivion—or rebellion.

Montford sent a significant glance after Frederick. "A troublesome age."

Rand nodded curtly. "Well, you would know."

Montford was famed for the unusual step of taking six of his wards under his own roof and bringing them up together. Rand suspected it hadn't been an easy road to choose. Any other man in Montford's position would have farmed the children out to other households in the family and concerned himself only with their financial welfare. He wondered why Montford had taken them under his wing.

"May I walk with you?" asked Montford as Rand received his hat and coat from a footman.

With a gesture that said *be my guest,* Rand allowed Montford to precede him into the night air. They descended the steps and turned in the direction of Rand's house.

The pavement gleamed wetly, washed by recent rain. The air was crisp and cold. Spring had not yet breathed warmth into London.

"He'll come about, I'm sure," said Montford, picking up the subject of Freddy where Rand would have preferred to leave it.

"I don't doubt." Despite his harsh reaction to the news of this latest debt, Rand would not discuss Freddy's affairs with anyone.

"A wife can be a steadying influence, even on one so young," remarked Montford.

Oh, no, you don't.

Montford was head of an organization nick-named the Ministry of Marriage, in which the heads of various aristocratic families negotiated and ap-proved marriages between members of their respec-tive dynasties. Technically, Rand was entitled to a seat in that illustrious circle. He'd never taken it up, however, and he didn't intend to allow either Freddy or himself to be caught in the ministry's clutches.

Rand flicked a sideways glance at the duke, who sauntered along, swinging his cane with his habit-ual elegant nonchalance. "Luring me to your pre-cious Ministry of Marriage to bargain with my ward's future, Your Grace? Not a chance in hell."

"Your vehemence does you credit," murmured Montford, not in the least perturbed by the sum-mary rejection of his overture. "But it was mere friendly advice. I dared not hope you would con-sider appealing to the ministry after such a long-standing and adamant opposition to our practices."

Rand made no answer.

"One wonders what *your* matrimonial plans might be, Your Grace."

Rand clenched his teeth. Montford was nothing if not persistent. And impertinent. No other man in England would dare ask Rand such a question. Only one woman would.

Montford continued. "Lady Arden seems des-perate to find you a suitable wife this season. And yet, there are those with equal experience and expertise in arranging such matters."

Rand decided to play along for the moment. "What could your precious ministry do for me that I can't do very well for myself?"

Montford waved a gloved hand. "Oh, all manner of things, I should imagine. We can select a young lady for you who has been brought up knowing how to conduct herself as a duke's wife should, one who entertains no romantic notions of love or any nonsense of that nature. The unmarried ladies of our families know how such marriages should be conducted."

"Indeed?" Rand injected a wealth of indifference into the comment.

In spite of himself, he acknowledged the idea had much to recommend it. Oh, he wasn't about to become involved in the complicated marital negotiations facilitated by the Ministry of Marriage—that group of power-hungry nobles bent on arranging the most advantageous marriages for their families. He most certainly would not subject anyone in his family to their rule. He believed young people should marry for love if they possibly could.

But for himself . . . He had never fallen in love, as the saying went. Perhaps he did not have the capacity for such violent, all-encompassing emotion. Freddy's words had struck true. Rand was, indeed, cold at heart.

He needed a wife soon, if only to nip in the bud any expectations Freddy might harbor of inheriting the dukedom.

Perhaps it was time to put away self-indulgent leanings and make a practical marriage. He was a duke, after all, and he owed it to his name and to his family to make a brilliant match. He owed it to Freddy to father sons before Freddy became one of those pathetic idlers who lived on expectations that would never be fulfilled.

However, it wouldn't do to let Montford gain the slightest whiff of his interest.

Abruptly, he said, "I'm obliged to you for your, er, concern. But if and when I decide to marry, I'll do it without assistance—either from Lady Arden or your precious Ministry of Marriage."

Chapter Three

Cecily shrank into the shadows outside the Duke of Ashburn's house as another carriage rolled to a stop.

She peered from behind a stone pillar that supported the grand steps to the house, wishing she could see better in the dark. Impossible to identify the duke's guests in this light as they traveled the short distance from their carriages to the foot of the stone staircase.

She could hear them, though. Cecily strained for snippets of information she might gather from the gentlemen's conversation as they passed. Anything that would give her the smallest clue about the purpose of the club, who its members were, anything that would help her make some sense of Ashburn's connection to her brother.

She couldn't distinguish much from the general murmur of voices. What she could make out seemed to range from philosophical debate to political gossip to astronomy. Fascinating, but of little practical use in her investigation and none at all in identifying the speakers themselves.

What sort of a club was this? Prometheus was the Greek who'd stolen fire from the gods and was tortured for his impudence for eternity. The name suggested a drive for advancement, new discovery, perhaps in a manner that was highly subversive.

That sounded exactly like Jonathon.

An unwelcome thought occurred: Perhaps the club had been founded for more illicit purposes than scientific advancement. Perhaps the fire to which the name alluded was *hellfire,* and the club was some offshoot or resurrection of Dashwood's scandalous Hellfire Club. Black masses and depravity.

No, she could not see Jonathon as a party to activities like that. Nor did tonight's host, the Duke of Ashburn, have the reputation of a satyr. Much as the ladies might whisper behind their fans of his prowess in the bedchamber.

The steady stream of arrivals slowed to a trickle. She'd not discovered nearly enough for her purposes. She needed to know more.

Cecily turned to slip inside but stopped short when she heard a distinctive, loud bray of a laugh.

The hairs on the back of her neck raised. She'd know that laugh anywhere. In fact, it was the one thing about him she absolutely could not abide.

That laugh was the sole property of her betrothed, the Duke of Norland.

What on earth was *he* doing here?

She thought it over and realized his presence was not such a strange coincidence as one might suppose. Norland was a notable scholar and he'd become something of a mentor to Jonathon after their father died. Perhaps he was the reason Jon had joined the club in the first place.

Any lingering suspicion that the Prometheans traced their origins to the Hellfire Club vanished. Her betrothed was far too mild-mannered and staid for that kind of thing.

Norland went inside and the wheels of his carriage crunched on the drive as it rolled away. Under cover of the sound, Cecily edged around to the back of the house.

She passed a kitchen garden redolent of herbs and the earthy scent of newly turned soil. Her courage wavered as she approached the kitchen door, but she steeled her nerves to go on.

She'd expended too much thought and preparation over what she was about to do to turn back now. It had taken weeks of careful planning, reconnaissance, and the dispensation of a considerable amount of money to reach this crucial point. Her next opportunity to spy on a meeting of the Promethean Club wouldn't come for another month.

Pressing her hand to the doorframe, she listened intently for any sound from within. She'd paid a footman an exorbitant bribe to leave this door on the latch.

The footman had assured her there'd be no one to see her slip inside the Duke of Ashburn's mansion at this hour. When the Promethean Club gathered, the duke invariably instructed his staff to prepare a sumptuous buffet in the dining room and make themselves scarce.

What did that suggest? That the society was secret—illicit, perhaps? That the duke's guests wished to remain anonymous?

Her heart pounding, Cecily tried the door.

It *was* unlocked, just as the footman had promised. With a rush of relief that spiraled into anticipation, she eased it open. The big, heavy door swung inward, silent on well-oiled hinges.

For some reason, that silence struck her as more ominous than an eerie creak would have done.

Oh, she was as jittery as a cat on hot bricks! But then, why shouldn't she be? Not only was she housebreaking, she was entering the Duke of Ashburn's domain.

Ashburn was renowned as hard and uncompromising, with a sharp intelligence that bordered on omniscience. His friends numbered among the most powerful leaders, the brightest wits, the greatest talents of the day. He was a true Renaissance man, accomplished at a vast array of pursuits, most notoriously amorous ones. One mistress of the duke's—a famous courtesan—had claimed *she* ought to pay *him* for his services in the bedroom.

Everyone knew who he was but no one seemed to know much about the man himself. Upon learning that the Promethean Club met here, Cecily had inquired about Ashburn. But when she tried to delve deeper into his character, she was stymied at every turn. The duke was a private man, it seemed, known to many but intimate with few.

Ashburn was an enigma. He was fast becoming an obsession with her—and not only because he and his colleagues might hold the key to her brother's death.

And here she was, stealing into his house at dead of night.

With excitement pulsing through her veins, Cecily crept inside.

She found herself in a kind of mudroom filled with pattens and boots and cloaks, umbrellas and walking sticks and other outdoor wear. She hadn't dared bring a lantern with her, but her luck held. A faint wash of light from the kitchens beyond this room allowed her to see well enough to avoid obstacles in her path.

She listened until she was satisfied no one stirred. Then she moved carefully through to the narrow passageway.

She'd memorized the rough map the footman drew for her and found the servants' stair without difficulty. Once on the first floor, she quickly located the saloon where the footman had told her the meeting would be held. There was a vestibule leading to the dining room, he'd said. There, she might conceal herself and spy on the proceedings.

The door to the vestibule stood slightly ajar. Cecily darted a glance around her, then stole up to the door to listen.

She couldn't hear anything. No murmur of voices or clink of cutlery on plate. Cautiously, she peered into the room.

A large hand gripped her shoulder. Another hand covered her mouth. With a muffled shriek, she struggled to free herself.

She was clamped against a hard male chest. A deep, cultured voice murmured in her ear, "At last. I've been expecting you."

Cecily froze. Confound that blasted footman! He'd betrayed her.

It had all been too easy, hadn't it? But good God, how could she have guessed he'd tell the duke of her plans? How many servants would remain loyal to their masters when offered the kind of bribe she'd intended to pay?

Or perhaps the footman hadn't informed on her, and the rumors were true. Perhaps the Duke of Ashburn *was* omniscient.

He was certainly exceedingly strong.

All this passed through her mind in an instant. She fought him, twisting ineffectually in his iron grip, jabbing with her elbows, kicking back with her heels. If she could get free, she'd make a dash for it. She was fast when she needed to be and tonight, garbed as a footman, she didn't have skirts to hamper her.

His hold was not vicious but it was implacable. Seeming not to notice her struggles, her captor swept her into a room that was not a vestibule, as the footman had informed her, but a library. With not a member of the Promethean Club in sight.

Once inside, he released her. She whipped around to face him, her lungs straining for air.

Ashburn.

He was very dark and very tall and he had the most uncompromising mouth she'd ever seen. His strange eyes regarded her intently, sending an unwelcome chill through her body. Then he moved to close the door and lock it.

When he turned back to face her again, she refused to show him fear. Instead of quaking or begging, she folded her arms across her chest and waited.

His grim lips relaxed slightly. Holding up the ornate brass key, he said, "A precautionary measure," and slipped the key into his pocket.

That almost imperceptible change in the forbidding coldness of his expression made her less apprehensive of physical harm. But the preternaturally acute way his eyes assessed her was far from reassuring. She'd never been more conscious of the close fit of her breeches, nor of the footman's peruke wig that perched, askew now, on her head.

He was hard and lean and broad shouldered. Not an ounce of frivolity or decoration softened the harshness of his aspect. Dressed soberly in a black coat and gray trousers and waistcoat, white shirt and cravat, he wore no jewelry save a heavy gold signet ring on the third finger of his right hand. His close-cropped black hair seemed to emphasize the hawkish lines of his nose and the sharp, almost Slavic contours of his cheekbones.

And his eyes. They were a stunning golden hazel with dark brown flecks, framed by thick black lashes. Amber ringed with onyx.

Unsettling, almost feline, those eyes. She wondered if they glowed in the dark.

"Take off your wig," he drawled.

The instruction was not quite a command but it was not a request either. More a suggestion with overtones of intimidation.

Of course he knew she wasn't a footman or a page boy. The disguise was never meant to fool anyone except at a distance and in the dark of night. Besides, his manhandling had brought him into contact with the softer parts of her person. The notion sent a hot spear of ... *something* through her body.

Forcing herself to give a casual shrug, Cecily lifted the peruke from her head and set it on a piecrust table nearby.

His brilliant gaze flicked over her.

She'd worn breeches enough times to feel neither shame nor embarrassment that he'd caught her in them. But somehow his impassive regard made her want to leap to the defensive, to justify her actions to him.

As the Duke of Montford's ward, she'd long since mastered control over such inclinations. Instead, she studied Ashburn as dispassionately as he studied her.

He was far younger than she'd supposed when she'd seen him at a distance. The harshness of his features, his arrogant air of authority, and the deference more senior members of the ton paid him had deceived her.

She resented that illusion, as if it had been a deliberate ruse on his part. Older gentlemen were so much easier to handle.

The silence lengthened between them until it became an object with her not to be the first to break it. She let her attention wander around the room, over bookshelves and tables, globes and maps. As if she'd appraised him, found him tedious, and now sought some other source of amusement.

"Your accomplice betrayed you," he said at last.

"I'd rather gathered that at the start of our acquaintance." She tried to make her tone cordial, but it came out with something of a snap. Now that her initial fear had abated, chagrin at her failure took its place.

Though perhaps she'd not failed entirely. She surveyed Ashburn with a speculative eye. Might she discover what she wished to know directly from him? If she was clever about it, then perhaps . . .

Drawing herself up, she donned her most regal air and waved a careless hand. "But I am keeping you from your guests, Your Grace. Do go ahead. I shall find my own way out."

Rand nearly laughed aloud at this summary dismissal. Who the Devil did the chit think she was? She couldn't be more than nineteen or twenty, but she waved him away with the careless aplomb of a dowager duchess.

"My guests go on most happily without me," he said, leaning one shoulder against the door and folding his arms. "Besides, you interest me far more than a meeting of the Promethean Club."

"I'm so happy to provide you with entertainment," she said.

Better and better.

He allowed his gaze to drift over his captive's person, lingering at the lush bosom that jutted unmistakably from her blue velvet coat, pausing again at the womanly flare of hips that made her knee-breeches stretch a shade too tightly across her thighs. He imagined her bottom would be as round and female as the rest of her and experienced a sharp tug of curiosity on that account.

It really was a very poor disguise.

He regarded her face. Wide brown eyes with a slight tilt at the corners, a pert little nose and the rosiest bud of a mouth he'd ever seen. Her lips reminded him of the dimpled lushness of a cherry when the stalk is plucked. Ripe and plump and sweet, begging him to bite.

"What is your name?" he said.

She watched him for a few moments without

replying; it occurred to him that she scrutinized him quite as critically as he examined her. From her expression, he did not meet with her approval.

A novel experience. A not altogether comfortable one.

Breaking off her inspection, she wandered over to a set of globes that stood by the desk. Tracing the arcing frame of the celestial globe with a fingertip, she said, "If I tell you who I am, will you let me go?"

"I'm more likely to convey you home to your papa so he can beat you," said Rand.

"But I don't have a papa," she said on a note of false mournfulness. "I am quite alone in the world, you see."

Quite alone. He suppressed a pang of predatory opportunism that was entirely out of character for him.

Ah, but she was lying, of course. And even if she wasn't . . . He'd never been the sort of evil lecher who took advantage of helpless, friendless maidens. He'd never ruined a woman in his life.

But he wanted her. And what the Duke of Ashburn wanted, he would have.

One way or another.

"If you won't give me your name, at least give me your direction and I'll take you home." He did not intend to take her anywhere, at least not before they became rather better acquainted. "You'll not walk the London streets alone at this hour."

"If I tell you," she said, "will *you* tell *me* something in return?"

Her effrontery knew no bounds. She didn't seem to comprehend that he had her at his mercy. That he had not even asked her what she was doing stealing into his house.

Rand angled his head and said in a soft, menacing voice, "I don't think you're in a position to bargain with me."

He wished she'd take down her hair. It looked dark and rich as mahogany, thick and soft and luxuriant. The kind of hair a man dreamed about trailing over his naked body, following the path of those cherry-sweet lips . . .

But she'd scraped her shining tresses back from her face and twisted and pinned them in a fat knot at the crown of her head. Little curling tendrils had fallen free, however, gleaming darkly against the pale, delicate skin at her forehead and temples. He wanted to reach out and twist one of those mad little springs around his finger.

Not at all disconcerted at the way he openly admired her charms, she strolled toward him. "Well, that depends. If you were an ordinary man, perhaps I wouldn't dare. But you, my lord duke, suffer from the eternal ennui of the pampered aristocrat. You're intelligent enough to perceive that I am no common housebreaker. *I*, in fact, am a novelty."

"You, in fact, are a criminal," he said.

"But you are curious about me," she murmured, staring up at him with those big brown eyes. "Admit it."

She was wrong. He was never bored. His interests were wide ranging and intensive. But . . . he failed to remember a time when he'd felt so *enlivened* by a woman's presence. Furthermore, his curiosity about her nearly consumed him.

He could have her hanged twice over for attempting to bribe his servant and breaking into his house. Quite apart from that, he had her here, alone, in circumstances that were entirely to his advantage. Who was this girl? She wasn't even slightly afraid.

"You are very sure of yourself," he commented.

She spread her hands. "Why go through all of this if you intend to hand me over to the law? Why not simply order one of your minions to deal with me? You do have minions, don't you, Your Grace? You look like the sort of man who has minions."

He favored her with an unpleasant smile. "Perhaps I merely seek to toy with my prey before I devour it—or in this case, hand it over to the magistrate."

She snorted. "No, I don't believe that. You are intrigued."

"I am," he admitted, his voice dropping deep and low. "Most intrigued. But you do yourself an injustice if you think it is your novelty that excites my interest."

He moved closer and had the satisfaction of seeing her eyes darken with apprehension. One side of his mouth curled upward. He let his gaze sweep down her curvaceous little body in a manner calculated to intimidate and confuse a virginal, gently bred female. Or excite an experienced one.

She gave a sudden gurgle of laughter, startling him so much that his attention shot back to her face.

"Oh, dear," she said, her brown eyes dancing with mirth. Her teeth were very white, framed by those deep red lips. "Pray, do not *smolder* at me so! You will set me off into whoops."

Disconcerted in spite of himself, he said, "I beg your pardon?"

"You needn't do that," she replied generously. "Though it *is* quite improper for you to stare at me in that odious way, of course."

Now, the predator in him awoke, stretched, unsheathed its claws. "My attentions would not be welcome to you?" he murmured. Reaching out, he stroked one fingertip down her cheek. "Somehow, I don't believe that."

Her skin was satin soft, and he let his fingertip linger at the hinge of her jaw.

Something in the flare of her eyes gave him pause. For a strange, heart-stopping moment, time seemed to hold its breath. . . .

As if a tautened thread snapped inside her, his fair intruder blinked. Then she put up her hand to lightly bat his away. "*I* am not one of your highfliers, Your Grace. Keep your hands to yourself."

Already, he missed the warmth and texture of her skin. A singular and unprecedented need filled him. He folded his fingers into a fist to stop himself giving in to it.

Most men in his position wouldn't hesitate. She was dressed scandalously in a footman's garb. She was alone, unchaperoned in his house at night. Entirely at his mercy. He knew he affected her on a visceral level. Though she did her best to conceal it, he saw the signs. He could easily give in to his inclinations and make his best effort to seduce her.

What stopped him? Not her clipped aristocratic accent nor her air of gentility. She might speak like a duchess but he'd known—and enjoyed—highborn ladies who were as earthy and sensual as any other woman.

No, there was some quality about this girl, some innate core of resilience, of feminine strength, that intrigued him. He responded to it in a way that ranged beyond his physical reaction to her, even as it seemed to heighten his desire.

And for some strange reason, it held her inviolate. At least for tonight.

"Why are you here?" he murmured. And why hadn't he asked that question sooner?

He could almost see the cogs whirring in her brain as she decided how much information to give him. "I wasn't burgling the place, if that's what you're thinking."

"I think you came to find out about the Promethean Club," he said. "Unless you have designs on my person," he amended, giving her a flashing smile. "In which case, I'd be most happy to oblige."

She stared at him wonderingly. "Do you know, you are quite the most conceited man I've ever met? And that's saying something when you consider my family."

"Ah. Yes. Your family," he said. "And who might they be? I thought you were all alone in the world."

Challenge sparked in her eye. "No, you didn't— and my family is every bit as powerful as yours, so I think you should let me go now."

Was it his imagination, or did he detect a slight squaring of her shoulders, a renewed courage when she mentioned her people? She was proud of her origins, then.

"You interest me exceedingly," he said, mentally sorting through any dukes he knew with daughters around this girl's age. "And will you not tell me who this so powerful family of yours is? I shall discover the answer whether you do or not, you know."

She looked for an instant as if she was debating whether to trust him. Then her chin lifted. "I daresay you will. My name is Lady Cecily Westruther."

Well, now. This was a surprise. And she was correct. The Westruthers were every bit as old and powerful as his family. But surely she was one of the Duke of Montford's wards. Two of the girls had married recently. Why, then . . .

His stomach clenched. Suddenly it all made sense.

Slowly, he said, "I knew your brother. He was brilliant. Some called him a genius."

"He would have scoffed at that notion," said Lady Cecily. Her voice was steady, her eyes dry. Only the convulsive movement of her throat betrayed any hint of grief.

"Yes," said Rand. "He could never be satisfied with the boundaries of his knowledge. There was always more to discover."

Her expression held a mixture of pride, sadness, and surprise at his understanding. That touched him as nothing had touched him in a very long time.

Guilt licked like fire at his insides. If he'd considered the matter at all, he'd thought of Jonathon, Earl of Davenport, as alone in the world. But he hadn't been alone. He'd had a sister. This plucky, clever-tongued girl who had dared to break into Rand's house.

"He belonged to the Promethean Club, didn't

he?" she said. "He'd been here, in this house, the night he died."

Where was she heading with this? "He attended a meeting here, yes. But the fire that took his life occurred in his laboratory many miles away. You know that." Gentling his tone, he added, "I am sorry. More sorry than I can express. But it was a horrible accident. Nothing at all to do with his activities here."

His assurance didn't seem to make an impression on her. What did she know to the contrary? Or think she knew?

She licked her lips. "I want to know about this club."

Rand said, "I am surprised that your brother should have mentioned the Prometheans to you."

"He didn't. I found his diary a few weeks ago and I—I read it." She colored faintly, as if the admission embarrassed her.

He experienced a hot flash of irritation, followed by a stab of horror.

"The diary. What's in it?" he said. "Do you have it? Is it safe?"

Her bewilderment seemed genuine enough. "It is safe, yes. But all it contains are appointments. There are scarcely any entries in it at all."

Relieved, he turned about and paced, raking both hands through his hair as he considered the implications.

Relief was premature, of course. There might still be something in that diary even if Lady Cecily couldn't recognize its importance. He had to get it away from her, out of fear for her safety, if for no other reason.

"You must give me that diary," he said. "It is important, do you understand?"

She shrugged. "I think you will be disappointed in its contents. Why should you want it so badly?"

"For the same reason I wanted Jonathon's papers," he lied. "I was commissioned to prepare an archive of his work for his university college. To do that, I need everything. Every scrap of paper he wrote on."

Her eyes brightened at the idea of her brother's research being preserved for posterity. Again, guilt crept over him. But it was necessary. Necessary for her protection. He'd hold fast to that.

"I see," she said. "Well, in that case, I will most certainly give you the diary. But I want to know about the Promethean Club, Your Grace. Is it meant to be a secret?"

"No, not at all." He spread his hands as if he were laying all his cards on the table. "If you were expecting cloaks and daggers, you'll be disappointed, I'm afraid. The Promethean Club is no more than a group of scientists, inventors, philosophers, and the like who meet once a month to debate and exchange ideas."

Seconds ticked by while Lady Cecily digested this, her clear-eyed gaze giving him the odd, disconcerting sensation that she saw far more than he wished to reveal to her.

"It *sounds* innocuous," she said. "Given what I know about my brother and my . . . another member of the club, your explanation makes sense." She narrowed her eyes. "But there's something you're not telling me, isn't there?"

"Perhaps there is," he said, refusing to show any

hint of his unease. "It is irrelevant to your inquiry, believe me."

"You have Jonathon's papers," she persisted. "The Countess of Davenport told me only recently that she gave them all to you when he died." She hesitated. "May I see them? There might be personal correspondence, things pertaining to the family. I—I should like to have those back."

"I will see what I can arrange," he said. The request seemed innocent enough. Natural for Jonathon's sister to want such keepsakes, wasn't it?

Jonathon's sister . . . Now that he knew who she was, for some reason her continued presence in his house and in that costume increasingly bothered him.

He cleared his throat. "Now, you must repay me for the information I've given you tonight by letting me take you home."

She took a deep breath and let it out slowly. "Very well, then."

What? No argument? The quick about-face surprised him. Was she truly so mercurial, or had she accomplished her real purpose in coming here without his realizing it? He did not make the mistake of believing Lady Cecily Westruther docile.

With an unsettling twinge of uncertainty, he rang for a servant. He did not mean to let her escape him completely. "We will discuss this at a more appropriate time."

Looking up at him with a gleam in her eye, she said, "I shall not be satisfied until you have told me all. Are you going to be like Scheherazade and spin out your tale over successive meetings?"

His lips twitched. "Something like that," he replied. In a soft voice, he added, "But my motives are not nearly so pure."

He had the dubious victory of seeing her eyes widen slightly with alarm. At last, he'd disconcerted her.

That vague spark of irritation flared to annoyance. He was not pleased to discover that while neither his physical intimidation nor his threats had scared Lady Cecily Westruther, the allusion to more amorous intent threw her off balance. A salutary notion, indeed.

While his fair intruder wrapped herself in a cloak he found her and pulled the hood down low over her face, Rand disposed of the peruke wig. When a footman came in answer to his summons, he gave orders for his carriage to be brought around.

He continued to question her as they waited, but she didn't give him any more information about herself. He suspected she would withhold personal details just as he withheld information about the Promethean Club.

Lowering to reflect that he needed to resort to trading information for a lady's company. The most effort he ever expended over a woman was in calculating how best to extricate himself from her arms at the end of an affair.

This one, however . . . Lady Cecily Westruther was neither intimidated by his manner nor impressed by his rank. She *was* novel, but not quite in the way she'd meant. And his immediate, powerful response to her . . . Well, that was unprecedented.

When he wanted something, Rand approached getting it with a single-minded drive and implacable determination. Lady Cecily Westruther was no exception.

He'd secure the diary. Then he'd go about the far more pleasurable task of securing her.

As he escorted Lady Cecily to his carriage, his brain seethed with plans.

There'd been an instant, an infinitesimal pause after she'd announced her identity when the Duke of Ashburn appeared thunderstruck. Cecily savored the memory as he handed her into his carriage.

That small satisfaction couldn't keep her mind from the breathtaking proximity of the man beside her, though.

He'd insisted on accompanying her the short distance to Montford House. Despite her outward protests, she was forced to acknowledge she felt safe while he was there to protect her. Far safer than if she'd gone home alone.

Difficult to believe anyone could best the duke in a fight. Cecily didn't doubt he'd be as competent at self-defense as he was reputed to be at everything else.

Was it ever tiresome to be such a paragon, or did it all come as naturally as breathing? She must remember to ask him next time they met.

The leap of anticipation in her chest at the thought of meeting him again made her frown. The Duke of Ashburn was dangerous. If only she didn't need to retrieve that letter, she'd avoid him like the proverbial plague.

After a tense silence, Ashburn said, "I believe I

still have some of your brother's papers in the attics at my country house. I'll send for them."

Hope surged inside her, but she tried to remain outwardly calm. "I should be grateful to you. But how might I see them?"

"I hold a masquerade next Friday evening. We can slip away then."

"The Duke of Montford decides which entertainments I may attend," said Cecily primly. Glancing at the large figure beside her under her lashes, she added, "His Grace does not approve of masquerades for debutantes."

Particularly wayward debutantes like Cecily.

Ashburn turned his head to look down at her. His eyes didn't glow in the dark, she discovered. They glittered. "Something tells me that if you wish to go somewhere, you will find a way. With or without your guardian's consent."

She supposed that conclusion was reasonable, given her intrusion into his house tonight. "Nevertheless, I shall not be at that masquerade. I—"

Words stuttered in her throat as he took her hand in his. The heat and assured firmness of his touch made her heart lurch in her chest.

"What are you doing, sir?" Her voice came out in an odd tone that was infuriatingly weak. Strangely, she couldn't make herself pull free.

He raised her hand and bent his dark head to brush a kiss over her knuckles. It was the lightest, most fleeting touch of his lips, but a tingling warmth spiraled inside her, wrapped around her, all the way down to her toes. Heat fluctuated in her cheeks. She couldn't stop the small, responsive gasp that escaped her lips.

He never took his gaze from her face, and even in the dim light, she could tell he registered her reaction. His eyes burned; his features lit with triumph, then darkened with intent.

Softly, he said, "You will devise a way to come to the masquerade. And I will find you."

His words resonated through her blood. His nearness, his air of power and assurance nearly overcame her will. In that moment, she understood why men obeyed Ashburn's merest suggestions. And why women scrambled over one another to climb into his bed.

She barely retained the presence of mind to withdraw her hand from his clasp. She tried to think of something flippant to say, but she couldn't seem to wrest a smart quip free from the tangle he'd made of her brain.

"I will do no such thing," she managed. But the protest sounded lame even to her ears. If a mere kiss on the hand had this power over her . . .

Suddenly, Cecily remembered she was betrothed to another man. All those warm, sweet, melting feelings soured and curdled in the pit of her stomach.

Disgust lay heavy in her chest. She'd behaved like the veriest trollop! And a dunce as well, allowing Ashburn to exercise his skills of seduction over her.

If she needed any more reason to stay away from Ashburn, her engagement to Norland was an excellent one. And why hadn't Norland been uppermost in her mind all along?

Yes, Ashburn was dangerous, but she needed to know more about why he'd come to collect her brother's papers from Lavinia, why it had been Ashburn and not some close friend or relative who'd broken the news of Jonathon's death. And she needed that horribly damning letter.

Asking him outright seemed foolhardy at this juncture. She'd prefer to further her acquaintance with him in a public location where there were limits and constraints on his behavior. Not now and certainly not at a masquerade.

At a masquerade, anything could happen. She didn't need Montford's warnings to realize that anonymity most often led to loose behavior.

Perhaps Ashburn only pursued her like this because he wanted Jonathon's diary. She couldn't see what harm it would do to give it to him. There was nothing personal or precious in it, after all. And if she handed it over, Ashburn's strangely compelling attentions would, in all likelihood, cease. That would be a relief.

Mercifully, before the duke could do anything else to disconcert her, the coach came to a stop.

"We are here," she said. Relief drenched her like cooling spring rain.

Cecily clutched the cloak Ashburn had given her tighter around her, enveloping her scandalously clad form from neck to toe. "Good-bye, Your Grace. Thank you for escorting me home."

If she'd been a stronger woman, she'd have put out her hand to shake his, but she couldn't seem to risk it. She wasn't as strong as she'd thought. Not in his presence, anyway.

Abruptly, she said, "I'll give you the diary, but you'll have to find another way to get it. I shan't attend your party, you know."

"You underestimate yourself, Lady Cecily,"

drawled the duke. "I'll see you at the masquerade." His tone deepened. "In skirts this time, I trust."

The low thrill of his voice echoed in her blood long after his carriage rolled away.

Chapter Four

When Rosamund found her, Cecily stood in the long gallery at Montford House throwing a ball for Ophelia, the family's ancient Great Dane. The ball bounced several times before it rolled to a stop beneath an elegant love seat by the wall. A circumstance that Ophelia only acknowledged with a deep, doggy sigh from her prone position by the fireplace.

"I fear it is hopeless," said Rosamund, gripping Cecily's hands and kissing her on both cheeks. "Ophelia's frolicking days are over."

Sighing, Cecily said, "Yes, you are right." She watched the massive, graying hound. "Poor old girl. Do you think her spirits seem depressed?"

Rosamund's blue eyes sparked with humor. "How on earth could one tell? All she ever does is sleep."

"Yes, but she likes her humans to be here when she does it. And I've neglected her sadly these past weeks."

Cecily retrieved the ball from beneath the love seat and bent down to offer it to Ophelia. The Dane's jaws opened to accept the toy. With a single thump of her tail she expressed her thanks, then settled back into slumber with the ball lodged in her mouth. She looked as if she ought to be served on a platter like a suckling pig.

Thank goodness for Rosamund. For the past week, Cecily had not been able to stop thinking of that night in the Duke of Ashburn's house, and even Ophelia had not proved an adequate distraction. Rosamund's cheerful company was just what she needed to put a stop to a really rather maudlin tendency to brood.

"Enjoy the season while you may," said Rosamund. "You'll be buried in the country with Norland soon enough."

"No, I won't." Cecily rose, shaking out her skirts. "Is that a new bonnet?" She scrutinized the confection that adorned Rosamund's exquisitely styled golden hair.

Rosamund pursed her lips at the change of subject but said, "Indeed. Do you like it? You know how I depend on your taste."

"You should not have bought it without me," Cecily said severely. She gave the bonnet serious consideration. "Turn around."

Rosamund complied, holding her hands out a little. She was as poised and graceful as a dancer.

"*Almost* perfect," Cecily pronounced. "But just let me . . ." She stepped forward to pluck one superfluous plume from the arrangement of feathers at the capote and retie the buttercup yellow ribbons more becomingly beneath Rosamund's chin. "There."

"Thank you, my dear," said Rosamund, taking the feather from her and twirling it between her fingers. "Now, do tell me what you have planned for today. I came to see if you'd like an excursion to the Museum, since the weather is so inclement."

"No such luck," said Cecily, trying to keep the groan from her voice. "My betrothed and his mama are due to arrive at any moment for tea."

The look of undisguised dismay that passed over Rosamund's features made Cecily chuckle. "My thoughts *exactly*. But you are here now and you cannot escape."

Rosamund glanced at the clock. "I'm sure there's still time if I use the servants' entrance."

"No, no. How can you desert me in my hour of need? Stay, dearest Rosamund. Please?" Cecily took her arm in both hands and tugged her toward the door at the end of the gallery.

"But she is so horrid! And *he's* so . . ." Rosamund broke off with a slight flush. As if Cecily didn't know very well her opinion of the Duke of Norland.

"Diffident?" she said. "Persuadable? Teeth-achingly dull?"

"Well . . . yes!" said Rosamund in an uncharacteristic burst of candor. "He is like, oh, like a lump of clay. You could mold him into any shape you chose."

Cecily nodded. "You are right. It's what makes him such a perfect husband for me."

"I know you believe that," said Rosamund, regarding her steadily. "But, darling, he is not a man who could make you happy; of that I am convinced. He's years and years too old for you, for one thing. Won't you reconsider?"

"He is barely past thirty!" Cecily threw up her hands. "You all act as if I'm marrying Methuselah."

"Yes, it must be the bald spot and that slight paunch that make him seem older," said Rosamund with gentle sarcasm. "Don't do it, my dear."

"I never suspected you were so frivolous, Rosamund." Cecily refrained from pointing out the man Rosamund loved was scarcely an oil painting. However, there was a hard, masculine virility to Griffin, Earl of Tregarth, that was wholly lacking in the Duke of Norland.

Instead, Cecily said, "Really, my dear. What happened to duty and honor above all? Do I need to give you the Speech?"

Rosamund's brow furrowed. "I don't mean to say it would be the honorable thing to repudiate the arrangement, not after all this time. But . . . but it's such a crime that you should be obliged to endure . . ." Biting her lip, Rosamund glanced around to make sure no one was in earshot. Lowering her voice, she said, "I simply cannot *imagine* how you would suffer his attentions."

"Oh, stuff and nonsense," said Cecily. "You make too much of all that. Besides, I shan't be obliged to endure anything at all. Norland will remain in the country and busy himself with his study of infectious diseases or whatever he does, and I shall make my home in Town. We are to live entirely separately. I've made that clear. The arrangement suits us both perfectly."

She hadn't told her cousin her intentions before, or not in so many words. Rosamund widened her eyes. "But what about . . . intimate matters? Surely every husband wants his wife in his bed."

"Oh, no," said Cecily. "He won't trouble me on

that score. With two sons from his previous marriage, he doesn't need an heir. And Norland has had a mistress for years and years. He won't give her up. Why should he?"

After a dubious silence, Rosamund said, "I suppose I am lucky that my duty coincided with my inclination. I never had to make the choice."

"Well, and so does mine," said Cecily. She patted Rosamund's hand and drew it through her arm as they walked the length of the gallery. "Norland might be dull, but he'll make a most excellent husband. Particularly for my purposes."

Rosamund pulled up short. "You are willfully misunderstanding me, Cecily," she said quietly. "I want—I wish you to fall in love."

Cecily refrained from rolling her eyes. "That is sweet of you and I perfectly understand that being so blissful yourself, you feel the need to . . . to *evangelize* love matches. Jane is exactly the same and I don't blame her, either. But I'm not like the two of you, Rosamund. I don't possess an ounce of sentiment—you know I don't. I shall rub along very well with the duke."

More than anything, she wanted to live her own life with as much freedom as it was possible to have as a member of the so-called inferior sex.

Long ago, she'd decided that the future her parents had mapped out for her would suit her very well. A duchess might do as she pleased to a large extent and wield a great deal of influence if she chose. And Cecily, Duchess of Norland, would choose to wield that influence to try to better the lot of females who were not so fortunate as she.

Of course, certain sins were unforgivable, even in duchesses. But as most of these involved indiscretions committed by brainless, besotted females like Lavinia over worthless libertines, she knew herself to be safe on *that* score.

"Loving someone does not make you weaker, darling," said Rosamund gently.

Cecily flinched. She couldn't help it. Oh, but she detested the pity she saw in Rosamund's heavenly blue eyes. For a bare instant, she felt the urge to hit back at her cousin, to inflict a commensurate amount of pain.

But she no longer gave in to such childish impulses. Rosamund did not mean to wound her. And the last thing Cecily would ever do was deliberately hurt her dearest cousin.

That hadn't always been the case. After losing Jonathon, Cecily had fought hard enough against forming an attachment to her Westruther cousins. She'd been prickly and wayward and difficult.

But even when Cecily was at her worst, Rosamund, Jane, and the boys had refused to leave her alone in her grief. They'd teased her, tormented her as if she were one of them, shown rare, precious moments of kindness. A group of privileged children who'd stood together because there was no one else in the world to show them love or tenderness.

They were hers and she was theirs. They were the only people in the world she loved. The bond they shared was the only thing in the world she trusted.

That, and the Duke of Montford.

Dredging up her old nonchalance, Cecily shrugged. "If I ever fall in love, it will not be with a man who has ultimate power over me, body and soul. I am simply not made that way, Rosamund. I couldn't endure it."

"Do you know, Tibby said something similar to me the day I married Griffin." Rosamund hesitated. "It is true that many gentlemen exact blind obedience from their wives. But do you think Griffin exercises such tyranny over me? Or that Constantine does over Jane?"

Privately, Cecily thought her cousins' respective marriages were a kind of mutual enslavement, but she knew better than to express that idea to Rosamund.

Thankfully, before she could frame a tactful reply, their discussion was interrupted by the butler announcing Cecily's guests.

Cecily shot Rosamund a triumphant glance. "Will you show them to the drawing room, Wilson? Thank you. Lady Tregarth and I will be down directly."

"Wretch!" said Rosamund with feeling. "Mark my words: When you least expect it, I shall make you pay."

Ordinarily, Cecily looked forward to her betrothed's weekly call without interest or enthusiasm. Today was different. She was determined to glean what she could from Norland about the Promethean Club. Better yet, she would persuade him to aid her in a new scheme.

The notion had leaped into her brain in the early hours of the morning when, once again, she hadn't slept for stewing over her encounter with Ashburn.

"Your Grace. How delightful," said Cecily, moving forward. "How do you do?"

Norland was a tall, barrel-chested man, fair of coloring and complexion. A high forehead and a rapidly receding hairline emphasized the ovate shape of his head. All the more room for his gigantic brain, she supposed. Rosamund was correct: He did have a slight paunch, but then Cecily was no waif herself. Who was she to take exception to a little avoirdupois in her spouse?

"Lady Cecily." Norland bowed with a jerky dip from the doorway. He saluted Rosamund and Tibby in the same fashion.

That had never bothered her before, but now it occurred to Cecily that she and Norland had fallen into a rather dismally formal mode of greeting each other. Not that she *wished* him to kiss her hand. Or any other part of her, for that matter.

The memory of another man's kiss streaked across her senses like forked lightning, shocking her pulse into a frantic race.

Oh, this would never do! Exasperated at Ashburn's continual intrusion on her musings, she shoved all thought of him aside.

Norland's touch did nothing to raise her temperature or make her heart beat faster. That was exactly how it should be.

He smiled but the expression in his gray eyes was distant, as if he regarded something beyond her that he found troubling. She turned, half-expecting his attention to be riveted to Rosamund. Norland was a man, after all.

But no, it was only Tibby whose movements had caught his eye as she took up the shirt she'd been mending for Andy and bowed her head over her work.

Cecily smiled. Norland looked forward to his intellectual discussions with Cecily's former governess. Today, however, Tibby had positioned herself firmly in the background, perhaps in deference to the presence of the duchess. Her Grace was known for her stern views on paid companions knowing their places.

Then and there, Cecily resolved to make a point of including Tibby in the conversation at every opportunity.

"Won't you sit down, Your Grace?" said Rosamund, indicating the sofa.

"Ah, no. At least, not yet. Er, Mama will be along directly. Must see to her, you know."

They exchanged the usual meaningless pleasantries while they waited for the familiar stomp on the stairs that heralded Norland's mama.

The Duchess of Norland entered the room, aided by two footmen, on whose arms she leaned heavily.

With a deep curtsy, Cecily said, "How do you do, Your Grace?" She was determined not to let her future mother-in-law provoke her this time. "We're so happy you could call on us."

The duchess was a heavyset, irascible lady, who was usually to be found reclining on some couch or other with a vinaigrette in one hand and hartshorn in the other. She was the terror of her family, particularly her eldest son, for despite her inertia, she ruled both them and the ducal estate with an iron fist.

Cecily had little patience with the duchess and

her megrims, for Norland assured her that his mother's health was, in fact, excellent. This astonished Cecily. Why would anyone lie about all day if they weren't forced by illness or infirmity to do so?

"Do sit down," said Cecily, gesturing to a group of chairs by the window. "I'll ring for tea."

"Are you *mad*, gel?" said the dowager faintly. "If I sat so near to that drafty window, I'd catch my death. But I suppose that would suit you to a nicety, wouldn't it? By the hearth, if you please," she snapped, perversely shaking off her footmen as they tried to assist her. "Norland, build up a fire. I'm likely to freeze in this cavern." She sniffed. "The place *reeks* of damp."

Cecily might be prepared to ignore the aspersion cast on what was in truth an elegant and comfortable salon, but she detested the way her prospective mother-in-law ordered her son about as if he were a lackey.

Norland didn't seem to mind, however, and dutifully settled on his knees on the hearthrug, wielding fire irons and bellows until he'd conjured a blaze.

The bald spot on his crown was clearly visible beneath straggling strands of sandy hair as he bent to his task. His scalp glowed pink; the rest of his face was similarly ruddy as he rose to dismiss his liveried footmen and guide his mother to a chair.

He was a good son, Cecily thought. It wasn't as if he believed in his mother's condition, yet he indulged her every whim.

Tactful as always, Rosamund said, "Are you not feeling quite the thing, Your Grace? The exertion of this visit has fatigued you, I daresay."

The dowager duchess's grim features softened slightly. She patted Rosamund's hand. "You are a good, sweet child, Lady Tregarth. *How* I wish I had you for a daughter."

In other words, she wished Rosamund and not Cecily was to wed her son.

Unable to stop herself, Cecily rolled her eyes at Norland. She ought not to have done that, for his eyes lowered and his cheeks reddened all over again. "Mama, please."

Taking pity on him, Cecily indicated the sofa. "Won't you sit down, Your Grace? I'll ring for tea."

The dowager duchess let out a bloodcurdling moan. "*Tea?* Are you trying to poison me, girl?"

Her brows snapping together, Cecily opened her mouth to respond, but Rosamund hastily intervened. "Would a tisane be more acceptable?" she suggested. "That might suit Your Grace's constitution better."

"Or perhaps a posset?" said Cecily sweetly. "A mustard bath? Some laudanum drops?" An entire bottle full of them, if she had her way.

The dowager closed her eyes as if the mere sound of Cecily's voice pained her. "A tisane would be adequate. Thank *you*, Lady Tregarth."

While her kindhearted cousin fussed over the dowager, Cecily seated herself next to Norland.

In a low, thrilling murmur, she said, "The duke has made a fascinating addition to his collection of rare fungi. Would you like to see it?"

She felt as if she were casting out improper lures to him instead of appealing to one of his many intellectual passions. Indeed, he reacted as most men would if she'd offered to show him her garters. The mere mention of a botanical discovery made him straighten, a spark of interest brightening his eye.

"Well, by Jove! I'd no notion Montford was a keen mycologist."

Airily, she waved a hand. "Oh, His Grace is very fond of mushrooms." *Sautéed with cream and a dash of brandy.* "The collection is in the conservatory. Would you like to see it?"

Norland huffed in disapproval. "The *conservatory,* you say? No, no, that will never do. Fungi should be kept out of the light. A cool, dark environment suits them best, you know."

"Oh, but he's not growing them," said Cecily, mendacity oozing from her pores. "They're, ah, mounted. In a case."

Did people mount fungi in cases? She had no idea. But as the case itself was nonexistent, she needn't concern herself about that.

Still shaking his head, Norland said, "I shall certainly have a look. Perhaps I might advise Montford on how better to preserve the specimens."

"Oh, *would* you?" said Cecily, rising. "The duke would be most appreciative, I'm sure. Do come along."

Norland leaped up with the alacrity of a man promised a high treat.

"And where do you think you're going?" demanded the dowager duchess.

Rosamund clearly wanted to ask the same. Cecily sent her a pleading glance and received a look of resigned exasperation in return. Rosamund would exact payment in full later. A price Cecily would happily pay.

"Lady Cecily is showing me her specimens, Mama," explained the duke without a hint of double entendre. "My lady, lead the way."

Stifling a snort of laughter, Cecily did as she was bid.

"I am glad I had the chance to speak with you alone, Lady Cecily," said Norland unexpectedly as they proceeded down the stairs. "I have something particular to propose to you. That is to say, I'd like to know your opinion . . ."

Cecily looked up at him in surprise. "What is it?"

"You are the last of your cousins to be wed and it occurred to me that Tibby . . . er, Miss Tibbs, I should say . . ." He cleared his throat. "Well, it occurred to me that Miss Tibbs might not wish to find employment elsewhere once you are wed. Do you think she would like to remain with you after we are married?"

Cecily blinked. "What a splendid idea, Norland! I should like that of all things. Tibby has forever said she will live with her sister in Cambridge when I marry, so I suppose I never thought of asking her to make her home with me."

She put her hand on his arm. "What a kind man you are. Even if she chooses not to come, she will appreciate such a generous offer."

Norland blushed and disclaimed. "Will you present the idea to her? I think it would be best coming from you."

"I will do it this very day," she promised.

When they reached the conservatory, Cecily halted. "And now I must speak with *you* about something of vital importance."

He glanced down at her and then at their surroundings. With a gleam of humor he said, "*Not* fungi, then."

She laughed in surprise. On the odd occasion when he emerged from his abstraction, Norland could be quite engaging.

"No," said Cecily. "Do forgive me. I fear that was a ruse."

"Oh? Pity. What is it, then, Lady Cecily?" he said pleasantly. "Having second thoughts, eh? Well, well, nothing has been announced yet. Not too late to call the betrothal off, you know."

"Good God, no!" she said, frowning. "Nothing like that. But there is something I would ask of you. Something very particular."

He had the sense to look wary. "Indeed? Happy to serve, as ever, Lady Cecily."

She fixed him with her most guileless expression, which any member of her family would know spelled trouble. "I wish you to tell me about the Promethean Club."

His face blanked. "The *Promethean* Club?"

He looked for a moment as if he'd deny all knowledge of the organization.

"Yes," she said hastily. "My brother belonged to the club, as you are no doubt aware. I read his diary and he—he mentioned you." That was a lie, but she couldn't admit she'd been at Ashburn House and identified Norland by his singular laugh.

"*Did* he?" Norland's expression turned thoughtful. "Ye-es," he said slowly. "I am a member, as it happens. Though I can't quite see what it has to do with you."

In a rush, she said, "Would you take me to one of their meetings, Your Grace?"

His head jerked up as if she'd slapped him. "Certainly not."

Cecily stared at her fiancé, utterly disconcerted. She'd never heard him express himself so decidedly before. If he stood up to his mother this way, he'd lead a much more comfortable life.

She couldn't believe he'd refuse her, not on a matter so important. "But—but surely—"

With an impatient shake of his head, he cut in. "The Promethean Club is for men of science, men of philosophy. We discuss new ideas and inventions. All dull stuff to you, but to us . . ." He puffed out a breath. "Oh, you would never understand."

His dismissive attitude stung but she refused to let him provoke her into a heated response. Evenly, she said, "How do you know what I might understand, Norland? You have never asked me about my interests or my education."

"Ha! Furbelows and folderol. That's all you young ladies care about."

A flare of anger nearly made her lose sight of her objective. But she'd run up against such prejudice often enough to know that argument would gain her nothing.

"I *am* interested in science and advancement and ideas," she said, striving for calm. "I didn't receive a formal education, but you may be sure that I am far from ignorant. How could I be? I am Jonathon Westruther's sister. Just because I do not wear my knowledge on my sleeve like a bluestocking or thrust it down other people's throats, just because I happen to like beautiful things, that does not make me an empty-headed ninny."

Blotches of pink swarmed Norland's cheeks as his choler rose. "I'll not have it, I tell you! The meetings of our society are not spectacles to be gawked at by frivolous young ladies with nothing more amusing in their social diaries."

He didn't raise his voice, but his tone was adamant. And more than a touch contemptuous. Cecily realized—rather belatedly, if she were honest—that even a man who was in general mild and compliant might have one conceit. Apparently, Norland's was his intellect. And intellect, unfortunately, didn't preclude stupid, blind prejudice.

Frustration consumed her. *She* had been the stupid one, in this instance. She'd approached the matter too bluntly. She'd underestimated his arrogance and his resolve, and now she paid the price.

Trying to retrieve her false step, she said. "*Please,* Your Grace. Give me a chance to show you I am in earnest."

"No!" But as he looked at her, he must have seen the pain and longing in her eyes, for the fire gradually died from his expression.

Avoiding her scrutiny, he waved a hand. "Your interest in our society might not be frivolous but it is far from earnest. You wouldn't even think of joining us if you weren't curious about your brother. I deeply regret his death and I am truly sorry for your grief. But you won't find whatever you're looking for at the Promethean Club."

Cecily refused to give up. "Would you at least tell me about what goes on there?" she said. "There are so many things I want to know."

"I will not!" Now his words had a bluster to them. She had the oddest impression that he was deliberately fueling his own anger. He stabbed a finger at her. "Y-you and I agreed we'd live separate lives, Lady Cecily. If you don't want me poking my nose into your business, do not interfere with mine."

Norland puffed out his cheeks. "Now, forgive me if I say that on this subject, I do not wish to hear another word. Indeed," he said, looking at his pocket watch, "indeed, I think it's best for both of us if I take my leave before we say things we might regret."

He snapped out a bow. "Good day to you, my lady."

Without giving her time to reply or even return his courtesy, he spun on his heel and strode from the conservatory.

Stunned and bewildered by this change in her betrothed, Cecily watched him go.

Seconds ticked past before she could marshal sufficient of her wits to think. She'd never dreamed the man would turn out to be so stubborn. Norland left her in no doubt of the firmness of his refusal. Ordinarily, she'd wheedle and cajole him into agreement, but the steel in his demeanor just now told her she would not succeed this time.

Who would have thought it? Her supposed milksop betrothed had a backbone. How inconvenient, how *bewildering* that he should show evidence of it now.

Indeed, it seemed she'd have far more success gaining information from the Duke of Ashburn. Oh, the irony of *that* realization.

A hot, urgent sense of desperation surged through her, a feeling of anticipation that was not precisely fearful but not at all pleasurable, either.

If she wanted to find out more about the Promethean Club, not to mention retrieve that confounded letter, she knew what she must do. Against her instincts and her better judgment, she must attend the duke's masquerade tonight.

Chapter Five

"Tibby?" said Cecily as she passed her former governess on the stairs. "Might I have a word with you before we dress for dinner?"

"Of course, dear." Miss Tibbs turned to fall into step with Cecily and mounted the staircase once more.

When they gained Cecily's room, Cecily said, "Let's sit down."

She took Tibby's hands and drew her to sit beside her on the blue cream satin couch by the window. "I have something important to ask you."

"You haven't been getting into mischief again, have you?" Tibby pressed the bridge of her spectacles to slide them farther up her nose. "My dear girl, I thought you'd outgrown all of that nonsense. Perfectly understandable that you had to fight for Montford's attention as a little girl, but you are to be a married lady now."

A trifle stung by that admittedly just reading of her past antics, Cecily replied, "It is nothing like that." She gave her companion's hand a small squeeze. "In fact, it is precisely because I am to be a married lady that I wish to ask you about *your* plans for the future."

"Oh!" Tibby looked taken aback at the abrupt change of subject. She flushed a little. "Well, it was always my intention to live with my sister once all of you were married off. You knew that."

"The duke *will* pay you a pension if you do that, won't he?" asked Cecily.

Tibby's features tautened in disapproval but Cecily persisted. "Oh, I know talking about money is vulgar but what point is there in clinging to that kind of nonsense while living on bread and water?"

"The duke has been most generous," said Tibby repressively. "I shall do a *little* better than bread and water, thank you very much."

Cecily would have expected no less of Montford, but it was as well to be certain. She understood the lure independence must hold for Tibby after all these years. Didn't she want the same thing for herself, after a fashion?

"In that case," said Cecily, "I daresay the proposition Norland bade me put to you won't be terribly enticing. But for my sake, Tibby, will you promise to consider it?"

Tibby's gray eyes widened. "Proposition? What proposition, pray?"

"His Grace wants you to come and live with us. Well, live with me," amended Cecily scrupulously. "Norland and I won't make our home together for most of the year, you know."

All of the year, if she could help it. Where Norland went, so went Norland's mama.

Tibby said, "But why . . . I thought . . . *Surely* you will wish to be a proper wife to the duke, Cecily."

Why did Cecily have to explain this over and over? She was tired of it, so she said crisply, "It's an arranged marriage, Tibby. He doesn't love me and I don't love him. In fact," she said, reflecting on his bigoted dismissal of her intelligence, "I'm not even sure that I like him very much at the moment. But I shall be content enough as his wife."

Tibby sat back, apparently appalled at this matter-of-fact assessment.

Cecily gripped Tibby's thin hand between her own. "But however out of charity with him I might feel, I must say he can be unexpectedly thoughtful at times. His Grace was the one who thought of asking you to be my companion."

"The Duke of Norland came up with the idea?" Tibby's bewildered expression touched Cecily's heart. There *was* good in Norland, wasn't there? Even if he was a dreadful misogynist.

Cecily nodded. "Was that not kind of him? I'd never expected he might anticipate what I should like so well. For I *should* like it, above all things! Just think, Tibby. All the good we can do once I have money of my own . . ."

She noticed her companion didn't seem to share her enthusiasm. She'd turned quite pale, and a faraway sadness touched her eyes.

"Tibby?" said Cecily. "Tibby, are you quite well?"

"Y-yes. Yes, I . . ." She forced a smile but her aspect remained bleak. Slowly, she said, "It is a very great surprise, that is all."

Cecily regarded her uncertainly. Perhaps she ought not to have confessed it was Norland's idea. Did Tibby think Cecily didn't truly want her? Or was she dismayed at the prospect of remaining in essence a paid employee rather than mistress of her own fate?

"Have I said something wrong?" Cecily asked. "I would not wish to insult you or—or place you under an unwelcome obligation."

That made Tibby quiver with agitation. "No, no, of course not, Cecily! How could you *think*— It isn't that. Indeed, I am so very grateful to you." She stretched out her hand to press Cecily's arm. "*Dearest* girl."

With a murmured apology, Tibby took out her handkerchief and dabbed at her suddenly moist eyes. "Will you let me think about it a little before I give you my answer?"

"Why, of course. You will wish to consult with your sister, too, I daresay. There is not the least need for haste," said Cecily, regarding her with concern. "But dearest one, you don't look at all well. Perhaps you ought to lie down."

"Yes. Yes, you're right. A rest will do me good," her companion said distractedly. "Yes, I'll do that."

Feeling as if she had made a grave error in presenting the invitation the way she had, Cecily watched her companion's straight back and bowed head as she left the chamber. What a horrid day it had been.

She could only hope her fortune changed before the evening. For her next encounter with the Duke of Ashburn she needed all the luck she could get.

Cecily made a number of cold, hard resolutions about the evening ahead. She would take the opportunity to search Ashburn's library while the duke and his staff were otherwise occupied. She would not join in the dancing, nor in any other pleasures that could be had at this masquerade.

Her aim was to give Ashburn the diary, discover as much information from him as she could manage in return, and then leave. If she could possibly get that confounded letter from him, too, all the better.

She would not show any sign of the embarrassing way Ashburn affected her. And she would not—most certainly not—allow him to touch her. Not even for the space of a dance.

On one hand, she was impatient for the evening to pass so that she could put her plan into action. On the other, she wished to Heaven she could ignore the promptings of curiosity and pride—not to mention Ashburn's sly provocation—and stay far away from his stupid masquerade. There must be a less . . . *dangerous* way of having private conversation with the man.

Ever since Diccon the footman had left the duke's service to become Rosamund's butler, Cecily had been without a reliable partner in crime. Montford watched her more closely, too. In fact, all her family did, particularly Andy and Xavier. It was as if Montford had known all along about her exploits and relied on Diccon to keep her safe.

She scowled as the notion solidified in her mind. So that was it! She'd been a fool not to see it before. Lord, how that rankled. She'd thought herself so very clever, and all the time, Montford had designated Diccon to be her keeper.

Despite the difficulties, or perhaps because of them, Cecily was determined to go to the masquerade. It seemed quite impossible to allow Ashburn

to label her a coward—or worse, lacking the ingenuity to escape her protectors and attend this entertainment. It seemed even less possible to let
Montford win their silent battle of wills.

She shivered, recalling the unnerving intensity
with which Ashburn had regarded her that night
in his library. No man had ever looked at her that
way before. Most gentlemen thought her an odd-
ity because she never simpered or flirted or troubled herself to flatter them. Which just showed
how silly females were, to let men fall into such
complacency.

But Ashburn was different. Ashburn had made
no secret that he admired her. Not only that, he
had listened to her, too. She'd often complained in
a joking way that men didn't appreciate her ster-
ling qualities. Now that one apparently did, she
was at a loss to know how to react to such pointed
interest.

She would go to this masquerade. But she would
remain on her guard.

The spirit was willing, if conflicted. Practicalities
were another matter entirely. Montford had accepted only one invitation on her behalf that night:
her cousin Bertram and Lavinia's ball. That turned
out to be the most excellent stroke of fortune imaginable.

She'd planned it all very carefully, visiting her
former London home that afternoon, where of
course Lavinia and Bertram now resided. She'd left
her costume and the diary with a maid and whee-
dled a promise from two of the footmen to be at
hand to carry her in the sedan chair to Ashburn's
house.

Cecily bit her lip. She'd be obliged to sacrifice the India mulled muslin gown she wore, but it was a small price to pay for what she might learn that evening.

Tibby, while assuring Cecily she needed only a decent night's sleep, said that she rather thought she was too unwell to accompany her tonight. Concerned but aware of Tibby's dislike of fuss, Cecily left her companion to solitude, with the threat that if she wasn't better by the morning, Cecily would summon the doctor.

All her relations had left the house to attend various engagements. After much persuasion, Cecily managed to convince Tibby that Lavinia would be an adequate duenna at the ball. Now, all she had to do was give herself an excuse to leave the ball early and immediately, rather than waiting for Montford's carriage to be brought.

"There you are, Cecily." Lavinia's cool, crisp voice came from behind her.

Cecily turned and curtsied, observing with thanks to Heaven that Lavinia did not wear her pink pearls with that horror of a buttercup yellow gown.

Lavinia's gaze flickered over Cecily, then darted away.

In a remote voice, she said, "I heard you called this afternoon. I was sorry not to receive you."

"Oh, that's quite all right," said Cecily. "I hobnobbed with the servants instead. I hope you don't mind, but it's an age since I heard all the gossip."

She'd meant the comment innocently but the freezing of Lavinia's features showed she had secrets she didn't wish her staff to pass on. Lord, did she think Cecily wanted to hear the sordid details of Lavinia's private life? Or that the servants would sully her ears with them even if she did?

"How kind," murmured Lavinia.

Cecily lowered her voice. "My purpose in calling was to ask for my pearls back, Lavinia." That had been the excuse she'd decided upon, should Lavinia chance to be at home. Her real object had been to prepare for tonight's escape.

Lavinia scratched at the back of her hand and bit her lip, sending another glance skittering around the room. "I don't have them."

Lavinia's tone was so low that Cecily wondered if she'd heard correctly. "I beg your pardon?"

"I don't have them, I tell you!" Lavinia clamped a hand around Cecily's wrist and dragged her to a deserted anteroom. "I lost your confounded pearls!"

"*Lost* them?" Horrified, bewildered, Cecily stared at her cousin's wife. "But . . . was the catch loose? Saunders checks it every time I—"

"Don't be obtuse!" hissed Lavinia. "I didn't *lose* the necklace. I mean, I know where it is. I lost it in play, Cecily! To Lord Percy."

Cecily's stomach clenched. Self-recrimination washed over her in a hot tide. Lavinia was right. She *was* obtuse. Thickheaded and stupid to have let those pearls out of her sight. Thunderously idiotic to have lent them to Lavinia.

She bent her formidable glare on her cousin's wife. "The necklace wasn't yours to stake. You must get it back."

Lavinia's blue eyes drowned in tears. "I can't, Cecily! I don't have any money to repay the debt! Bertram keeps me in penury, I swear it. And if he finds out about this, he will *kill* me!"

That might have been a little melodramatic. However, Cecily knew Bertram from old and she was aware of both his fanatical penny-pinching and the thin streak of cruelty that ran through his character. She didn't waste her breath arguing.

"What was the sum you lost?" Perhaps Cecily might redeem the debt herself and no one need be the wiser.

"Th-three thousand pounds." The words came out on a sob.

The air expelled from Cecily's lungs in a whoosh. *"Three thousand?"* That was too vast a sum for Cecily's savings to cover.

"I never thought he'd make me pay him in m-money!" wailed Lavinia.

"You stupid girl, how else would he want you to pay—? *Oh.*"

Cecily flushed at her own gaucherie. No matter how she pretended to be thoroughly sophisticated, she had little experience of real decadence. She could scarcely conceive of using her body to pay a debt. Yet, in Lavinia's circle of acquaintants, it probably happened all the time. The notion made her queasy.

She thought furiously but she could come up with no better solution than to ask for help. "Lay it all before Montford. He will aid you. Even Lord Percy wouldn't stand a chance against him."

Lavinia's eyes grew large. "Oh, but how could I? He will guess that Percy . . . that I . . ."

"Knowing Montford, he is already well aware of that," said Cecily. "You will have to swallow your pride, Lavinia."

"But he would command Davenport to keep a

tighter rein on me, and that would be worse than *anything*."

The fear in Lavinia's blue eyes was not feigned. A shocking notion now occurred to Cecily. She knew of Bertram's vicious side, but she'd always thought of Bertram and Lavinia as a common enemy and therefore that they acted in concert. She'd never considered that Bertram might mistreat his wife. The intimate, horrible ways a husband might do so flashed before Cecily's mind.

She shuddered. She disliked Lavinia. At this moment, she could happily have slapped her for being such a bird-wit. But she wouldn't wish the silly woman to suffer for her actions at Bertram's hands.

"Stop crying." She handed Lavinia her handkerchief. "You will make your nose red."

With a soft shriek of consternation, Lavinia dabbed at her cheeks. "But what are we going to *do*?"

Cecily had no idea. She set her teeth. "I'll think of something."

Cecily had still not come up with a solution to the conundrum of the missing pearls when she realized she'd dallied far too long at her cousin's ball.

Mr. Babbage, one of Rosamund's swains before her marriage, claimed his dance but Cecily convinced him to take her to the refreshment parlor instead.

Obedient to her command, her escort procured her some ratafia and champagne for himself. Cecily preferred champagne, too, but ratafia would serve her purposes better.

Lavinia had converted what she now called the

green salon into the refreshment parlor this evening. She'd decorated the chamber in the Egyptian fashion, in a glaring combination of gilt and green and yellow, with so many crocodile-footed furnishings, Cecily half expected them to spontaneously animate and scuttle away.

Cecily declined a lobster patty with an inward grimace. If her appetite hadn't already deserted her, the bilious décor was enough to turn her stomach.

But that didn't matter now. What she needed to do was put her plan for escape into action.

Cecily swirled the ratafia in its glass and waited for her opportunity.

A glance at the ormolu clock on the mantelpiece told her it was nearly midnight. She made herself sip her ratafia and listen and nod and make polite conversation with her companion as her heart accelerated and her breathing quickened.

Silently, she apologized to poor Mr. Babbage for what she was about to do. As someone moved behind her, she stepped back and allowed her elbow to jog.

"Oh!" With a flick of her wrist, she sent sticky chestnut-colored liquid splashing over her white muslin gown.

"Lady Cecily!" Mr. Babbage reddened with embarrassment. "Oh, how unfortunate. Here, let me." He fished a handkerchief from his pocket and began pawing awkwardly at her bodice with it.

Then he seemed to realize what he did, for he snatched his hand back, with abject apologies.

That was the excuse Cecily needed. She could not possibly remain at the ball with a great brown stain on her gown. With assurances to Mr. Babbage that her own clumsiness was the cause of the accident, Cecily excused herself from the party.

She refused to have Montford's carriage called. It was but a step to Montford House. She was positive her cousin would lend her the sedan chair.

Finally, she managed to escape the refreshment room. But it was not a demure debutante with a soiled gown who gave the footmen the order to take her to Ashburn House. It was a mysterious lady in a purple taffeta domino and mask.

Rand knew he appeared cool and aloof from the guests who filled his vast public rooms and spilled out onto the terrace.

Well, he was aloof, certainly. He had no interest in engaging with anyone here tonight. But he was far from cool. Frustration burned so hotly inside him, he was likely to incinerate before the night was through.

Damn it, where was she? Surely she should have arrived by now.

Had he missed her in the throng? But no, he couldn't have. Costumed or not, he would know his fair housebreaker anywhere. He must have considered and rejected every lady here tonight—and remembering Lady Cecily's predilection for breeches, some of the men.

Besides, she'd have no reason to attend the masquerade unless it were to approach him. To that end, he'd taken care to don only the lightest of disguises—a black domino and the narrowest black velvet strip of a mask. She couldn't fail to recognize him. For good or ill, he'd made an impression on her. Of that he was certain.

He might be forced to accept that the lady had been sincere in her refusal to come tonight. The notion whipped up his annoyance every time it struck him.

He'd planned for this evening, quite meticulously. The possibility that the intrepid and resourceful Lady Cecily Westruther would not find a way to be here had not occurred to him.

He'd relied on the challenge of it to pique her interest as much as her desperation to know more about the Promethean Club. He thought he'd discerned in her a fascination for him that reciprocated his growing obsession with her.

She couldn't have remained oblivious of what had lain thick in the air in his library that night. Each flare of those dark, velvety eyes, every nervous gesture seared themselves upon his memory.

Those reactions had not denoted fear, but an awakening desire in an innocent but otherwise remarkably self-possessed young woman. The contrast was delicious, intriguing. He couldn't get her out of his head.

Had she thought about him in the intervening days?

So many duties and pursuits had occupied him in the week since they'd met. Yet, Lady Cecily's face, so vivid and striking, was rarely absent from his thoughts. He turned over their conversations in his head, took them out and viewed them with the critical appraisal of a playwright watching actors perform his work.

He wished now that he could rewrite that script, that he'd taken what he wanted instead of holding himself so sternly in check.

But no. His instincts about Lady Cecily Westruther's interest in meeting him here might have been faulty, but his judgment about her lack of experience was accurate. He needed to take her in slow measures, to hold back every ounce of his own desire while he teased hers forth slowly, delicately, like silk thread from a cocoon.

His lips twisted, mocking such self-delusion. He had fooled himself about many things, it seemed, including his power to compel her. He couldn't recall ever being surprised by a woman before.

It occurred to him that he wasn't entirely sure of anything where this young lady was concerned. Where did he want it all to lead, anyway? His interest in her was far from platonic; yet, she was an innocent. Moreover, she was a gently bred lady. As such, she was forbidden.

Why couldn't he seem to remember that?

Logic did not make so much as a dent in his determination to know more of Lady Cecily Westruther. Perhaps this strange infatuation would fizzle and die on closer acquaintance. Yet his character was not capricious. His first impressions of people were generally sound.

When another half hour passed, Rand finally accepted he would not see her tonight. The evening held not the slightest allure for him now. He propped his shoulders against the wall to await the dawn and wished these people would get the hell out of his house.

Five minutes later, one of the footmen brought him a note.

The library. Hurry!

He read it with a surge of triumph. Crushing the note between his fingers, Rand nodded his thanks to the footman and slipped away.

Was there ever anything so unfortunate? Cecily crouched, frozen, behind Ashburn's desk as she waited for two very tedious lovers to finish their business and leave the duke's library.

She'd searched this room for nearly an hour before the library door opened and a man and a woman came in.

Cecily had dropped to the floor, praying they hadn't noticed her. But she needn't have worried. Soon, it became clear that this pair's attention was wrapped up in each other.

A lady's low, suggestive laughter thrilled across the room, followed by a masculine gasp.

Oh, good God! That's all she needed. She blew out an exasperated breath and waited for the lovers to do what they'd come in here to do, then go.

Although on second thoughts, the gentleman didn't seem all that loverlike.

"Really! No, *really,* ma'am. I don't think we ought. I mean, deeply flattered. Most beautiful woman I've ever beheld, but—"

Whatever the besieged fellow had been about to say was cut off, presumably by the lady's mouth. He continued to make muffled noises indicative of his wish to finish his sentence, but the lady was persistent.

A low, husky female voice said, "You want to get back at him, don't you, darling? You want to prove to him that you're a man and— *Oho!*" The voice broke off with a low, husky laugh. "You are, *most definitely,* a man."

The gentleman sucked in a sharp breath. "Yes, I am angry. I do want to show him, but, er, n-not quite like this, d'you see. M'cousin's a crack shot, you know, besides having the most punishing right hook. He wouldn't take it at all kindly—"

There was a deep groan, followed by a string of halfhearted protests from the hapless gentleman.

"I'm sure I can make you forget all about Ashburn," purred the lady. "I know *I* have."

Ashburn? That made Cecily prick up her ears. Cautiously, she peered around the desk.

The pair were sprawled on a low-backed couch by the fireplace, apparently engaged in an elegant wrestling match. The couch faced the door, so from this vantage point, Cecily could see little more than a stray leg, or a hand, or the lady's profile as she occasionally came up for air.

She saw the gentleman's hands close on the whiteness of his seductress's upper arms, but he wasn't pulling her close; he was trying to separate the woman's body from his own.

The lady quickly overcame such feeble resistance. And a man, Cecily supposed, was only flesh and blood, after all.

Soon the gentleman's negatives became less forceful, until *no* became *Oh, God, not here.* A sentiment with which Cecily thoroughly agreed.

"Yes, *here*," the lady insisted.

And then the library door opened and His Grace, the Duke of Ashburn, walked in.

The tableau Rand found in his library winded him like a punch in the gut. For several seconds, his mind reeled. He'd been so fixed on Lady Cecily Westruther that for a fleeting instant, he thought it was she on that couch with another man.

Fury blazed through him, darkening his vision. A possessive, animalistic urge made him want to rip the man apart with his teeth. Rand had started forward, fists clenched, before he recognized the woman. Not Lady Cecily. *Louise.*

In a tangle of half-clad limbs, long dark tresses, and petticoats, his former mistress was enthusiastically servicing another man.

His cousin Freddy, to be precise.

Emotions swiftly flooded Rand. Relief that it was not, after all, Lady Cecily on that couch. Anger at Freddy for this petty piece of revenge. For his former mistress, he felt only disgust tinged with regret.

He'd been as gentle as he could when breaking it off with Louise. Guilt had made him absurdly generous over the parting gift he'd bestowed on her. But he had ended the affair all too soon after beginning it, and that must have been a blow to Louise's pride. He'd intended their association to be a long one when he took her as his mistress a month ago.

But a month ago, he hadn't met Lady Cecily Westruther.

A cold sense of calm pervaded his body. He watched the couple struggle up from their undignified positions and did not allow himself to feel even the slightest hint of betrayal. He'd be foolish to lay claim to either party's loyalty or affection, not even Freddy's. He ought to know by now that people always acted out of self-interest. Particularly members of his family.

Louise fixed him with a triumphant, defiant stare and did not trouble to cover herself. *See what you're missing,* she seemed to say. As if he'd ever want her now.

Freddy, on the other hand, looked as if he might cry. His fingers fumbled over buttoning the fall of his pantaloons.

Rand was searching his brain for something remarkably witty and devastatingly cutting to say, when a voice called from behind his desk, "Oh, thank Heaven! They've been at it for such an age. I thought I'd be trapped in here until dawn!"

Chapter Six

Rand froze. A string of oaths went through his mind but he managed to stifle the urge to curse aloud.

In an hour or so, he might bring himself to smile at the way Lady Cecily's entrance on the stage transformed the scene from tragedy to outright farce.

Louise's smugness turned to horror. Shrieking with outraged modesty, she scrambled to cover herself. Freddy flushed a deeper shade of red, if that were possible. He sprang to his feet, trying even more desperately to straighten his clothing.

Ashburn moved to open the door wide in a mute invitation to leave. Without another glance in his direction, Louise fled in disarray.

To his credit, Freddy stood his ground like a man, albeit a man who faced execution. Well, that was something. At least the young idiot wasn't such a fool as to run.

Rand put up his brows. "As usual, Freddy, you're a little late."

He kept his body relaxed, his voice even, though his nerves were taut. He couldn't shake the grip of a deep, cold anger. Damn it, hadn't he vowed he wouldn't let this matter?

"Shaking in your shoes, coz?" he drawled, eyeing Freddy up and down. "Did you expect me to fly into a rage over your dalliance with my former mistress?" He placed only the slightest emphasis on the word *former*.

A soft gasp from Lady Cecily reminded him of his company. Damn it to hell! What a sordid business.

"It wasn't like that!" Freddy protested.

Rand observed him without expression. "You mistake, Freddy. I know exactly how it was."

Louise had used the boy to punish Rand, to make him jealous. But he didn't feel one particle of pain or jealousy on her account. Their liaison had been entirely free from finer sentiments. He *was* dismayed that she'd found it necessary to go to these lengths to punish him; it showed he was not such a good judge of character as he'd supposed.

Regardless of whatever physical intimacies they'd shared, Louise simply did not have the power to hurt him.

But Freddy . . . Well, that was different.

His cousin took a step toward him, one hand lifted in supplication. "Rand, I—I can explain."

A civilized man would listen and try to understand. A careful one would take advantage of the situation to mend a bridge. Rand couldn't bring himself to do either of those things.

"Go away, Freddy," he said, his attention fixing on Lady Cecily. "I have far more interesting things to do than listen to you."

* * *

When the young gentleman named Freddy had gone, Cecily eyed Ashburn warily. He stood tall and silent near the doorway, watching her through the slits in his mask.

When the hint of a smile tilted one corner of his grim mouth, Cecily's heart jumped about in her chest. The most shaming and ridiculous melting feeling spread through her stomach.

To make up for such weakness, she scowled back at him. Not that he could see her scowl with her mask covering most of her face, but it made her feel better.

"I apologize," he said unexpectedly. "You should not have been obliged to witness that." He cocked his head as he moved away from the door, adding silkily, "Of course, you would not have witnessed it at all if you hadn't been skulking in my library, up to no good."

She'd hoped he'd forgotten that with all the drama that surrounded her appearance on the scene. "I was not skulking, precisely."

"No, you were not skulking," he agreed. "Skulking implies lack of purpose. You were searching. What did you hope to find?"

"Actually, I came in here to hide," said Cecily mendaciously. "I saw one of my Westruther cousins in the ballroom, and I couldn't risk staying there in case he recognized me."

That was partly true, as a matter of fact. Not that Lydgate was at all likely to have noticed her, much less identified her in the throng. He only had eyes for the lush blond lady he'd taken as a waltzing partner.

A little self-conscious, she added, "I was—er—waiting for you."

He held up a screw of paper. "But you didn't write this note."

"No."

"Of course you didn't," he muttered. He went over to toss the paper in the fire.

Ought she to tell him what had transpired in this room? Clearly, the young man called Freddy had been a reluctant participant in that hurried liaison. Would that matter to Ashburn?

He'd probably resent her for raising the subject. She'd had enough dealings with her male cousins to understand that one must tread carefully around masculine pride.

But in the grim lines of his face and the rigid set of his shoulders, she sensed the fury behind his apparent indifference. And she knew that such anger could only stem from hurt.

"She threw herself at him, you know," offered Cecily. "And she is so very beautiful. I don't think any man could resist."

You did not, she added silently. It had not been altogether pleasant to see the lady Ashburn had chosen as his mistress and realize how greatly she herself suffered by comparison. Not that she wished to supplant the mistress. It was just that she knew now Ashburn's admiration for her comparatively ordinary appearance must have been false. He wanted the diary; that was all.

The duke's right hand clenched and released in a reflexive movement. Then his features seemed to relax an infinitesimal amount.

But he made no answer. Instead, he moved unhurriedly toward her, with that lithe, easy gait that rang of masculine confidence. Oh, he had confidence in spades, along with a dash of pure arrogance.

Ashburn's thin mask was inadequate to hide the contours of those sharp cheekbones, the lazy sensuality of his mouth. It did reduce his eyes to a hard, formless glitter, however. She couldn't decide whether that made him more or less intimidating.

How had she ever thought that he might require comfort, or that she might give it to him?

In silence, he reached behind his head to remove the black strip of slitted velvet from across his eyes, then held it dangling from his long fingers.

With a wave of his hand, he indicated a couch. Not the one Freddy and the mistress had used. "Shall we?"

Apprehension fizzed in her stomach like champagne. She seated herself and clasped her hands in her lap.

"I thought you wouldn't come," said Ashburn in a low voice, taking a seat beside her.

"I nearly didn't," she admitted. "I had to go to great lengths to deceive my guardian and get here with no one the wiser." Cecily let her tone speak for her. *This had better be worth my trouble.*

He dipped his head in a slight bow. "I am honored. And also . . . relieved. I'd toyed with the idea of going after you if you hadn't turned up."

Surprise made her eyes widen. "Really?"

She almost wished she'd failed to find a way to be here tonight just to see what he might have done. "How would you have gone about it? Ridden into my cousin's ballroom and fetched me up on your saddle like Young Lochinvar?"

He must have thought that the most hilarious thing he'd ever heard, for he actually smiled. "That method has its appeal, certainly. Though I hope I would have more finesse."

A little dazzled by that sudden, brief gleam of teeth, Cecily said faintly, "Indeed."

She rallied. "You told me you would have my brother's papers sent up from the country. May I see them?"

"The diary first, if you please."

Cecily eyed him speculatively. "You seem awfully desperate to get your hands on my brother's diary."

"Pure academic interest," he said. He held out his hand and repeated, "If you please."

She shrugged and went to retrieve it from where she'd left it on Ashburn's desk. Handing it to him, she said, "And my brother's papers?"

He flipped the diary open and began to leaf through it. At her question, he hesitated, as if debating whether to tell her the truth.

Then he laid down the diary on the table beside him and said, "I am afraid my staff have not been able to locate them yet."

He spread his hands, a gesture meant to convey openness, but it didn't fool her. He added, "I am sorry to have brought you here under false pretenses, but there was no way I could send you a message."

She suspected he was very well able to find a way to communicate such news to her if he wanted. She'd wasted her time coming here; risked her reputation and Montford's wrath for nothing.

He moved closer, until she smelled the intriguing hint of his cologne.

"May I?" Before she knew what he was about or could answer him, his hands had pushed back her hood and his fingers delved into her curls to locate the ties of her mask.

She felt the cool rush of air against her heated face as the mask fell away and tumbled to her lap.

His fingertips trailed down to the ties at her throat.

She experienced the oddest sensation, light-headedness and a sharp tug of excitement in her viscera.

She ought not to allow this. "Your Grace, I didn't come here to—"

"Call me Rand," he murmured, working at the strings that held her domino together.

"I don't think that would be appropriate." She put up her hand to bunch the ends of her domino together and remove them from the deft manipulation of his fingers.

Why she needed to do that or was so panicked at the notion of his removing her outer garment when she had on a perfectly respectable gown beneath, she didn't know. She counted herself a practical person, unfettered by missish rules and illogical conventions.

Yet it was not the well-schooled debutante who objected to this intimacy but the instinctive, animal part of her. It felt frightening, thoroughly exposing, as if he peeled away more than an unnecessary outer garment.

"Are you afraid of me, Lady Cecily? I would not injure you."

The perceptiveness of his gaze nearly undid her wits. Not injure her? She felt as if she danced on a precipice with him, that together they'd fall at any moment.

"I did not come here to—to flirt with you," she said in as strong a voice as she could manage.

His lips twitched. "You think this is flirting?"

She ignored that. "You know why I came."

Ashburn regarded her steadily. "I think that even if you did not acknowledge it to yourself, you knew why I wanted you here tonight. And I also think," he added, holding up a hand to silence her protest, "that in your heart of hearts, you want what is going to happen now."

His voice had taken on a deep, husky timbre, almost hypnotizing in its mellifluence. His face was close to hers; his breath, sweet with wine, feathered over her lips. Those amber eyes captured hers; then his eyelids lowered and his gaze fixed on her mouth.

Her lips tingled under that compelling inspection. He wasn't even touching her, yet he commanded her utterly. Her usual flippancy deserted her like a rat from a sinking ship.

Inwardly, she cursed herself for sitting there frozen and wide-eyed like a startled deer, but some greater force seemed to hold her in its grip. *Had* she wanted this to happen? No, surely she'd thought only of that letter, of Jon.

A protest clanged in her head like a ship's bell, but it didn't strike louder than the drumming of her heart.

With an amazing effort of will, she drew back a little. "You promised me intelligence about the Promethean Club tonight."

"All in good time," Ashburn said softly, moving closer still.

His sharp, handsome features swam in her vision. Her brain ordered her to protest, to move away, to run, but her insubordinate body stayed where it was. Her breath suspended in that silent moment of anticipation.

Ashburn set his mouth to hers. The world rocked beneath her, and everything she'd ever known about herself was upended in an instant.

The sensation was an extraordinary mélange of heat and excitement and uncertainty. His lips were hot and firm, gentle and provocative, calling forth an answer from her that she'd never suspected she was capable of giving. Her response was untutored, inexperienced, embarrassingly clumsy, but that did not seem to bother him.

With a soft groan, he smoothed one hand up her back to her nape, pressing her closer to the growing firmness of his kiss.

Desire surged through her in a dizzying rush, made her revel in his growing urgency, made her seek to match it with equal power and fire.

She ought to call a halt to this. In some vague, distant corner of her mind, she knew that. But no man had ever kissed her like this before and perhaps no one ever would again. Curiosity as much as the unprecedented feelings he evoked stopped her from stopping him as she ought.

His arm stole around her waist; his tongue delicately teased her bottom lip. She made an involuntary sound of shock and pleasure and allowed her head to fall back against the arm of the couch.

She sensed a change in his mood then. His mouth left hers, drifted over her cheek, to her ear; then he kissed the side of her neck. He murmured something as she shivered with helpless delight. His body half covered hers and his hand—oh, Lord!—his hand smoothed up her bodice beneath her domino to caress her breast.

She couldn't seem to draw air into her lungs. The warning bell clanged louder, penetrating her dazed senses. She must not let this go any further.

"No. Stop," she whispered, struggling to sit up. "You must stop now."

Ashburn froze. Then he expelled a harsh sigh and drew back, raking a hand through his cropped hair. Frustration rolled from him in waves.

Cecily scrambled to her feet, pulling the edges of her domino together as she backed away from him. "I did *not* come here for this, whatever you might think."

She thought he might laugh at that. She'd certainly given a convincing impression of a woman who had precisely such an amorous purpose in mind.

Ought she to tell him about Norland? But no, she rather thought that would make her appear even looser in her morals than she did already. Besides, she doubted news of a rival would cool Ashburn's ardor.

"I know you didn't come here for this," he said, surprising her. His tone was anything but apologetic, and the heat had not left his eyes. "You ought not to stay if you don't want a great deal more. Cecily, you present far too great a temptation for me to withstand."

His words left her fluttery and shamefully pleased. But she said, "A true gentleman ought to be in control of his baser desires. I hope you do not seek to blame *me* for your lack of—"

"Of course I don't blame you," he said impatiently. "But if you remain in this room looking like that, I'm going to do it again."

Instead of fleeing like any sensible person, Cecily said, "Looking like what, pray?"

His eyes glittered. "Like cherries and cream and chocolate," he said. "Like a sweet, soft banquet waiting for me to feast."

That sentiment shocked her but it intrigued her, excited her, too. A subtle shift in the lights in his eyes told her he knew it.

In a leisurely fashion, he rose and moved toward her. She stood her ground, but she couldn't seem to tear her gaze from that firm-lipped mouth, nor her mind from speculating on what that mouth might do to her if given the chance.

She ought to find a way to steer the conversation back to the reason she'd come, but she'd completely lost control of this voyage of discovery. Ashburn had staged a neat form of mutiny tonight.

Had he kissed her solely to frustrate her purpose? She would not like to think him so calculating, but she couldn't discount the possibility. He was a man entirely capable of such an act.

If it weren't for that letter, she hoped she'd have the sense to stay away from the Duke of Ashburn. But she had to retrieve it. And she had to know more. Why had Ashburn taken Jonathon's papers? What had he done with them? And what role had the Promethean Club played in all this?

She didn't trust Ashburn. Not enough to explain

the truth of her quest. She couldn't ask Ashburn outright for that incriminating piece of correspondence. That letter could ruin all her hopes of marrying Norland if it got into the wrong hands.

The danger in Ashburn's eyes convinced her she'd not learn any useful information from him tonight.

He took another step toward her. It was an effort not to flee.

Hurriedly, she said, "Very well, I shall leave now, but you must send word to me when those papers are found." She did her best to ignore the unsettling way he stared at her. "Sh-shall I see you at my come-out ball?"

He smiled down at her, another gleam of white teeth. "I wouldn't miss it."

Cecily moved to snatch up her mask from the floor where it had fallen, but he was there before her, scooping up the stiff concoction of beaded satin.

"Turn around," he said.

She had an impulse to argue that she would tie the mask herself, but that seemed petty and craven. She obeyed, but her heart jumped into her throat when he moved to stand close behind her. She felt his heat all down her body as the mask pressed against her face. His fingers were in her hair again, fastening the ties.

An agony of embarrassment flooded her. Would she ever meet him now without remembering that kiss?

"Is it tight enough?" His voice sounded a little hoarse.

"Yes. Thank you." Cecily fought the stupid urge to sink back against him. Instead, she stepped away.

"You must promise to behave yourself at my ball," she warned. "My cousins will watch me, not to mention Montford."

"I think my self-control extends to refraining from ravishing you in public, my lady," said Ashburn, amused. "With or without your fearsome relatives in attendance."

"Well, how should I know what you would do?" said Cecily, exasperated. "I am inexperienced in such matters."

"Most women count that as a virtue." He cocked his head, as if making a discovery. "But not you, Lady Cecily." He regarded her with dawning sympathy. "Ignorance in any form bothers you, doesn't it? You so hate to concede the advantage."

The truth of his statement struck home. How had he, a man who'd met her only once before, understood how greatly she disliked being unenlightened on this or any important subject? Even more irksome, her lack of experience left her at a loss in her dealings with him.

She might have been prepared to flout most constraints on a lady's education and occasionally to court danger in her nocturnal adventures. But even she'd never plucked up the courage to rebel against the tenet that a lady must remain pure for her husband.

Of course, no one had ever offered her the opportunity to be impure before.

But even setting aside the morality of it, there were too many risks involved in those sorts of liaisons. Despite her sheltered upbringing, she'd heard tales about fallen women. The man always walked away unscathed and blameless, leaving the lady pregnant and disgraced. Well, Cecily might be innocent, but she was not a fool.

That didn't mean she wasn't burningly curious about the sort of intimate relations both her married cousins so obviously enjoyed.

Ashburn nodded as if she'd spoken her thoughts. "I suppose I need not tell you that the best remedy for ignorance is *education*."

Though the severity of his expression hadn't changed, his deep voice warmed with amusement. He was laughing at her!

Cecily looked him straight in the eye and dropped a disdainful curtsy. "My thanks, Your Grace, but in this case I believe ignorance is bliss."

He returned her courtesy with an elegant bow, but there was an unholy gleam in those brilliant amber eyes. "Bliss can be a relative term, Lady Cecily."

His low laughter followed her as she turned on her heel and fled.

Chapter Seven

Rand did not move for many moments after Lady Cecily had gone. His heart had not yet resumed its normal pace after that astonishing kiss. His body remained hot and urgent. It had taken all his will to obey her command to stop.

He'd given no idle warning when he said it was better for them both if she left.

Laughable the way his careful plans had flown from his head the moment he'd laid eyes on her. The debacle with Louise and Freddy had shaken him; that was true. But Lady Cecily herself was the cause of far greater disturbance to his equilibrium.

The romantic waltz he'd planned, the moonlit walk in the garden, all of it had vanished from his mind as soon as he'd seen her. He'd thought her striking when garbed in a page boy's costume. He hadn't been prepared for the vision she presented when clothed as a woman, with her feminine curves molded and revealed so enticingly. The deep, shining purple of her domino made her eyes appear like pools of gleaming chocolate in the pale cream of her face. And those lips . . . God. His body gave a reminiscent shudder.

Lady Cecily had taught him another salutary lesson tonight. He was not at all in the habit of denying himself when it came to carnal pleasures. But then his interest had never alighted on a gently bred virgin before.

It was a damnable predicament.

Or was it? His heart picked up pace again as the idea struck him like the slap of another man's glove.

Had he in fact found the perfect wife?

The most powerful and swift sense of rightness overtook him at that notion. He had an insane impulse to go after her this very moment and make his proposals.

No, that would not be wise. Despite the overwhelming certainty *he* felt, she would need convincing.

A duke generally assumed that if proposed, the lady in question must say yes. But Rand would lay steep odds that if he ran after her now, she would not have him. That only made her more attractive.

Despite her predilection for breaking into his house, Lady Cecily Westruther was a perfect candidate for his bride. She was the ward of a duke, the daughter of an earl. She had poise and confidence. He'd no doubt of her ability to run a household, to act as hostess to his guests in all their infinite variety.

Most of all, he needed an heir. His vision darkened as heat swept through his body. It would be no hardship to bed Lady Cecily Westruther as often as possible in furtherance of that aim.

Would material considerations weigh with such

a girl? Certainly, she seemed unimpressed by his rank, his wealth, and his family. She was not indifferent to *him,* however. He could use that.

He must persuade her that she had as much to gain by her marriage to him as he did. And yes, he could be very persuasive when he wished.

True, there were obstacles beyond the lady herself. Montford might prove a problem; the duke might have chosen Cecily's mate already. Rand's jaw tightened. He would deal with Montford and any prospective bridegroom.

But the business with Jonathon must always stand in the way. If Lady Cecily found out the truth, she'd never forgive him. Nor would she forgive him for doing all in his power to prevent her pursuing her mission.

Clever and quite ruthless of her to search his library rather than seek him out at this masquerade. He admired her the more for that bit of deviousness. But there was nothing to find in this room and he would make sure she did not discover anything he didn't want her to know.

Jonathon's secret was safe.

Cecily's heart expanded with joy as she looked around the drawing room where her family gathered before dinner.

All her Westruther cousins were there tonight. Well, all except one. But then Beckenham never came to town. It was useless to expect him.

Eight-year old Luke wormed his way through the Westruther cousins to Cecily. "Thank you ever so much for inviting me to dine, Cousin Cecily. Aunt Jane says I can't stay for the ball and I shouldn't wish to anyway, on account of there's *dancing* and *girls*." He gave a small, eloquent shudder that made Cecily laugh.

Constantine, Luke's guardian and Jane's husband, glanced down at him and sighed. "How much you have to learn, my boy. Dancing and most particularly *girls* are quite the best things about balls."

After an admonishment from Jane, Luke made his bow. It had a touch of the swagger about it that was so reminiscent of Constantine that Cecily exchanged a laughing glance with Jane over the boy's head.

"Ought you to be here?" Cecily asked Jane in a lowered voice. "I cannot thank you enough for coming, but is it wise, this close to your confinement? I worry about you, dearest."

Jane, big with child, waved away her concerns. "Why should I miss all the fun?" she said. "I'm as healthy as a horse, though *some* people might think I'm made of spun glass." She said the last with a meaningful glance at her darkly handsome husband.

"You look marvelous, my dear," said Cecily. Was it pregnancy or marriage to Constantine that made Jane's fair skin glow with health, her gray eyes sparkle, her hair a richer, deeper auburn? Whatever elixir Jane had found ought to be bottled and sold.

Embracing her cousin gingerly over her formidable bump, Cecily looked up at Jane's husband. "I hope you are taking good care of her," she said severely.

"And good evening to you, too, brat," said Constantine, leaning in to kiss her cheek. "I've yet to hear of any riots or even mere scandals of your making. I confess I'm disappointed. What *have* you been doing with your time?"

"I'm lulling you all into a false sense of security," she said lightly.

But Constantine had made a pertinent observation. Since the business with Lavinia and Jonathon and Ashburn, Cecily had had little leisure for making idle mischief and little inclination for such antics, either.

Any risks she took now were for the purpose of avoiding scandal, not creating it. Not because she feared notoriety so much. Westruthers never cared what people said about them, after all. But because that dratted letter would hurt Norland if it came to light, not to mention putting her betrothal to him in jeopardy.

Rosamund and Griffin claimed her attention then. Though he was an earl, Griffin would never be totally at ease in elegant company. It would be a pity if he lost all his rough edges, however, for this was exactly how Rosamund liked him.

Cecily watched Griffin critically as he bowed to her. "You've been practicing," she said approvingly as she curtsied in return. "I trust you will break your rule tonight and dance with me. I am the guest of honor, after all."

The big man flushed and glanced about, presumably for assistance. When Rosamund simply widened her eyes at him and let him sink or swim on his own, he cleared his throat. "I, uh. Ahem. I don't—"

"He'd be *honored*," said Rosamund, turning the full power of her smile upon her hapless husband. "Wouldn't you, Griffin?"

It was a fascinating phenomenon to observe the effect of Rosamund's smile upon her lord. The great colossus of a man melted on the spot.

He did not even glance in Cecily's direction. "Yes, of course. Honored," he repeated absently.

"I'll hold you to it," said Cecily, but she wasn't sure if he'd heard her. Clearly, Griffin expected to be a very lucky man later this evening.

"Cecily, where is Tibby tonight?" asked Rosamund.

"Oh, didn't you know? Tibby was called away to her sister in Cambridgeshire. I believe the poor thing is ill."

"What a shame," said Rosamund.

"Yes, rotten luck," agreed Cecily. "I do feel for her. Particularly when—" She broke off as the male contingent shouted greetings to a newcomer.

A smile burst over her face as she saw who it was. *Beckenham*. Her cousin Beckenham, who never, ever came to London, stood in the doorway, looking gravely handsome in his evening clothes.

"Becks!" She ran to her cousin and flung her arms about him in a tight bear hug, ignoring Jane's admonition to mind her gown.

"Oh, Becks! I am so glad to see you." She squeezed his hands, bouncing on her toes. "Thank you for coming."

Beckenham's stern features relaxed a little as he returned the grip of her hands and held them wide so he could see her finery. "You look very grown up," he said softly.

Cecily interpreted that mild statement as approval of no mean order. Tears stung behind her eyes.

In an effort to collect herself, she curtsied grandly. "Why thank you, my lord."

They had locked horns on many occasions over the years, for her wayward behavior provoked the staid Beckenham to no end. Nevertheless, he held a special place in her heart. For Becks to make the sacrifice of returning to Town to attend a ball in her honor was a gesture she'd never forget.

"Beckenham, you oaf! Cecily is *exquisite*," corrected Andrew, Viscount Lydgate. He eyed her white silk gown with approval. "You might not have Rosamund's beauty, Cec, but I'll say this for you: I never met another woman who could match you for taste."

"What an evening for backhanded compliments," murmured Xavier, pouring the last glass of sherry. When the drinks were distributed, he said, "To Cecily. Unleashed, at last, on an unsuspecting society. The ton will never be the same."

Her cousins took turns roasting Cecily mercilessly. She laughed harder than anyone at the jokes at her expense and the many stories that began with *Do you remember the time she . . .*

Laughter and love surrounded her like a warm embrace. She was glad that she'd insisted on a small, private dinner this evening.

The Duke of Montford came in, accompanied by Norland, and their party was complete.

A small hand found Cecily's and tugged. Obedient to Luke's wordless command, Cecily bent down to give him her ear.

"Is *that* him?" he whispered.

"Yes, darling," she whispered back. "That's the man I'm going to marry." Why did she feel a trifle reluctant to admit that to Luke? She was not ashamed of Norland, was she?

"I know that," breathed Luke with a touch of scorn for her slow-wittedness. "But that's him, isn't it? That's Sir Ninian Finian." He snorted and his shoulder shook beneath her hand. "Oh, Lord! How f-funny."

Cecily's heart sank. She recalled now that Jane had read those silly stories to Luke. Dear God, if a mere child could recognize her caricature of Norland in all that nonsense . . .

Before she could answer him, her attention was claimed by the butler's announcing dinner. All she could do was throw Luke a minatory look. In response, he sobered and ostentatiously pressed his lips together. She hoped to goodness that meant he knew not to breathe a word about that dratted book.

On tenterhooks, she caught Luke observing her betrothed keenly throughout the evening, like a dog watching for scraps its master might throw from the table. A small smirk of private enjoyment appeared on Luke's face whenever Norland said or did something Sir Ninian–like. Cecily died a thousand deaths, anticipating some indiscretion that would expose her.

Thankfully, none came. Indeed, she could not blame Luke for his enjoyment of the situation. Norland looked sadly out of place in this gathering. Cecily winced several times as he failed to understand her cousins' jokes or recounted an incident to do with one of his experiments that could not be of interest to anyone but him.

Norland looked completely discomfited by the

casual way the family talked across the table to one another. She rather feared he was shocked by some of her exploits that her cousins couldn't resist recounting over dinner.

It wasn't poor Norland's fault that he was so awkward. He'd had a formal upbringing with no siblings close to him in age. He couldn't understand the exuberance and eccentricity of the Westruthers. She doubted if he'd ever be absorbed into their circle the way Constantine and Griffin had.

But then, that made it easier for her to keep him at a distance, didn't it?

A clutch of apprehension made Cecily's smile waver for an instant.

She dismissed it. At the ball this evening, Montford would announce her betrothal to Norland. After tonight there would be no going back.

"My compliments," said Lady Arden, glancing around the ballroom. "I could not have done better myself."

"High praise, indeed," murmured the Duke of Montford. The ball he'd thrown for Cecily's debut was as spectacular as befitted a lady who was not only a Westruther heiress but also his ward.

It was nearing the supper hour, when he'd undertaken to announce Cecily's engagement to the Duke of Norland.

The truth was, he approached that task with something akin to dread. Once the betrothal was public, it was to all intents and purposes irrevocable.

"Something troubles you, Your Grace?" Lady Arden's voice was gentle.

Montford produced his blandest expression. "Troubled? I? Perish the thought."

Her low laughter sounded in his ear. "I know you quite well by now, my friend. Do not seek to deceive me." She tapped her chin. "Let me guess. You are having second thoughts about allowing the spirited Cecily to marry that dreadful bore."

He was silent, which was all the confirmation she needed.

"Don't do it, Julian." Her hand touched his arm. "Dance with me and we shall discuss the matter."

But he never danced; she knew that. Montford did not answer that part of her command.

Instead, he said, "You will not alter my decision. This match was made long before I had guardianship of Lady Cecily. I cannot, in conscience, put a stop to it. Particularly when Lady Cecily is content to have it so."

Though every fiber of his being urged him to forbid the betrothal, his hands were tied by his own principles. Hoist with his own petard, in fact. Wouldn't his adversaries at the Ministry of Marriage laugh themselves sick if they knew it?

"What does a chit that age know about marriage?" scoffed Lady Arden. "Oh, I grant you, Lady Cecily is not your average simpering debutante. She has character, that one. But at a mere twenty, she is ill equipped to determine her own path."

Her words were like a shower of darts in his flesh. A line from Shakespeare ran through his head: *If it were done when 'tis done, then 'twere well / It were done quickly.* He'd delayed Cecily's debut for two years, waiting for her to come to her senses, but she held fast to the understanding her parents had forged with Norland's years before.

It was an effort to reiterate, "I shall announce the engagement at supper."

He felt, rather than saw, Lady Arden shake her head at him. "Then I shall be very sorry indeed," she said softly, and drifted away.

Rand never bemoaned his exalted position nor the responsibilities that went with it, but tonight he'd happily consign them all to the Devil.

His aunt had come to him in a rare taking that afternoon with the news that Freddy had not returned to his lodgings at all after the masquerade and in fact had not been seen by anyone since.

If it weren't for the affair with Louise, Rand might well have dismissed his aunt's hysteria as overreaction.

Young men tended to be erratic. They went on drinking sprees that lasted days; they jaunted off to the countryside without warning if a friend suddenly decided that it was a jolly idea.

Ten to one, Freddy was sleeping off his excesses in the arms of a luscious woman or, indeed, on the couch at a crony's lodgings. He might have taken it into his head to drive down to his property in Kent or made a bet that he'd walk backwards to Brighton, for all Rand knew.

Then why was Rand trawling Freddy's usual haunts, looking for the boy? He tried to shake off the nasty, uneasy feeling that wrapped around his chest like armor.

His inquiries finally led him to a gin shop in a disreputable part of town, and there the trail went cold. If the boy had imbibed much of the rotgut they served in this place, he could not have gone far without assistance.

Yes, the young gentleman had a companion. No, they couldn't rightly say what he looked like. Only that he was older and a toff, too, by the way he was dressed. But no one had any idea where the two men had gone when they stumbled out some time after dawn that morning.

Rand took out his watch. Hell! It was past eleven, and he'd need to return home to wash and change before he attended Lady Cecily's ball.

In one last effort, he retraced his steps and returned to Freddy's lodgings on Half Moon Street.

"Freddy?" Rand pounded on the door. If Freddy had gone home to sleep off his libations, perhaps he hadn't heard Rand's knock earlier.

He pounded again and heard a crash within, followed by mumbling and a shuffling of feet. Relief broke over Rand, mingled with a good dose of annoyance. While he'd been out combing the hells and sluiceries of London, Freddy had been tucked up snugly in his own bed.

The door opened a crack and Freddy's face appeared, white and owlish. "Wha—? Oh! 'S you, Ashburn. Come in. Wanted to—" He swallowed with difficulty, winced, and put a hand to his head. "—'pologize."

But Rand already had his pocketbook in hand. He took out the draft for a thousand pounds, picked up Freddy's hand, and slapped the draft into his palm. "Here. Pay your damned debt."

Incomprehension and wonder broke over Freddy's haggard features.

"This is the last time, Freddy. If it happens again, I'll personally put those nags of yours on the auction block."

Freddy still stood there, staring at the bank draft in disbelief. With the strong, discomfiting feeling he'd failed the boy once again, Rand turned on his heel and left.

But his concerns over his heir soon faded, overtaken by elation and the sharp pounding of excitement in his blood. The prospect of seeing Lady Cecily again made him pick up his pace.

Damn that boy for making him miss half the ball! She must have given him up by now. A fine prelude to a proposal of marriage.

Ought he to reconsider his plan to pay his addresses tonight? But no. Now that he'd fixed on Lady Cecily as his future bride, he didn't want to wait.

Anticipation burned in his chest. If he played his cards right, by the end of this evening, Lady Cecily Westruther would be his.

Chapter Eight

Butterflies waged war in Cecily's stomach as she moved through the steps of a country dance with her cousin Bertram. She could not seem to rid herself of the most absurd sense of impending doom. Which was utterly ridiculous, considering how steadfastly she'd refused to draw back from a formal betrothal to Norland.

Tonight, the betrothal would be announced. Tomorrow the best legal minds in England would negotiate marriage settlements.

Cecily had made a point of being present at the preliminary discussions between Montford and his advisers. It was the duty of every woman to understand her finances and the duty of every heiress to ensure that the fortunes of all her children were secured, not just the firstborn son. She didn't intend to have children, of course, but one never knew. It was as well to be prepared for eventualities.

All was in train to make her the Duchess of Norland. The announcement tonight would seal her fate.

She ought to be jubilant. Yet, she couldn't help an absurd tendency to glance over her shoulder.

But no, the Duke of Ashburn wasn't here, after all. That sinking realization ought not to affect her so keenly.

What did she expect? That he'd ride in on a white charger and rescue her? She didn't wish to be rescued. If she'd wanted to escape this engagement, she could have done it without Ashburn's help. Montford had given her every opportunity to withdraw.

She turned her attention to her partner. Her cousin Bertram was a handsome man—or at least that was what many ladies claimed. Cecily couldn't see it herself. He had all the dark good looks of her branch of the Westruther family, but his mouth was too red and too fleshy for her taste and his complexion a shade too florid. But then his character completely spoiled any charm his looks might have held in any case.

Had he been a thoroughly pleasant fellow, Cecily might still have resented him for stepping into her brother's shoes. Bertram was not a pleasant fellow, however. He was a pompous prig and an avaricious one, besides, and Cecily did not hide her dislike as well as she ought.

"So, little cousin, your duke has launched you into Society in rare style," said Bertram in his sneering way as they wound through the set. "I daresay this evening cost him a pretty penny. It hardly seems worth it when you are already spoken for. He would have done better to invest his funds."

"How like you to express concern for my guardian's purse, Bertram," said Cecily. "His Grace would be most gratified to hear it."

"Never understood why the duke should take a parcel of brats under his wing in the first place," said Bertram, as they circled each other and separated again.

"No, I suppose you wouldn't," muttered Cecily.

She was not at all certain of the reason either, but she did not question Montford's integrity as Bertram seemed to do. She'd long suspected the duke of a hidden streak of altruism, though of course she'd never dared to question him about it. Even her precocity had limits.

She wondered if His Grace knew the reason himself.

Oh, it was usual for the head of a family to be made guardian of its children in the event of their parents' death. But Montford could have easily placed them all with other relations rather than undertake their upbringing personally. He'd rescued Jane from virtual slavery and taken Xavier and Rosamund from a vicious mother. He'd saved Cecily from being obliged to live with Bertram and Lavinia until her marriage—a fate that didn't bear thinking of.

Something seemed to catch Bertram's eye at the end of the ballroom. He so far forgot himself as to mutter an oath under his breath.

From the corner of her eye, Cecily saw Lavinia lay her hand on Lord Percy's arm and disappear with him onto the terrace. Perhaps Lavinia was trying to persuade Percy to return the pearls. Cecily did not hold out much hope in that direction.

Bertram seemed to recollect where he was and put on an air of unconcern. He made conversation with Cecily throughout the rest of the dance, but his attention kept flicking back to the terrace.

When the dance ended, she caught his elbow, effectively preventing him from going after his wife. "Will you escort me to the refreshment parlor, cousin? I'd give my eyes for some claret cup."

Rand arrived at Montford House to see Lady Cecily with the Duke of Norland, whirling sedately about the floor to the final strains of the supper waltz.

She looked every inch the aristocratic virgin, decked out in white, with her hair piled high and a pearl choker clasped about her slender neck. Tiny pearls dotted her coiffure, nestling among those luxuriant curls. The gems were no more lustrous than her skin, which seemed so fine as to be translucent, a dramatic contrast to her dark features and rosy lips.

Watching her closely, Rand cocked his head. Was it his imagination, or did she seem a trifle pale? Composed, yes, with that queenly tilt to her chin that spoke of a self-confidence he found immensely attractive. But he couldn't rid himself of the notion she was unhappy about something.

Norland was not a close acquaintance, but Rand knew him well enough through their mutual involvement in the Promethean Club. A dull dog, certainly, but as inoffensive and bland as whey. What could the fellow have done to make her look like that?

The music stopped; Lady Cecily and her partner

joined in the applause. Resting her hand on his proffered arm, Cecily made as if to accompany him to the dining room.

Suddenly, as if someone had called her name, she turned her head and her eyes locked with unerring precision on Rand's. A strange force pulled him, like a magnet attracting a piece of metal. He resisted it, testing its power.

A blush warmed the pallor of Lady Cecily's neck and cheeks, and he knew without a shadow of doubt she relived their kiss.

He started toward her.

With a tiny shake of her head, she turned her back on Rand and moved with Norland to join the flow of guests leaving the ballroom.

He couldn't allow that. Without seeming to hurry, Rand let his long legs eat up the space between them.

"Mind if I join you?"

The couple stopped and looked around. Norland's eyebrows were raised in surprise; Lady Cecily's dark brows lowered in the beginnings of a scowl.

Rand kept his own eyebrows where they were and attempted to look benign. It was not an expression he had ever cultivated, so he wasn't sure if it was successful.

"I have arrived late, I'm afraid," he said, bowing to them both. "Too late to form a party for supper. Might I join yours?"

Lady Cecily opened her mouth, but Norland's answer forestalled her. "Yes, of course, Ashburn. In fact, it's a good thing you're here. I want to talk to you about funding for my latest project."

"Certainly." Rand gestured toward the dining room. "Shall we?"

The last thing he wished to do was listen to Norland drone on about infectious diseases all night. What a slow-top, to think of science when he had Lady Cecily Westruther on his arm!

Rand slanted a glance down at her. Clearly the girl wasn't as up to snuff as she seemed to think if she allowed herself to be saddled with Norland as a supper partner. Instead of sending Rand those dagger looks from her remarkable eyes, she ought to thank him on bended knee for saving her from a period of unalleviated boredom.

When they'd found somewhere to sit, Norland said to Cecily, "I'll fetch you a plate, my lady. Is there anything you'd prefer?"

Lady Cecily said, "Whatever you choose will be perfect, Your Grace."

Rand cut in. "A couple of lobster patties will do for me, thank you, Norland."

The duke looked a little startled but said, "Oh. Yes. Yes, right. I'll, ah, attend to that now."

As Rand watched him go, he felt the heat of reproach in Lady Cecily's regard.

"What do you think you're doing?" she demanded in a low, impassioned tone.

Rand lifted a finger to a passing footman and procured them champagne. "Anticipating my supper, as a matter of fact. I missed dinner and I am quite hungry."

"That's not what I meant," she hissed. "What is your object in seeking me out like this? We are not supposed to know each other."

"But Norland introduced us."

"No, he didn't!"

He smiled. "Oh, I think you'll find that he did. Never fear. He's so absentminded, he will believe us if we assure him it's true."

Lady Cecily bit back a hasty response. She swept a furtive look around, as if she were calculating how frank she could be, based on their proximity to the other guests.

"You've placed me in a most awkward position," she said quietly. "I—I deeply regret what happened last night—"

"My only regret is about what *didn't* happen last night," he murmured.

Her dark eyes flashed at his effrontery. He was enjoying himself immensely.

"In fact," he murmured, "I regret that I cannot do it again, here and now. You look—" He paused, considering her. "—quite delicious, you know."

Her face turned bright pink. "If you came here to tease me with such nonsense, I can only say that I am disappointed in your character, Your Grace. I'd thought you were a gentleman."

The slightest tremor of emotion in her voice made him frown. He searched her face, and the deep trouble he saw there dismayed him. "Forgive me. I didn't mean to distress you."

"Distressed? I?" She cut her gaze away and bit her lip and tapped her fan on the table in a fast rhythm. "You mistake, sir. You have no power to distress me."

"That is a relief," he said dryly. "Cecily—"

He realized he'd reached for her hand only when she snatched it away. In a strangled tone, she said between her teeth, "Kindly recall that we are in public, Your Grace, and refrain from addressing me so familiarly. Are you *determined* to ruin me?"

No, I'm determined to marry you, Rand thought. *And I cannot wait a day longer to make you mine.*

Damn this ball! "I must speak with you in private," he said. "I'll wait on the terrace. Slip away when you can."

"I *won't*—" She stopped, as if startled at having raised her voice. She continued more quietly, "I will not meet you anywhere. This has gone too far."

"Not nearly far enough," he corrected, capturing her eyes with his.

A current passed between them, just as it always did. The zing and sizzle of their attraction was too powerful even for an untried maiden to deny. She felt it. He knew that by the small gasp she gave and by the fact she'd not given him the cold setdown he knew he deserved. He'd wager Lady Cecily Westruther was not often lost for words. Or for cold setdowns, for that matter.

Before she could find an answer, Norland returned. He was all flustered and bothered, as if the simple act of putting a few plates of food together were some sort of Herculean labor.

Why would Lady Cecily keep company with such a fellow, even for the space of a supper dance?

Norland handed them their plates and seated himself on Lady Cecily's other side. Leaning across her as if she wasn't there, he waved his fork about. "Now, Ashburn. About that little matter of mine . . ."

Norland launched into a dry monologue about his latest line of research and the funding he needed to further his aims. Out of politeness as much as boredom, Rand would have turned the subject back to matters of more general interest, but he saw that Lady Cecily gradually relaxed under the lull of a conversation that did not require her participation.

That was a good thing. He did not wish her to be so on edge when he broached the subject uppermost in his mind. He did not want her to reject him summarily out of pride or fear or sheer contrariness.

So he listened to Norland, all the while conscious of Lady Cecily's every movement and mood.

Before the scientist could become entirely lost in his own circuitous explanations, the butler's mellifluous voice announced that the Duke of Montford wished to say a few words.

An expectant hush fell over the crowd. Intrigued, Rand glanced at Lady Cecily. The girl paled and tensed. Her gloved hand came up to run a fingertip along the pearl necklace at her throat, as if it felt too tight.

"Ah. The announcement," said Norland, as if he knew what was coming.

A strange feeling of presentiment filled Rand. He had the ridiculous urge to leap to his feet and shout at Montford to stop.

The duke surveyed the assembled crowd. His lips spread in that thin smile of his. "My lords, ladies, and gentlemen, it gives me great pleasure to hold this ball tonight in honor of my ward, Lady Cecily Westruther."

He paused for the polite applause that ensued. "But there is another reason to celebrate. Tonight, Lady Cecily has become betrothed to His Grace, the Duke of Norland."

In that moment, Rand knew precisely how his ancestors must have felt in a jousting match, when the lance connected with their guts and sent them flying to the ground.

A gasp swept the room. A Babel of conversation and exclamations broke out.

Paralyzed, Rand watched Norland take Lady Cecily's hand and help her rise. As she got to her feet, she looked back at Rand.

It was a swift glance, but in that instant Rand read the emotion in those dark eyes as if she spoke directly to him.

You should have listened when I told you I didn't want you. And it's your own damned fault that you didn't.

I am sorry.

It seemed to take forever for Norland to lead Cecily forward to where Montford stood. Rand felt as if he were in a nightmare where everything moved slowly, yet he was powerless to stop the progression of events.

As one, Lady Cecily and her betrothed turned to face the guests. Norland still held her hand, damn him! Damn him to hell.

And *she* . . . Lady Cecily Westruther looked pale but composed. Her lips trembled as if she tried very hard to smile but couldn't quite manage such hypocrisy. She didn't look again in Rand's direction, much as he willed her to do so. Nor did she regard her fiancé.

Rand wanted to stride over there and shake some sense into that clever brain of hers. How *could* she? How could she throw herself away on Norland, of all men?

Didn't she know Rand had laid claim to her last night with that kiss?

All around him, glasses were charged and a toast drunk to the happy couple. Rand drank, too. He drank, all right. Drained his champagne glass, wishing very much it were brandy and not this fizzy French wine. He'd need a gallon of it to get as drunk as he'd like.

Supper drew to a close as the crowd converged on the couple to congratulate and wish them happy.

Rand sat alone among the steadily emptying tables as the resolve hardened in his mind and in his soul.

This betrothal was a farce and a tragedy. He could not allow it to stand.

He would make Lady Cecily Westruther his wife. If that meant deceit and seduction and even scandal, so be it.

He didn't care what it took.

Chapter Nine

Cecily was ready to shatter by the time Montford stepped in to stem the flow of congratulations and draw her away from the crowd. With some suave words of thanks and excuses, he led her back to the ballroom.

She managed to say, "I have yet to thank you for this evening, Your Grace. The ball has been a marvelous success, don't you think?"

"I wish I could say the pleasure has been unalloyed, Cecily," he returned. "I must say, I find myself strangely disappointed. I'd expected fireworks of some sort when you finally hit the ton. And yet, here you are, accepting your fate like a lamb. Indeed, you have given me less trouble than either Jane or Rosamund."

Please don't.

She knew the sentiments that underlay his words. He thought her a poor creature for accepting her duty so tamely. He'd wanted her to renege on the arrangement with Norland. She hoped he didn't intend to try persuading her at this stage. She didn't think she had the strength to fence with him now.

But she ought to have known the duke would not repine uselessly when the deed was done.

Eyeing her with more understanding than she wished him to have, he sighed. "You would benefit from some air, my dear. Perhaps a stroll on the terrace?"

"Thank you," she managed.

Montford was nothing if not perceptive. She hoped no one else discerned from her demeanor that she was anything but pleased with her engagement. And why should she be *dis*pleased? That was a question, indeed.

He frowned. "I cannot leave my guests, but—Ah! There is Rosamund. I'll fetch her for you."

Cecily battled with an absurd desire to burst into sobs. She'd never thought of herself as the sort of ninny who wept at trifles. In fact, she'd always prided herself on her resilience, hadn't she?

She wished she'd never gone to Ashburn's house that night.

"Cecily." Rosamund took her hands, her blue eyes suspiciously bright. Her smile seemed effortful. "Well, it is done. I must wish you happy."

"Yes." Cecily squeezed her cousin's gloved fingers, grateful at least that Rosamund had now stopped trying to persuade her to throw Norland over. "Yes, it is done and now I should like to go somewhere. . . . Oh, I don't know where. I want to be alone for a while, but I can't go back to my bedchamber. My maid will be there. The servants will talk."

Rosamund glanced to the long windows at the end of the ballroom. "Shall we take a turn on the terrace, as the duke suggested?"

"No!"

Rosamund blinked and Cecily realized she'd spoken too vehemently. If she walked on the terrace, Ashburn might think she courted his attention—or worse, that she'd obeyed his autocratic command to meet him there.

Cecily pressed her stomach with one hand, smoothing the silk that covered it over and over. "No, there are too many people there already."

Rosamund considered. "What about the summerhouse?"

"Won't it be locked?" said Cecily.

Was it a trick of the light or did Rosamund blush a little? "It so happens that I have a key." She patted her reticule as if to indicate the key's current location.

That caught Cecily's interest. *"Oh, really?"* she drawled. "Planning a moonlit tryst, were you, my dear?"

"It is something of a tradition with Griffin and me." An uncharacteristically naughty twinkle sparked in Rosamund's blue eyes; then a grin broke over her face as if she could not contain it. That look enhanced Rosamund's exquisite features until her beauty became almost unbearable.

All at once, Cecily felt burningly envious. Not of Rosamund's beauty, but of the excitement and passion and soul-deep trust she shared with her husband.

"Well, as long as I won't be in the way," she said, wishing she hadn't sounded so wistful.

"Of course not." Rosamund slipped the key from her reticule and Cecily unobtrusively palmed it.

"Shall I come with you?" asked Rosamund.

Cecily shook her head. "No. I want to be alone, just for a while. It's not as if I need a chaperone in my own home, after all. Nothing can happen to me in Montford's garden."

A reckless statement. She knew very well what might happen to her if Ashburn found her there. But on reflection, she thought it better to have this confrontation than to let resentments fester and conversations go unfinished. If tonight's announcement hadn't dissuaded him, she needed to end Ashburn's pursuit of her, once and for all.

Besides, she still needed that letter.

Rosamund kissed her cheek. "If you are not back in half an hour, I will send Griffin looking for you," she said.

For the sake of discretion, Cecily did not leave by the central terrace steps but through the library and down the side staircase. Screened from the ballroom by a high yew hedge, she hurried down to the summerhouse at the edge of the garden.

Her confidence in Ashburn's ingenuity was not misplaced. Only a few minutes passed before he walked in.

His face was in shadow, its harsh angles limned by moonlight. He looked even more enigmatic than usual, if that were possible.

"Why?" His expression might remain impassive, but his voice betrayed him. It seemed strained, perhaps even a little hoarse.

She didn't pretend to misunderstand him. "The alliance was arranged between our families many years ago."

"And you did not see fit to inform me of that last night?"

"Why should I?" she said. "What business is it of yours whom I marry?"

That statement should have been enough. But something compelled her to add, "I told you I did not go to your house for any amorous purpose."

"Your words told me you were not interested," he said. "Your response to my kiss said something entirely different." His voice deepened. "Indeed, it spoke volumes, Lady Cecily."

She felt the heat of his regard as if she stood before a roaring hearth. "Whatever you perceived, or thought you perceived, that is irrelevant now. I am pledged to Norland."

The mention of her betrothed's name seemed to act powerfully on him. Ashburn loomed over her. Tall, deep-chested. Overwhelming in a very masculine way.

He took her by the shoulders, not as if to shake her, but as if he braced her while the world tumbled around her. "You cannot marry him."

She must. She drew away from him and repressed a shiver of loss as the warmth of his hands left her skin. She felt as if he *had* shaken her. Right down to her soul.

No. That was ridiculous. One did not fall in love or even form a mild attachment after a scatter of short meetings. She admired Ashburn's intellect; Lord knew his manner coupled with his dark good looks made him immensely attractive on a physical level, too. He had a powerful presence. How could any woman remain unaffected by him?

And yet . . . Honesty compelled her to admit there was more to it than that. There *was* a connection between them. She'd felt a sharp tug of recognition from the first instant she'd laid eyes on the Duke of Ashburn.

But she didn't want to explore that connection. She knew down to her bones that if she gave in to him, the Duke of Ashburn would make demands on her she wasn't willing to fulfill.

Regrouping, she called on all her Westruther pride. "The fact that you were presumptuous enough to kiss me does not give you the right to dictate whom I marry."

That statement was self-evident, and yet somehow she felt the justice of his accusatory glare. Shame at her own behavior that night washed over her.

Frustration seemed to pour from him. He expelled a harsh breath and ran a hand through his cropped hair. "Rights? What do rights have to do with it? There is something between us, and you know it, Cecily. Instead of facing that, you are running away. Into a safe, dull marriage that can only end in your misery. *Norland*, for God's sake!"

"Do not speak of him like that! He is a good, kind man and he will make an excellent husband."

"Not in the ways that matter," he said softly. "Don't ever think it."

She flinched. Was he talking of marital relations? Again, her lack of experience set her at a disadvantage. If she knew what she was missing, it would be easier to dismiss.

Or did he mean he could offer something deeper

than physical satisfaction? She could scarcely believe he meant that.

Love, as she understood it, took time and close acquaintance to develop and mature. She and Ashburn had met a grand total of three times now. Besides, Ashburn was no silly debutante but a man of experience. He could not possibly believe in love at first sight.

What it came down to was this: His Grace, the Duke of Ashburn, was a proud man accustomed to getting his own way. He'd been thwarted, that was all. He'd intended to pursue her and set her up as his flirt for the season and make her fall in love with him because that's what men of his stamp did.

Now, however, she had taken on all the luster of the forbidden. A man of Ashburn's temperament must see her betrothal to another first as an affront, but ultimately as a challenge.

And if she succumbed and broke her engagement at his demand, what then? When he'd made her as desperate for him as he now appeared to be for her, he would lose interest as such men always did. He would leave her with nothing but the knowledge that she'd behaved badly toward a very good man.

"I want to marry you, Cecily," he said.

The world spun around her. *"What?"* she said faintly. "Will you stop at nothing to get your own way? How can you possibly wish to marry me?"

The buttons of his coat flashed as he made an impatient gesture. "I don't know how. I simply know that I do."

She put her hand to her cheek, then to her temple,

which had begun to throb. This was all about his pride, surely it was. How could a sane man wish to marry a woman he hardly knew?

Unless . . .

Her eyes narrowed. "You have not lost your fortune, have you?" She was a considerable heiress, after all. And she thought she might as well drown herself in the Serpentine if he wanted her for her money.

His brows twitched together in incomprehension, as if she'd just spoken in Mandarin. "Of course not."

"Then I—" Oh, it was all too much! She squeezed the bridge of her nose, but the burn behind her eyes wouldn't go away. She was tired and overwrought and this truly could not be happening to her. Not when she felt so low already.

He moved close to her again, and the touch of his hand was warm against her cheek. It was a gesture of comfort, even if his words gave her no quarter.

"Look at me," he urged, using his fingertips to tilt her chin so she must meet his gaze. "Tell me you don't feel that thrill of excitement when I touch you. Just being in the same room with you makes me forget everything else. When I'm not with you, you fill my thoughts. I can't sleep for thinking of you."

He bent his head closer, until his warm breath feathered over her lips. She knew a fierce longing for his mouth on hers again, for him to claim her, feast upon her as he'd threatened to do the previous night.

Cherries and cream and chocolate . . .

Cecily choked out the words. "I don't. I don't feel anything for you!"

"No?" His head angled slightly, as if he were attempting to gain better access to her mouth.

And while her attention was focused with painful anticipation on the tantalizing nearness and promise of those firm, skilled lips, his hand swiftly captured hers and held it. A sneaking, shabby thing to do to her, because she'd steeled herself for the kiss.

The warm, gentle clasp of his large hand slipped through her defenses. It felt insidiously intimate, even though they both wore gloves.

When he raised her hand to his lips, that weak, melting sensation threatened to overtake her. She fought it with a growing sense of desperate frustration, but she did not stop him. She could not.

He drew her against him. Heat sizzled and spread where their bodies touched. He bent to her, as if to follow through with that kiss.

The sheer gentle strength of him, the way his eyes compelled her to stay in the circle of his arms even while his hold on her did not, made her afraid. Afraid enough to summon the will to resist.

At the last second she turned her head, denying him that kiss. She placed her palm firmly against his hard chest and pushed away from him.

He stared at her. In another man she might have thought she detected pain.

"Let us talk of more neutral topics," she said shakily, taking another step back. "The papers. Jonathon's papers. Are you any closer to locating them?"

The duke's entire body seemed to vibrate with

tension. The time he took to answer her told its own tale. Despite her own confusion, she sensed the disarrangement of his cool, smooth presence and found some small wonder in it.

He recovered soon enough. With only a slight strain in his tone, he said, "There are acres of attics at my house and it is many years since I ordered Jonathon's papers to be stored up there. It is likely to take some time."

Her disappointment must have shown, for he amended quickly, "However, if I don't receive word next week, I'll go myself. If that would please you."

Anxiety made her throat tighten. If Ashburn read that dreadful letter she'd written to Jonathon, he'd have ample ammunition against her. He could smash her betrothal to smithereens. She must get to those papers before he did.

"I wish I could look for them myself," she blurted out, well aware that she was practically inviting herself to his house.

He frowned, considering. Slowly, he said, "What if I gave an impromptu house party? Then you can help me look."

When she hesitated, he murmured, "I'll even invite Norland."

She eyed him suspiciously. Why should he want Norland there? He was probably forming some Machiavellian plan to prevent their marriage, but she couldn't think how he might do that without her cooperation. It was well known that the gentleman couldn't break an engagement without ruining the lady.

Certainly, Ashburn was up to no good. But she needed that letter.

"You'd better speak to Montford, then." She moved to the door.

She was so agitated, it took her several fumbles with the handle before she wrenched the door open.

"Cecily."

"Yes?" She ought to admonish him for using her given name but she could not. Nor could she resist turning to look back at him. She saw a man hell-bent on a mission, determined in the face of insurmountable odds.

"When's the wedding?" he said. "Is the date set?"

"Yes. Three weeks from now," she answered. That might make him accept the inevitable.

He fixed her with a hard, vital stare that pierced her as cleanly as a sword point. "Then I have three weeks to make you change your mind."

Chapter Ten

When Rand left the shelter of the summerhouse, he took a different path from the one by which Lady Cecily had fled. The last thing he wished to do was to compromise her. If he did, he'd fling her into her betrothed's arms even sooner than she'd planned.

The wind had picked up and clouds scudded across the sky. A light drizzle fell, tiny drops sparkling in the moonlight as they powdered down. He quickened his pace and nearly collided with someone coming the other way.

He stepped back with an apology and made to proceed when a big, meaty hand fell hard on his shoulder. "Not so fast."

"Who is it, Griffin?" A low female voice came from behind the massive male form. Rand couldn't see her, but he assumed it was the man's wife.

"Oh. It's you." Tregarth released Rand's shoulder but he didn't move aside. "It's Ashburn," he said over his shoulder.

Lady Rosamund peeked out from behind him,

then edged around her colossus of a husband. She curtsied, seeming oblivious of the rain that misted down. A great beauty, the former Lady Rosamund Westruther. He'd danced with her many times in the past.

Rand bowed.

"Did you meet anyone down here in the garden, Your Grace?" asked Lady Tregarth. "Only I sent my cousin to the summerhouse to retrieve my handkerchief, you know. I wonder if you saw her."

"I saw no one," he lied. "But then I did not stroll as far as the summerhouse before it came on to rain."

Lady Tregarth's shoulders sagged just a little, as if she were relieved.

Rand smiled. "Well, I won't detain you. I must get back to the ballroom."

Tregarth didn't even return his bow. He seemed eager to be off. Why was finding Lady Cecily so pressing? She was hardly in danger here.

Rand watched the couple as they continued on sedately down the path. Then there was a low growl from Tregarth and a smothered laugh from his lady. Tregarth caught her hand and pulled her to him and kissed her passionately.

Ah. So that was it.

With a stab of envy for a man who held the woman of his choice in his arms, Ashburn turned and walked back to the ballroom.

Inside it, he had no trouble locating Lady Cecily. He seemed to home in on her as effortlessly as a pigeon flew back to its loft. But he gained no satisfaction there. She was dancing, yet again, with her betrothed.

With the taste of ashes in his mouth, Rand sought out the Duke of Montford.

They exchanged a great deal of suave small talk before Rand said, "When last we spoke, you suggested I avail myself of the ministry's services."

"Yes." Montford evinced no more than a polite interest in Ashburn's opening gambit, but the air seemed to still around him. Montford would crow about this coup for years to come.

Well, that couldn't be helped.

"I might be interested," said Rand. "I'll call on you tomorrow to discuss it."

Montford inclined his head. "I should be most happy to receive you, of course."

Rand smiled grimly to himself. Montford might not be quite so smug when he heard what Rand had to say.

Cecily spent the rest of the evening with her heart in an unprecedented state of agitation. The Duke of Ashburn did not leave after their encounter in the summerhouse as she hoped he might. He watched her all evening. She knew it without seeking him herself. She sensed his regard by the hot tingle at the nape of her neck.

The tension built inside her like a storm about to break. She had to laugh and flirt and dance and make inane conversation with that hum of anticipation thrumming through her body.

It was almost a relief when Ashburn finally approached her.

As she sipped lemonade with Beckenham and Lydgate, she spied the duke moving purposefully toward her. His tall, lean form sliced through the crowd like a knife through butter.

Quickly, she muttered. "Becks, I am engaged to you for this dance."

He looked down at her with grave amusement. "No, you're not."

She turned to Lydgate, putting a hand on his arm. "Andy, then. You must partner me for the next waltz."

Lydgate eyed her over his wineglass as if she'd run mad. "Dashed if I'll stand up for a second time with my own cousin. I have a reputation to uphold."

He turned his golden head to survey the crowd. "Whom are you trying to avoid?"

"But Andy—"

"Ah! Ashburn." Beckenham bowed, cutting off Cecily's protest. "Come to claim your dance?"

Cecily sent Beckenham a glare that promised retribution later.

Ashburn's attention was fixed on her. "Indeed." He held out his hand to her. "Lady Cecily?"

Andy plucked the lemonade glass from her unresisting fingers and made a shooing motion. "Don't mind us, dearest cousin. Off you go."

Outmaneuvered by her horrid relations, she had no choice but to lay her fingertips on the duke's proffered arm. She placed them there gingerly, as if he were made of live coals.

Something burned hot in his eyes as he looked down at her. "I'm honored," he said, and led her from the refreshment parlor.

This ball won hands down as the longest evening of her life. Her heart, which had been rocketing about in her chest since Ashburn appeared on the scene, took up a hard, steady hammer in her throat. She might choke on it if she spoke.

Why had she never registered before how intimate a dance the waltz was? She'd thought herself in danger in the isolation of the summerhouse. Here, in the ballroom with dozens of people looking on, she felt no safer.

When Ashburn's arm encircled her, she became acutely aware of the solid power of his muscles, the heat and pressure of his gloved hand at her waist.

His other hand clasped hers lightly, but the latent strength and dexterity of his fingers, the size of the palm engulfing hers struck her anew.

And when she rested her hand on his shoulder and they moved into the dance, all she could think about was the circle their bodies made. Or rather, the space inside that circle. A no-man's-land into which his legs might intrude as he stepped into a turn or her skirts might billow, but no part of their upper bodies would cross.

She contemplated that interesting, fraught space in silence, shamefully aware of her cowardice in avoiding his regard. Then she lifted her chin to look up into his face. And all she could think about was his kiss.

The yearning in her body was stupid and painful and traitorous. The more she fought it, the stronger it seemed to become.

So *this* was desire. How extraordinary. How confoundedly inconvenient!

She told herself it was a physical reaction, an appetite, the same as hunger or thirst. Hadn't Jane explained to her long ago that men could feel desire with no corresponding affection at all?

Surely that must be true of women, too. For Cecily did not feel at all affectionate toward Ashburn. Particularly when he watched her in that insufferable, knowing way.

"Stop looking at me like that," he murmured in a pleasant, conversational tone. "People will talk."

She jumped. "Like what? How did I look?"

"As if you can't decide whether to kiss me or kill me," he answered. "You might as well surrender to the inevitable, Lady Cecily. You will never marry Norland."

She plastered a society smile on her face and spoke between her teeth. "Not only are you mistaken, you are impertinent. This conversation is highly improper."

"Not half as improper as I'd like it to be," he said. "But I promised to behave myself in public, didn't I?"

"It's a good thing for you we are in public or I'd punch you in the nose," said Cecily, smiling relentlessly.

His lips twitched. "You will have ample opportunity to practice your pugilistic talents at my house party next week."

"That's if Montford approves." She feared her guardian's consent to the house party visit as much as she needed it.

"Oh, Montford will approve," said Ashburn, whirling her down the room. "I'll see to that."

She eyed him incredulously. "You do not know the duke very well if you can be so sanguine."

"On the contrary," he said. "I have long been

acquainted with Montford's methods." She felt the slight shrug of his shoulder beneath her palm. "Handling His Grace is very simple. One has but to show him how his own interests might be served by agreeing to what one wants."

She narrowed her eyes. She'd never met a man who could manipulate the duke, but it seemed Ashburn might make a decent attempt.

Rallying, she answered, "In politics, perhaps. But do you truly think he would put his own interests above my happiness?" She knew people saw Montford as a cold, unfeeling man, but that went too far.

"I think he will support my suit," said Ashburn, neatly sidestepping the question. "You have called me conceited. That may be so. But anyone can see you will be happier as my wife than as Norland's. Montford could wish that this had all transpired before your engagement to Norland was formally announced, but he will be fully alive to the advantages of changing grooms."

She feared he was right. Oh, not about being happier with him. What nonsense! But Montford had urged her more than once to reconsider marrying Norland. He might welcome Ashburn's high-handed interference.

She felt the ground shift beneath her feet. "You speak of our marriage as a foregone conclusion," she said. "But I will not bend to anyone on this, not even my guardian. I will *never* marry you."

He smiled down at her. "Would you care to wager on that?"

She wished that rare smile of his didn't make her giddy, even when she was frustrated with him and his high-handed ways.

Between her teeth, she said, "Why can't you leave me alone? Why, of all the ladies you could have, do you want me?"

"I don't know." His arms were like steel as he spun her down the room. "I only know that I do."

Chapter Eleven

Cecily begged Rosamund to go with her to Ashburn's house party as chaperone, but Rosamund expected a visit from her sister-in-law, Jacqueline Maddox, so she regretfully declined.

"So unfortunate!" said Rosamund as they walked together in Hyde Park. The sun shone from a blue sky, and a light breeze ruffled Rosamund's golden curls. "I should dearly love to go, if only to see the sparks fly."

"I can't imagine what you mean," said Cecily airily. "I shall behave with utmost propriety, as I always do."

"Ha!" said Rosamund. "You could not even dance with him last night without fighting with him. *I* saw those dagger looks of yours, even if no one else noticed."

"Nonsense! We engaged in lively debate about impersonal topics, that is all," said Cecily. She could not possibly explain her association with Ashburn. Rosamund was a born romantic. She'd resume urging Cecily to reconsider her betrothal.

"I wonder what is behind the invitation?" said Rosamund.

"Behind it?" said Cecily innocently.

"Oh, come now, Cecily," said Rosamund, laughing. "Ashburn was clearly smitten with you."

"I'll smite him," Cecily muttered. She dearly wanted to smite *something*. "He sees me as a challenge because I am already spoken for. There is no true feeling there. Why, I hardly know the man!"

Rosamund frowned. "One would think he'd at least wait until the knot was tied between you and Norland before approaching you. I cannot like the way he is pursuing you so openly." Rosamund gave her parasol a thoughtful twirl. "I confess I am surprised at him. I never thought he was the sort of man to prey on innocents."

Rosamund thought Ashburn wished to strike up a liaison with Cecily? Startled, she put her hand on her cousin's arm. "No, no, you mistake!"

She didn't know why she felt the need to defend Ashburn's honor. God knew he had little enough of it to pursue another man's affianced bride, but . . .

"He—he wants to marry me," she blurted out.

"*What?*" Rosamund stopped short, staring at her.

Cecily darted a quick glance around. "Ashburn asked me to marry him in the summerhouse last night. Well," she amended pedantically, "he didn't ask, precisely. It was more of a command."

"And what did you say?" asked Rosamund in a hushed, awed tone.

"I said no, of course! What do you think I said? I'm engaged to Norland."

"Yes, but . . ." Tact probably held Rosamund

silent, but it was clear from her expression that she compared the two men in her mind—and Norland came a very poor second, no doubt. That made Cecily scowl all the more.

She erupted into speech. "You know, I think it very hard that I'm the only one of us all who hasn't made the least fuss or bother about accepting the man chosen for me. Everything was going smoothly until Ashburn came along. And now you all want me to throw Norland over for that—that *coxcomb* of a duke!"

Rosamund's astonishment gave way to a considering look. "Cecily?"

"Yes?"

"When did you meet the Duke of Ashburn? I didn't know the two of you were acquainted."

"We're not. Well, we are only slightly acquainted." Cecily tried not to remember that kiss, because it would make her blush and then what would Rosamund think?

"And the duke proposed marriage, just like that?" Rosamund frowned. "He must be in love with you. Or at least, he must believe himself in love."

Love? The mere mention of it terrified Cecily. "Good God, no! Ashburn needs a wife and for some odd reason, he has decided I will do. Like any man, once he gets a notion in his head, he won't give it up for anything. Indeed," she added, "I'll wager he had no thought at all of marriage until the betrothal was announced."

The perceptive way Rosamund eyed her made Cecily uncomfortable. "You make him sound quite stupid and pigheaded," Rosamund said. "And yet I hear his intellect is extraordinary."

"What has his intellect got to do with it?" said Cecily. "Lord knows when it comes to women, even the cleverest men do the stupidest things. Not that I accept he is clever. *I* have seen no evidence of superior intelligence in my dealings with him."

"To be sure," said Rosamund, blinking a little. "If that is your opinion of him, why are you going to this house party? Don't you have engagements in Town?"

Cecily sighed. "The duke canceled them, giving out that I was fatigued by the season and needed country air."

Cecily hesitated. "Rosamund? When Jonathon died, who told Montford the news?"

Her cousin took a while to answer her, and Cecily belatedly remembered that Rosamund had been very fond of Jonathon. He might have been Cecily's brother, but he was Rosamund's cousin, too.

"I don't recall," Rosamund said at last. "At least, I doubt I ever knew. The duke seems to hear these things on the wind. Why?"

Cecily shook her head. "Never mind."

Rosamund gave her arm a comforting squeeze. And with a swiftness that took her unawares, Cecily's throat ached. The pain of losing Jonathon was like an old wound that would never quite heal.

She couldn't talk about it, so she smiled brightly and changed the subject. "But do tell me, dearest, since I shall not be there next week: What will you wear to Lady Bamfrey's picnic?"

As soon as he returned from Lady Cecily's ball, Rand wrote to the steward at his country estate, giving orders for his house to be prepared for a small party of guests.

He had no qualms about the ridiculously short amount of time he'd granted his staff to make the necessary arrangements. That's what they were trained for, after all. That's why he paid them such handsome wages.

His servants saw to the mundanities of life while he kept his mind on higher subjects.

Matters of state, for example. The welfare of his tenants. The management of no fewer than five estates and various properties in London. The progress of his protégés in their scientific and exploratory endeavors. The manifold demands of his extensive family.

He had a mountain of important, high-minded work he must see to at once if he wanted to devote himself to Lady Cecily at the forthcoming party.

And yet . . . He scrutinized his surroundings with dissatisfaction.

Was that really the best they could do with flowers in the great hall? He didn't know the first thing about floral arrangements, but it seemed to him that he'd seen far more impressive displays at other gentlemen's houses.

Those gentlemen had wives, he reminded himself, or sisters or daughters. Ladies who listed flower arrangement among their accomplishments. Not busy, efficient housekeepers who strove more for propriety than artistic flair.

It would be tactless and possibly futile to request Mrs. Juteney to improve upon her work.

But what about the furniture, now? All at once, the dark mahogany upholstered in deep green and burgundy seemed heavy and somber, though he'd lived comfortably with these pieces all his life.

There was no time—not even for him—to refurnish the house before his guests arrived. But as he strode about the place, he saw it through new eyes. Eyes that grew increasingly critical the longer he looked.

Anglesby Park was splendid in its proportions and grand in its appointments, but it lacked a certain almost indefinable something: The feminine touch.

His stringent appraisal took on an edge of rueful self-mockery. He'd wanted to impress Lady Cecily by inviting her here, hadn't he? Perhaps she'd be appalled instead.

He was not one to wring his hands over what he couldn't help, however. If and when she married him, he'd give Cecily carte blanche to redecorate the house to her taste. And it was a magnificent house, even if its grandeur might be considered a little old-fashioned.

His butler and his housekeeper had matters well in hand, so Rand went to his library and threw himself into work. He needed to clear his schedule completely to make room for a far more pleasant task: wooing Lady Cecily Westruther.

Despite all his preparations, Lady Cecily's arrival took Rand by surprise.

He had issued the invitation to this house party in the vague manner in which these things were usually done. Nothing so precise as a date was ever set, for that would be vulgar in the extreme. One opened one's house, and guests came and went as they pleased.

Why it had been fixed in his head that no one would arrive until tomorrow at the earliest, he had no idea. Perhaps because today was a Sunday?

He'd underestimated Lady Cecily's enthusiasm, it seemed. He only wished that enthusiasm was for him and not the contents of his attics.

Her early arrival was not the only surprise in store for him. An older lady, fearsomely elegant in a bronze carriage dress, accompanied her.

"Lady Arden." He bowed. "What a delightful surprise."

Her fine eyebrows flexed at that. The last time their paths had crossed, his primary concern was to deflect her attempts to marry him off. Now, those attempts would be more than welcome, if channeled in the correct direction. He must contrive to have a private conversation with her.

Lady Cecily curtsied, but there was a frown in her eyes. She looked from him to Lady Arden "You are acquainted, then?"

"My sweet child," said Lady Arden, smiling benignly upon them both. "I am the dear boy's aunt."

"First cousin once removed," corrected Rand, smoothly ignoring Lady Cecily's hot, accusatory look. "On my mother's side."

Resentment settled over Lady Cecily's face and he'd no doubt it was directed solely at him.

He regarded her in amusement. He didn't know what the girl thought *he'd* done; he'd not the least idea she intended to bring Lady Arden as chaperone. If anyone had deceived her, it was Lady Arden herself. Or Montford, perhaps.

Now, there was a thought.

"I don't know why you ought to be so surprised,

Cecily," said Lady Arden. "I am related to half the peers in the country, after all."

"That is true," Rand said apologetically.

And he would take the utmost advantage of his relationship with Cecily's chaperone, assuming he'd find an ally in that lady.

One never knew, though. Lady Arden would do almost anything to further her family's interests, particularly when it came to marriage. There was a ruthlessness beneath her charm that so many men underestimated—to their peril. But she also believed strongly in honor and duty. She might refuse to upset a betrothal that was already in place.

Well, time would tell which way she might bend. If she came out against him, he didn't doubt his ability to match wits with Her Ladyship and win.

Belatedly, he recalled his invitation to Norland. "And where is your betrothed, Lady Cecily? Seeing to the horses? My grooms will do all that." He glanced beyond her through the front door but saw no sign of the duke.

"Oh, His Grace is not here yet," said Cecily. "He had business in Cambridge that will delay his arrival a day or two."

"Neglecting you for dull research, Lady Cecily?" said Rand.

"Not at all," she returned with a bland look. "He has a commission to execute for me, that is all."

There wasn't a trace of defensiveness in her tone and he accepted that his shot had hit wide of the mark. Her alliance with Norland wasn't a love match, after all. The lady had no reason to be possessive or particular. She was unlikely to be needled by any lack of feeling her fiancé might display toward her.

For the first time, he wondered what it said about Lady Cecily that she should so readily accept a marriage that had no basis in love. Not only accept it, but steadfastly hold on to it in defiance of the undeniable passion she felt for Rand.

Lost in remembrance of that passion, he wasn't aware of his housekeeper's presence until Mrs. Juteney gave a discreet cough.

"Ah! Yes. And here is Mrs. Juteney to show you to your chambers."

"Thank you." Lady Arden smiled at the housekeeper and stripped off her gloves. "Then tea, I think?"

Rand bowed. "Yes, of course. Tea on the terrace, please, Mrs. Juteney. Shall we say, in half an hour?"

Cecily longed to steal up to the attics and search for Jonathon's papers as soon as she'd arrived at Anglesby Park. But that would be neither polite nor practicable. As Ashburn had remarked, there must be acres of attic in this house.

So she washed and changed her traveling costume for a cherry-striped gown and donned a chip straw hat with a wide ribbon that tied beneath her chin. Then she went down to join her host and her chaperone on the terrace.

She resisted the urge to avoid Ashburn's brilliant gaze. He surveyed her with appreciation, even amusement. Did he guess how she champed at the bit to get down to the business of her visit. Did he know how utterly suffocating she found the conventions that bound her?

As she sipped tea out of a translucently delicate china cup and made genteel conversation, Cecily realized she'd rarely felt more discomfited in her life. Every phrase Ashburn uttered, no matter how innocent, seemed charged with innuendo.

Lady Arden might rattle on about town gossip, but Cecily wasn't fooled. Despite her air of nonchalance, Lady Arden watched them both closely, as if awaiting confirmation of an opinion. Had Ashburn informed her of his intentions? Perhaps Montford had set her to watch them, perhaps even promote Ashburn's cause. That would be just like the wily duke.

Whatever the case, Cecily felt harried, challenged, measured, and scrutinized, none of which soothed her temper.

Ashburn, on the other hand, appeared at ease, which she hotly resented. She realized with surprise that this was the first time she'd seen him in daylight.

He had gallantly taken the seat facing the sun, so that when he turned his head to look at her, the sunlight danced in his eyes, burnishing them to gold.

Those eyes, Cecily thought with a faint, delicious shiver. They looked almost wild in their glittering intensity. By contrast, the natural light gentled the sharp contours of his face, making him appear younger and more relaxed. A young, virile lion lazing in the sun.

So at ease was their host, he even went so far as to laugh at one of Lady Arden's witticisms. A burning streak of jealousy shot through Cecily. She wished *she'd* made him laugh like that.

Oh, confound it! She wasn't developing a tendre for him, was she? Physical attraction was one thing; she'd be lost if she started fancying herself in love with the Duke of Ashburn.

Resolutely, she turned her thoughts back to the reason she'd accepted this perilous invitation. Jonathon's papers were here somewhere, waiting for her. When might she have a chance to speak with Ashburn alone? When could she begin the search?

Would he and Lady Arden chatter on about nothing forever? Cecily's impatience built and built, until she felt like a volcano, ready to hurl rocks and steam and lava in every direction.

Ashburn regarded her with a degree of amused understanding that made her want to hit him. "Perhaps if you ladies are not too fatigued by the journey, I might conduct you on a tour of the house."

He glanced toward the magnificent vista that spread like a jeweled tapestry before them. "Or there are some pretty rambles if you are feeling more energetic."

Lady Arden smiled. "I have letters to write, dear boy." A large sapphire flashed as she flicked her fingertips in a shooing motion. "But you young things ought to take advantage of the clear weather while you can. Run along, both of you. Just be sure to return before dark."

This was Cecily's chance. She was on her feet before Lady Arden finished her last sentence. "I should like to see the house, if you please, Your Grace. I hear you have a fine . . . porcelain collection."

It was a safe bet, since almost every noble household had a fine porcelain collection.

"Indeed." The smallest tic at the side of his mouth

showed Ashburn's appreciation of this particular gambit. "I believe there's a nice little assortment of knickknacks somewhere."

He bowed and waited for Cecily to precede him into the house.

"Your subtlety never fails to astonish me," he murmured as they stepped through the long windows into the relative cool of the library. "This way."

Without further explanation, he led her up a flight of stairs and along a corridor to a saloon papered in pale green silk damask. The walls were lined with cabinets full of exquisite, eggshell-thin porcelain.

Breathtaking. Quite simply . . . Cecily looked about her in wonder.

She had never been an aficionado of art or music, but porcelain, now . . . The delicate beauty, the shapes, the luster, the way the colors came vividly to life on that medium, had always fascinated her.

Here was a room she could spend days in. Or she might if she did not have a far more vital mission at this house than to dwell in artistic appreciation.

"*A nice little assortment,*" she echoed, dryly ironic. "But you know I did not come away with you to look at porcelain."

However, as usual, Ashburn missed nothing. He had caught her expression of surprised wonder. With a curious quirk to his lips that she now took to be his version of a full-blown smile, he said, "Nevertheless, I think you ought to spend some time here, if only to answer Lady Arden when she quizzes you about it."

Ignoring her protest, Ashburn drew her hand

through his arm and led her from one cabinet to the next.

His touch, his nearness, sent her senses careering. Her body went first hot, then cold. Her heart skipped and jumped in her chest.

Stop it! She commanded her wayward self to fall in line with her reason. The mind, her cousin Xavier had always told her, was a more powerful instrument than the body. Why couldn't hers seem to seize control?

Ashburn was about to pass by the largest cabinet in the room when she stopped him.

"What about this one?" She indicated it with a wave of her hand.

"Ah." Ashburn remained silent for a time, while Cecily inspected the contents.

She immediately identified the service as Sèvres. Predominantly turquoise, the collection of plate showed a series of vignettes.

While she might appreciate the excellence of the artist's technique and the sheer decadence of the gilt decoration, the ornate extravagance of this pattern was not to Cecily's taste. The Chinese porcelain farther along better pleased her sense of harmony and restraint.

"This," Ashburn said at last, "is my favorite part of the collection."

She regarded him with a sinking feeling that had no business striking her at that moment. She had marked him as a man of great taste and discernment; certainly his appreciation for the rest of the collection in this room showed him to be so. Yet, this rather overdecorated set was the one he preferred?

Even if she were the greatest devotee of Sèvres, she could not think this service a superior example of that factory's wares. She thought the subject rather banal, for one thing: a pair of lovers, all powdered and patched. They were clothed in the dress of a bygone age in shades of pearl gray, pink, and pale blue—a rather insipid combination, she thought.

Ashburn turned to her, and that faint glimmer of a smile was in his eyes again, taking the edge off her disapproval. "Your expression is an excellent mirror of your feelings, Lady Cecily. I am forced to defend my choice."

"Not at all," she said politely. "It is a very fine set."

"But that is not the reason I like it." He hunted in his waistcoat pocket, then produced a small key.

Cecily wondered why he kept that key with him rather than leaving it in the lock as he left the others. She watched Ashburn's hands as he unlocked the cabinet and opened the glass doors. He wore no gloves. She became acutely aware of how large and strangely rugged those hands looked against the delicateness of the plate as he selected one and brought it out to show her.

His handling of the piece was dexterous and light and practiced, as if he did this often. She regarded him with renewed interest. She'd thought he cared only for steam engines and automatons and other innovations.

"Do you see the two lovers?" he said, tilting the plate so the sunlight did not glare from its surface. How ridiculous that the mere mention of that word *lovers* from him should set her pulse fluttering madly. Trying to appear unconscious of what lay thick in the air between them, she nodded.

Cecily examined the brushwork with critical, reluctant appreciation. "They are beautifully executed."

He gave an odd, almost embarrassed laugh. "They are my parents."

Her gaze flew to his, her lips parting in surprise. For some reason she could not name, she flushed.

She looked again at the plate in his hands, then turned to stare with fascination at the rest of the set.

It was some moments before she could bring herself to speak. She sensed him next to her, heard his breathing, felt the warmth from his body. She even smelled him, an indescribable masculine scent of mingled horse leathers, shaving soap, wool, and something she thought might be his sun-warmed skin.

Oh, dear Lord, was she so weak that she was drawn to the way this man *smelled*? How utterly ridiculous!

Determined to master this awful jumble of emotions, Cecily focused her attention on the collection of vignettes, following the narrative as it progressed from one plate to the next.

"It is the tale of their courtship," he murmured.

She nodded, for in those vignettes a saga of love lost and reclaimed unfolded as clearly as if it had been written in words.

Her throat seemed to close up. "They must have been very much in love."

Her voice sounded unsteady. She didn't know

why the notion that Ashburn's parents had known such passion and tenderness should unsettle her so much. That a collection of plates she'd immediately dismissed as prosaic could convey such a wealth and depth of emotion troubled her more than she could express.

Softly, Ashburn said, "Other men own plate commemorating the battles they've fought, the nations they've conquered, the trophies and honors they've won from their king. My father commissioned this. Because winning my mother was the crowning glory of his life."

As he spoke those words to her, she felt a monumental shift inside herself. His parents had experienced something precious and oh, so rare. Theirs was a great love story, a story worthy of being immortalized in porcelain. Each piece spoke of hope and pursuit, surrender, separation. . . .

"This one," Cecily said, pointing to the plate depicting a ship sailing away from shore, a small male figure on deck staring back toward land. "Where did he go?"

"My grandfather shipped Papa off to France. In the hope, I believe, that my father would forget his infatuation among the delights Paris had to offer."

"And the next?"

He returned the plate he'd been holding to its stand. "Ah, the next shows my mother, boarding the packet to go after him."

"Oh!" She laughed. "I think I should have liked your mama."

"A most determined lady," he agreed. His voice changed timbre. "Or so I believe."

She looked up at him, a question in her eyes.

He didn't meet her eye, but stared into the china cabinet, his attention far away. "My mother died in childbirth with me. My father soon followed her. They say he died of grief but that is not true. He succumbed to a deadly fever several months later." He glanced down at her. "I am told he used to bring me here."

Her reaction was barely a breath. "*Oh . . .*"

His lips twisted a little, as if the notion gave him an equal amount of pleasure and pain. She sensed he did not often show vulnerability to anyone, but this loss was too deep even for him to conceal.

Did he blame himself for his parents' deaths? Such a reaction was not logical, but when was the heart ever governed by reason?

Almost without her volition, she laid her hand on his forearm and pressed it.

His arm seemed to grow rigid at her touch. She saw his jaw work once, twice. Then without fuss or ceremony, he laid his hand over hers, as if accepting her offering of comfort.

And Cecily felt a curious sense of peace in that silent gallery, though the current of excitement never entirely left her. She suspected it never would while she was in his presence; she almost grew accustomed to this sharp edge of anticipation whenever the Duke of Ashburn was near.

She sensed somehow that the feeling of peace was the more dangerous of the two.

He gestured. "Do you see the final one?"

Cecily looked at the larger piece he indicated. A spill jar this time. When he removed it from its niche and placed it in her hands, it was cool to the touch. She felt the weight of it, and saw that it was singular, not only in shape, but in subject as well. The painting included a third figure. A baby. A chubby, healthy babe cradled in his mother's arms.

"You," said Cecily.

Ashburn's face was carefully blank, but she knew better than to trust his expressions by now. His eyes didn't lie, she discovered. They'd darkened subtly, turning from that golden brown to a mysterious tortoiseshell. She saw sadness there. Of course he would feel sorrow for the parents who had loved so passionately and whose love he had never known.

She examined the brushwork on this piece and discovered that while the subject matter was the same, the style was distinct from the others, as if a different artist had painted it years after the rest of the service was complete.

In the painting, each parent had one arm thrown up in an expression of joyful welcome and wonder at the blessing of this small life.

"That was my father's gift to me," he said quietly. "The most valuable part of my inheritance, in fact."

She turned the jar around to see what the cartouche on the other side of it depicted. A cherub with a harp, leaning one dimpled arm on the family escutcheon.

This design was repeated on the back of the other plates, she'd noticed that. But it seemed like an odd piece of prescience to show the solitary figure of a small boy with the family shield now firmly in his grasp. A responsibility that was his alone.

What must it have been like, to have grown up as Ashburn had, without even the memory of his loving mother and father? With no siblings, nor, she suspected, anyone who was truly his?

At least for the first six years of her life, she'd known what it was like to be cherished by doting parents. At least for ten years, she'd had Jon.

And later, her Westruther cousins had become as close to her as siblings. She did not know this for a fact, but she sensed Ashburn wasn't particularly close to anyone.

She turned the spill jar once more, revolving it in her hands until the three glowing figures faced her again. She stared at it a moment longer, then carefully replaced it in the cabinet.

"Thank you for showing me," she said. But she did not feel grateful, precisely. She felt . . . raw. As if it were her soul and not Ashburn's that had been stripped bare with this new revelation.

Ashburn closed the glass doors of the cabinet and locked them, pocketing the key. He took a deep breath, then exhaled it and rubbed his hands together. "Now, let us attack those attics."

Much as she'd longed to look for that incriminating letter, it seemed obscene to insist upon it now.

Instead, she lightly touched his arm again and said, "We do not have time enough to search before dinner. Why don't you show me the rest of the collection while we're here?"

Chapter Twelve

Later that evening, as he led Lady Cecily upstairs to the attics, Rand surprised himself by revising his former strategy.

He'd lured Lady Cecily Westruther to his home on false pretenses, allaying any qualms of conscience by telling himself he did it with the purest motives.

That justification no longer sat well with him.

Something had altered between them today. The strange elation he'd felt at having her so close had all but swamped the pain of talking about his parents. The mere touch of her hand had given him a solace he'd never expected to find.

Not only that, it had also given him hope.

She'd judged his mood so well that she'd given him precisely what he needed. Less would have indicated her disinterest; more would have embarrassed him. Could she truly be indifferent to him if in that moment she had provided what he didn't even know he sought?

He didn't think so. But then the story of that

dinner service would melt the hardest female heart, would it not?

Cynically, he thought that must have been his intent in relating the tale. He did not ordinarily speak of his parents, and he'd never told anyone about the dinner service and its significance. Yes, Machiavellian instinct must have guided him to tell that tale, even if he had not thought of it at the time impulse struck.

He halted. The notion turned his stomach a little.

She had caught him up as he paused in thought. He heard her breathing a little more heavily than usual. He supposed it was from the exertion of climbing four flights of stairs.

Excitement tugged at Rand's insides as he continued the ascent. The darkness, the need for secrecy, perhaps . . . He didn't know what it was, but the atmosphere seemed to make the sound of her quiet pants supremely erotic. He imagined her breathing hard in his ear as he covered her body, made love to her, kissed those sweet, ripe lips, that soft, creamy neck. . . .

He stopped and looked back at Cecily.

By the lantern light, her eyes appeared larger than ever, rich pools of darkness, with a glossy sheen like freshly milled chocolate.

He held out his hand to her, a mute offer of assistance.

She spent what seemed to him a long time considering this gesture. Then she shook her head and motioned for him to continue.

Disappointed but far from surprised, he did.

When they reached the attic, Ashburn set down

his lantern, closed the door behind them. Then he turned to her. Without a word, he reached for her and drew her into his arms.

This time, Cecily surrendered. All evening, she hadn't been able to get that story Ashburn had told her about his parents out of her mind. After dinner, she'd allowed her maid to undress her and put her to bed. All the while she'd thought of him and of all that he had lost. All that he'd never had.

When Jonathon died, she'd felt that same pain. Not only grief at his passing, but a bone-deep sense that she was now irrevocably and completely alone. Everyone who truly belonged to her, everyone she loved was gone.

She wouldn't wish that feeling on her worst enemy.

True, she'd been extraordinarily lucky to find a new family to love. Even if they weren't hers the way her parents and brother had been, a special bond had formed between her and her Westruther cousins.

But Ashburn's own cousin had just betrayed him with his former mistress. Worse, she'd sensed Freddy's behavior had not greatly surprised the duke. Did he have such a low opinion of Freddy, then? Were his other relations any better? He seemed to live all alone in this vast palace of a house.

Here, now, in the quiet of the attics with one lantern to light the cavernous space, she felt as if they dwelled in another world, where ordinary things did not exist. A time out of time, where if a woman wanted a man, she could have him without shame or consequences.

So when he reached for her, it seemed churlish and small-minded to push him away.

Instead, she put her hands up to his lapels and gripped them so that she might draw him closer.

With a hoarse exclamation of her name, he slid his arms around her waist and swept her into his kiss.

Emotion broke over her like a great, dumping wave, knocking her senseless, dashing her against the rocks. His kiss was like the pull of the current, drawing her to deeper waters. She all but drowned in sensation as his mouth devoured hers.

She smoothed her hands up his lapels to his shoulders, then caressed his nape, pulled him closer still.

He gave a quiet gasp, such as a man dying of thirst might give when offered water. Then he accepted her invitation, licking into her mouth, probing deeply.

Unpracticed as she was, she soon become proficient in this art. Tonight, her fears and pride seemed to fall away. Only the raw essence of her remained, responding eagerly to him, seeking connection with that lonely soul inside the impossible magnificence of the man.

His arm tightened about her waist. She stood on tiptoe to reach him; her breasts pressed against his chest, her nipples tender and sensitive to every movement.

He still wore his evening clothes, while she was clad in a simple round gown she'd managed to put on by herself after her maid thought she was abed.

Ashburn slid a hand up her rib cage, and there was no corset to dull the feeling of his touch. When his hand closed over one breast, she gave a ragged gasp that turned into a moan. All at once, it seemed natural to want his hand on *her,* large male palm to soft female skin.

He continued to tease her through the fine, soft cambric. Gently touching, stroking, molding the shape of her breast, he caressed her until she could have pleaded with him to do something to ease the hunger, the tension that built inside her.

When he finally rubbed his thumb firmly over her nipple, she thought she might die from the exquisite relief. His mouth left hers. He kissed the side of her neck and she gasped and froze beneath his hands.

"Cecily," he murmured, as if reminding her who she was.

She didn't wish to remember. Perhaps she ought to speak some form of endearment or even encouragement, but even if she were so inclined, words were beyond her. She let him carry her along, willed him not to stop.

His hand slipped into her bodice and closed possessively over her breast. The warm, liquid feeling between her legs hardened to a hot throb as he stroked her nipple. The intimate pleasure of his caresses was so strong, she thought she might die of it.

He drew down her bodice, baring her to the night air. To her shock and surprise, he bent his head to kiss first her décolletage, then the soft mound of her breast.

And now she knew what he meant when he said he wished to feast upon her. His lips drifted over her breast until his mouth closed over her nipple with hot, wet suction, sending a spear of pleasure through her body. He laved and teased and sucked until she was out of her mind with ecstasy, until she shuddered and convulsed and threw her head back.

When the waves of delight ebbed, she realized dimly that he had ceased his attentions. Confused, dazed, vibrating with pleasure yet barely sated, she let her eyes drift open.

Cecily watched as Ashburn drew her gown up to cover her again. She was not so lost to bliss that she didn't realize his hand shook as he did so.

Instead of letting her go, he took her in his arms again, stroking her back in a soothing motion until her shivers and quakes died away.

That rocked her as his more exciting physical attentions had not. A shudder that had little to do with passion racked her body. For one, fraught moment, she thought she might weep.

The prospect of breaking down in his presence and in such circumstances horrified her so much that she pulled away with more force than tact.

A fleeting glance at his face told her his jaw was set in hard lines. Was he angry with her? Well, better that than . . . She didn't know what. What *did* he feel for her, after all, besides a sense of possessiveness and his obvious desire?

She could only pray he'd see his error and stop.

Determinedly slamming the lid on her own tangled emotions, she gestured toward the maze of boxes and trunks that filled this section of attic.

"Well, then. Perhaps we ought to get on with what we came for?"

Chapter Thirteen

For that piece of cowardice, Rand was tempted to leave Cecily to perform her search alone. But that would be churlish of him, wouldn't it? Besides, he had not meant to kiss her when he'd accompanied her up here tonight. Such impetuous folly was likely to have stymied him, set him back to *point non plus*.

Who could have guessed she'd respond with such exquisite sensitivity, such fire? As if despite her reason and her loyalty to her betrothed, she couldn't help but match Rand's passion. She felt it, too, the power of this force between them. And that was little short of miraculous.

The rapid beat of his heart and the absence of blood in his brain told him his own judgment was far from cool and collected at this moment. Perhaps he ought to let the matter rest; hadn't he won the first skirmish in this battle between them?

But dammit, he couldn't allow her to carry on as if nothing had happened. She deserved to be punished a little for not having the courage to face him after that kiss.

"Your Grace?" she began, but he interrupted her.

"Call me Rand," he said suavely. "At least in private."

She stared at him. "I couldn't use your name. Not even in private."

"Why?"

Her lips quivered. "It's too intimate, that's why! I don't wish to be intimate with you."

He lifted his eyebrows, mocking her. "You let me do wicked, lascivious things to your body and yet you are too prim to call me by name?"

She flushed, glaring at him. "That was . . . an error in judgment. I am going to pretend it never happened and wish you will do the same."

"But I can't pretend that, Cecily," he said softly. "Not with the taste of you still on my tongue."

Ignoring her shocked gasp, he moved toward her. "In fact, you taste even better than I'd imagined."

Her dark eyes blazed. "Stop it!"

He shrugged. "I will if you call me Rand."

"Oh, confound it! *Rand,* then." She gestured at the paraphernalia that occupied this section of the attic. "Rand, please tell me where I should start."

He decided to accept this small victory. Best not to push her too far. "Well, *Cecily,* I've managed to narrow it down somewhat."

He indicated a collection of ten large steamer trunks over by the dormer window. "Those contain the papers I took from your cousin's house that day."

"Minus the ones you gave to Jonathon's college."

"Yes. Minus those," he said evenly.

Without another word, she marched forward

and threw open the lid of the first trunk. A shower of dust billowed around her, but she didn't pay any heed, just knelt before the container with a singular air of concentration and purpose.

He went to the next trunk and crouched before it. Clearly, Jonathon, Earl of Davenport, had treasured every piece of correspondence anyone had ever written to him. Or, more likely, he'd simply never bothered to throw anything away.

"Anything in particular you're looking for?" he said.

"No, nothing in particular," she said in an off-hand tone that he didn't find the least convincing.

Out of the corner of his eye, he saw her sifting through the papers rapidly, glancing at them but not reading any in depth. Which of course meant she knew precisely what she sought but she didn't wish him to find it first.

"I'm afraid I cannot help you if I don't know what I seek," he said with spurious regret. He wanted her to take her time with this quest. The more time she spent up here, the more often he'd get her to himself.

Her busy hands stilled. He could see the cogs whir in that clever mind of hers.

She must know there was too much here for her to sort through in her short visit to his house, particularly considering how seldom she'd be at liberty to slip away. With his help, she'd cut that time in half.

She seemed to understand this, for she said, "Very well, then. Specifically, I am searching for letters I wrote to Jonathon as a young girl. They should be easy to find. You only have to look for the childish handwriting."

She glanced at him and made a self-conscious little moue. "I have all of Jonathon's letters to me and I should like to keep the full set. You will think it absurdly sentimental of me, I daresay."

"Not at all," he responded politely.

He didn't believe her—or at least, not entirely. Why should she go to so much trouble and sacrifice over letters she wrote when she was a mere child? For it *was* a sacrifice for her to remain in the same house with him, much less the same room. Alone. At night. Immediately after he had done unspeakable things to her body.

He pondered that question as he worked beside her. Again, he was acutely conscious of her movements, the sound of her breathing, of her voice as she muttered distractedly to herself.

Cecily, on the other hand, appeared to forget his existence.

She did not strike him as someone who was overly sentimental about things like letters she'd written in childhood. Yet he'd observed how close her relationship was with her cousins. He'd seen ample evidence of her attachment to them at the ball. And he'd heard the emotion in her voice when she spoke of her brother.

She might guard her heart with the ferocity of a tigress, but where Lady Cecily Westruther loved, she loved deeply.

The notion made his insides thrash about with guilt. He ought not to conceal the truth from her. If—once—they married, he would find a way to tell her. He simply couldn't risk telling her now.

Suddenly, she said, "You must have been through these already, I suppose."

Startled, he looked at her.

"For the archive," she explained, not meeting his eye.

"Oh. Yes, of course." He'd forgotten he told her that lie. "It was reasonably clear which papers more properly belonged to Jonathon's work, however. I did not pry into his personal affairs."

He tried to think back nearly ten years, to when he'd sorted through these papers to isolate the domestic and business-related material from the scientific. Had he come across anything that might account for Cecily's fervor now? He couldn't remember if letters from a little girl had registered with him at all. He'd been so intent on the matter at hand.

"It was a Herculean task," Ashburn said. "Your brother was not terribly orderly in his filing methods."

"No," she agreed with a reminiscent smile. "I recall the housekeeper complaining that if an idea came to him, he'd take out his pencil and scribble it down on the nearest available surface, whether it was a piece of foolscap or a napkin."

"Your annual linen bill must have been high," said Rand. "I found several fascinating tablecloths among his notes as well."

And he'd burned them all.

"*Fascinating?* You understood them?" She did look at him then, with surprise. But before he could form an answer, she said, "How silly of me! Of course you must, or the college would not have requested you to catalog it all."

Did he detect a veiled skepticism in her remarks? Perhaps she hadn't believed him when he told her the reason he'd purchased those notes from Lady Davenport.

She would be correct, as far as that went. But the truth was far too fantastical for anyone to guess at.

They worked on in silence for an hour or more before the frequency of Cecily's yawns told him it was time to call a halt.

"That is enough for one night, I think," he said, closing the lid of the trunk he was working on.

"I suppose you are right," she said. "I can scarcely keep my eyes open."

"Here." He passed her the key to the attic. "This way, you may come and go as you choose. With guests in the house, it might be difficult for me to slip away as much as I'd like."

Her eyes widened. Clearly she had not expected such a gesture. Raising her softened gaze to his, she said, "Thank you. I—I'm obliged to you."

The sweetness of her expression took his breath away. It cost him all his resolution not to snatch her up in his arms and kiss her again.

Instead, he decorously took her hand and assisted her to rise. But he did not let her go immediately.

"It cannot be just me," he said, looking down at her. "I might be conceited, but I am not blind. Sweetheart, you feel as much desire for me as I feel for you."

Cecily looked him full in the eye and her lips parted, as if to refute his statement. But at the last moment, she looked away.

"I have every intention of marrying Norland

next week." She swallowed hard. "I ought not to have let you kiss me. I apologize if I—"

"Good God, don't *apologize*." His voice dripped with sarcasm. "You are bent on ruining all three of our lives, but Heaven forbid you should feel *responsible*."

She gave a quick shake of her head as if to negate his words, to dislodge them.

He stared at her, trying to fathom what made her hold so steadfastly to this disastrous course. "Why are you so afraid?"

He knew she prided herself on her courage and daring, so he was unsurprised when his challenge lit a spark in her. The dark eyes flashed. "I am doing the honorable thing, which is more than I can say for you, my lord duke!"

"Believe me," he said harshly, "if it were not for my honor and yours, I'd have seduced you ten times over by now. And you would have loved every minute of it."

She flushed at his blunt speaking, but she did not shy away. "That is not honor. That is strategy!" she hit back. "I'm well aware of the game you're playing, *Rand*. You are trying to breach my defenses by degrees, by stealth and persuasion. I'm like some fortress you've vowed to conquer. Well, I hope you're well provisioned, my lord duke, because it's going to be a long, cold siege."

Cecily woke the next morning feeling cross, the heat of her exchange with Rand still burning in her chest.

She was tempted to avoid Ashburn's company altogether for the duration of her stay. That would be the wisest course. Now that he had bestowed the key to the attics upon her, there was no reason she needed to seek him out or to speak with him beyond the common civilities. However, she could well imagine his reaction if she made efforts to avoid him. He would accuse her of cowardice. Sadly, he would be right.

Just because Rand provoked her did not mean she wasn't madly attracted to him. Just because she would rather poke her eye with a stick than be tied in marriage to such an autocratic, compelling man did not mean he wouldn't make a devastating lover.

But no matter how deeply sympathetic she might feel toward him, no matter how much common ground they might find, she was pledged to Norland, and there was an end to it. She was not going to throw that away for the sake of this dangerous passion.

The best course would be to act toward the Duke of Ashburn with indifference. She would resist his overtures—both the physical kind and the far more dangerous emotional ones. She'd never have so willingly embraced him last night if he hadn't primed her well beforehand with the story of his parents' courtship and the tragedy of their deaths. His own aching loss.

Had that been a calculated move on his part? The notion was a corrosive one; it ate away inside her as she washed and dressed for the day. Surely even Ashburn could not be so cold and manipulative as to play upon her sympathies in such a shameless fashion.

Her temper was not improved by the steady rain

that would deter even the keenest horsewoman from her usual morning ride. Nor did her mood lift when she found her host in the breakfast parlor, partaking of a plate of ham and eggs.

Ashburn seemed disgustingly cheerful, though she didn't know quite how she gauged his state of mind. His expression remained as impassive as ever. But there was an air of alertness, almost of jauntiness about his movements that she found deeply suspicious.

And then she realized that they were not alone. The man currently perusing the spread of steaming silver chafing dishes on the sideboard was her betrothed.

She could not help but compare the two dukes: one so harshly handsome, debonair, and smoothly dangerous; the other so bland and vague and altogether malleable—except when it came to the Promethean Club.

Ashburn rose to his feet and bowed. "Lady Cecily."

She accorded Ashburn a careless nod. "Do sit down, Your Grace."

Norland looked up from the sideboard and waved a serving fork in her general direction. "Ah! There you are, Cecily."

Cecily managed a brilliant smile. "Yes. And there *you* are, Norland. I'm so pleased you are here at last."

She moved toward him. "How do you do, sir?"

Lightly, she touched his arm, giving it a small squeeze in a gesture a betrothed lady might reasonably use toward her fiancé. Norland started as violently as if she'd pinched him, so unexpected was this small token of affection.

Furious with herself, Cecily avoided Ashburn's eye. She did not need to look at him to register his amused satisfaction at the failure of her small gambit. Why had she tried to show her preference for Norland in this manner? She'd only made herself look like an idiot.

Without asking her what she would like, Norland took a fresh plate and absently loaded it with an assortment of hot viands from the chafing dishes and handed it back to her.

"Thank you." Cecily blanched a little at the sight of the heaped plate, but she made no comment as she joined Norland and Ashburn at the table.

She saw Ashburn glance at her plate and lift an eyebrow. Irritation buzzed within her like a fly trapped behind glass. Irritation at Ashburn's swift, accurate assessment; exasperation at Norland's overt carelessness. In all of their years of acquaintance, had Norland never noticed she took only a buttered bread roll and a cup of hot chocolate at breakfast? Her stomach turned at the thought of fried food at this hour.

But now that Ashburn had noticed, she'd have to eat it, wouldn't she?

Cecily took a determined bite of black pudding, chewed, and swallowed. Then she slapped a pleasant smile on her face as she addressed her betrothed. "And how was your journey, dear sir?"

"Tolerable," said Norland without looking up from his plate. "Though if the rain keeps up like this, the roads will soon be a mire."

She wanted to ask him about his detour to Cambridge, but she couldn't do it in front of Ashburn. That would have to wait.

"I called on Miss Tibbs and her sister while I was in Cambridge," added Norland unexpectedly. "Just happened past, you know."

"Oh, that was well done of you!" said Cecily, a little guilty that she'd not thought to visit her companion herself. But it had been less than a week since Tibby left, after all, and Cecily had other things on her mind.

"If I'd known, I would have sent a basket with you," she said. "How did you find Tibby, Norland? Is she well?"

He set down his plate and pulled at his chin as if the query warranted deep cogitation. "I rather thought her spirits somewhat depressed," he said finally.

"Oh, no! I am sorry to hear that." On a note of explanation, Cecily said to Ashburn, "My companion, Miss Tibbs, was obliged to remove to Cambridge to look after her sister, who is ill. Was that not kind of His Grace to see to her comfort?"

As usual, Ashburn's expression was unreadable. "Very kind," he agreed. "But perhaps Miss Tibbs might like to join us here for a day or two if her sister can spare her. Cambridge is not far and a little relaxation and amusement here might be just the thing to set her up again."

"By Jove, that is good of you, Ashburn," said Norland, looking much struck by the offer. Then he shook his head. "But I fear it would not do. The sister is too ill to be left alone, I believe. I snatched only a few moments' conversation with Miss Tibbs before she was obliged to return to the sickroom."

"I shall call on them tomorrow," said Cecily. That would have the twofold advantage of allowing her to see her dear old governess and getting her away from Ashburn's provocative behavior for a full day.

"You will?" Norland's brow cleared a little. "I shall escort you."

Ashburn said, "Ah. As to that, Norland, tomorrow might not be such a good time. I have arranged a meeting for you with Soames Grimshaw for the afternoon. But perhaps you would like to cancel it—"

"Grimshaw!" Norland straightened in his chair, his mouth dropping slightly in astonished surprise. "Ashburn, that is awfully good of you. Why—how did you manage it? But then you are so well connected, I shouldn't be surprised—"

Norland set down his knife and fork with a clatter. "Well, I must lose no time in preparation. Ha! Oh, I wish you'd informed me sooner, Ashburn. Then I could have . . . But no time to waste. How fortunate I brought my papers with me! I'll just—"

Before Norland lost himself entirely in a tangle of half sentences and exclamations, Cecily demanded, "But who *is* this Soames Grimshaw?"

"Who is—?" Norland looked thunderstruck, then burst into hearty chuckles, as if she'd asked who the Duke of Wellington was, or the Prince Regent. "Why my dear girl, he is the man who can make all my dreams come true!"

Her brow furrowed, Cecily looked at Ashburn.

"An investor," he explained. "Norland needs

money to fund a rather expensive experiment. The results, if we can replicate them, will be not only a scientific breakthrough, but a very lucrative one as well. For a percentage of future profits, I believe Grimshaw is willing to invest capital."

Norland threw down his napkin on the table, his breakfast forgotten. "It is too good of you, Ashburn. No, really, I say—"

Ashburn waved away his gratitude. "Perhaps I might suggest you ought to gather together the necessary documents to offer Grimshaw a complete proposal on the morrow. He is a man of business and he will be more impressed if you approach him in a businesslike manner."

"Yes, yes, yes. Of course, of course." But Norland hardly seemed to listen. He was out of his chair before Ashburn had finished speaking. Without even excusing himself from Cecily, he charged from the room.

Ordinarily amused by Norland's total disregard for anything but science, Cecily felt a flush of humiliation rise to her cheeks. How utterly petty and stupid of her. She'd never cared a jot for Norland's lack of regard for her. She'd welcomed it, in fact. Why should his careless behavior embarrass her now?

The reason was Ashburn, of course. She didn't wish to appear scorned and pathetic in his eyes.

Ashburn settled back in his chair, circling the rim of his tankard with one fingertip. The air of smugness that mantled him seemed to deepen as he watched her. The faintest smile played around the edges of those firmly cut lips.

Images and remembered sensations from that kiss last night flashed over her like lightning.

She didn't need to see Rand's expression to deduce he'd rid them of Norland on purpose. Now, her betrothed would be so caught up in his schemes, he would be of little use in her battle to hold Ashburn at bay.

She was beginning to think she'd need all the help she could get.

"Would you care for some chocolate, Lady Cecily?" Ashburn reached for the elegant silver chocolate pot and lifted it in offering.

He kept his voice deliberately bland, but from the flare of those big, dark eyes of hers, he knew she recalled his words on the night they first kissed as well as he did.

Cherries and cream and chocolate . . .

She choked. "A little coffee, perhaps."

"Craven," he murmured, reaching for the coffeepot. He poured a cup and passed it to her.

She set it down on the table with a snap.

"I expect my other guests will arrive today," said Rand. He waved a hand. "One or two close friends I'd like you to meet. My cousin Freddy, whom you've already, er, encountered, my friend Mr. Garvey, his sister and my aunt, Lady Marsham."

"How delightful," Cecily said. Her words sounded sincere, although she must wish the rest of the party at Jericho.

She hesitated. "Your Grace—"

He lifted a hand. "We agreed you were to call me Rand when we are in private."

"This is not private!" she hissed, darting a glance around the parlor. "Someone might come in at any moment."

"Not unless I ring for them," he said tranquilly. "Lady Arden ordered a breakfast tray to be brought to her room and will not be down before noon. And sad to say, I doubt your betrothed will recall your existence for another day or two."

With dignity, Cecily replied, "I should not wish His Grace to neglect such an opportunity out of misplaced consideration for me." She hesitated, then added, "I am a little confused, however. Why should Norland require investment in any of his schemes? He is one of the richest men in England, is he not?"

Rand regarded her for a moment, then said, "Can it be that you don't know?"

"Know what, pray?" She tried to sound unconcerned, but she didn't fool him.

Rand shrugged. "Norland might hold the title, but his mama holds the purse strings. He wouldn't dare spend his inheritance on something of which the dowager disapproves."

"And she does not approve of his scientific interests," Cecily said.

Rand inclined his head.

Cecily was quick enough to see immediately how the dowager's interference would affect her position, also. Her fortune would become Norland's upon their marriage. In practice, that would mean her fortune was at the dowager's disposal.

In a more generous spirit, Rand added, "To be fair to Norland, it is far better business practice for him to attract investors to his work than to fund it himself. That way, if the experiment fails, it is not his money he has gambled."

Cecily looked discomfited. "It is better to gamble

with someone else's? I should not like to be responsible for another man losing his shirt."

Rand shrugged. "A man like Grimshaw does not invest what he cannot afford to lose. He calculates the risks and demands a high return. Believe me, your sympathy is wasted on someone like him. In my experience, those with any kind of talent ought to be left to get on with their passion and leave the financial side of things to someone like me."

She looked inquiring. "Is that *your* passion, then? Finance?"

He watched her steadily. "What do you think?"

She narrowed her eyes as she considered him. "No. I believe it goes deeper than that. I believe . . . You enjoy your role as fairy godmother." She gave a gurgle of laughter at the inappropriate metaphor. "You like to bestow your riches on deserving people."

The notion disconcerted him as much as it disgusted him. "I don't do anything without profiting by it myself."

"If you say so." A small smile played about her mouth.

He relented. "It is not about the money; you're right. But it *is* a far more selfish motive than you give me credit for. I enjoy seeing brilliant minds in action. They come up with a hypothesis or an idea, but it takes money—often a great deal of it—to turn those ideas into something tangible. Often it takes influence, too. So that is where I step in."

"You invest your own money, then?" she asked.

He spread his hands. "That depends. Often, I am the conduit through which finance is arranged."

"You cannot be seen to dirty your hands in trade, I suppose."

Was there a touch of scorn in her voice?

He shrugged. "Land ownership is a business like any other, could our peers be brought to recognize it."

The animation this remark brought to her face made his heart give a sharp pound.

"Yes!" She slapped a small hand on the table, making the cutlery jump. It was the first time she had ever made a gesture that wasn't entirely elegant and controlled and polite.

"I was brought up with the notion that talking about business is vulgar," said Cecily, her dark eyes sparkling. "And yet it's a topic that interests me exceedingly. Not making money for its own sake, but so that I might do some good with it. Montford allowed me to participate in running the estate that forms the main part of my inheritance, you know. I helped him introduce a number of economies which increased profit without increasing rents. In return, he allowed me to dedicate a percentage of the income to my causes."

Rand sat very still as he listened to this speech. He hoped his astonishment did not show on his face.

"Oh?" he said. "And what causes might they be?"

She flushed and bit her lip. "How horrid! I sound like one of those ghastly females who is forever prosing on about their own beneficence. Do not regard it. All I meant to say was that I enjoyed applying my mind to the task."

"I asked the question because I want to know," he said gently.

"Well . . ." She chewed her lip. "I have always been concerned for the plight of unfortunate women. A large part of the funds are spent in the local parish, as is proper, but some of it goes to assist indigent females in London through various charities."

"And how do you select those charities?"

"That is the difficult part. I drew up a list of criteria and I rate each institution," she said. A shadow of her ferocious scowl appeared. "I am forced to rely on Montford's judgment on many of these matters and upon the investigations conducted by his man of business. The boards of such institutions would scarcely answer the interrogation of such a young lady as I am."

"And yet, a *duchess* would command their attention, no matter how young," Rand said.

She stared at him. Coolly, she responded, "Yes, I suppose you're right."

All at once, one missing piece of the puzzle that was Lady Cecily Westruther clicked into place.

"And so this is your particular passion, Cecily. What project occupies you now?"

Her mouth twisted a little ruefully. "Something different from the usual run of things. I daresay it will sound frivolous or ephemeral, perhaps. At this stage it is only a dream. I have not mentioned it to anyone, not even Montford."

And certainly not to Norland, Rand surmised. "Believe me, Cecily, I do *not* think you frivolous."

She picked up her napkin and pleated it. "I have always wished to establish a place for women who are of a creative bent to flourish. It seems to me that the only way most women can survive is to marry, and then all of their time is taken with the household and their babies. There is no time or—or mental space to write or to paint or to compose music. Only wealthy women or the men who gain patronage or earn their living in some other fashion can afford to do those things."

"So you wish to support women in those endeavors." He was fascinated. "How will you go about selecting candidates? How would you know where to find them?"

"I have made my selection for this particular trial," said Cecily. "There is already a community like the ones I hope to build in one of the villages on the Harcourt Estate, where I grew up. It was the need I saw in these women that made me decide to help others like them. But you are right. I don't know how I would go about discovering who most merits my assistance."

Rand experienced that gut-clenching sense of excitement that told him a project was worthy of his time and money. Oh, not for any financial return it would yield but because of an intrinsic sense of rightness in the cause.

His first inclination was to offer suggestions and support.

But if he did that, would she not suspect an ulterior motive? And besides, he did not wish her to marry him out of gratitude or hope that he would help her achieve her dream. He did not barter his influence and material advantages in return for affection anymore. He'd learned that lesson early in life.

So he said, "I don't know either, but I shall watch what you do with great interest."

A statement calculated to both dismiss and approve of the conversation in the most unexceptionable manner.

She looked rather like she'd been slapped in the face. "Thank you. But pray, do forgive me! This endeavor is rather a hobbyhorse of mine. I tend to run on if given the slightest encouragement. So few people are interested, you see."

The impulse to draw her into a practical discussion about the whys and wherefores of her project nagged at him. But he reminded himself that his resistance was in a just cause.

"There is nothing to forgive," he assured her. "I sincerely wish you the best in your mission. It is a worthy one."

Rising, she curtsied, her lips pressed together as if to contain further speech on her favorite subject. "I believe I shall take the opportunity to return to your attics now, Your Grace."

She seemed so crestfallen that he again repressed the urge to relent. He wanted nothing more than to delve further into a mind that seemed to burgeon with ideas and originality. But he wanted her to want him for himself. He would help her, but he wouldn't dangle his assistance like a carrot.

So he tamped down the fire her inspiration and drive set inside him and regretfully let her go.

Sipping his ale, he thought of the bundle of letters he had found when he doubled back to the attics last night and let himself in with the spare key.

Was he missing something? There was nothing in these to warrant Cecily's desperation, nor her urgency. Just a collection of amusing anecdotes and thumbnail sketches of family, neighbors, and servants.

Did he mean to hand the bundle over to her? Of course he did. Perhaps she might find them nestled at the bottom of the very last trunk.

He'd make sure he was there for the discovery. For he very much wanted to know what was missing from this small collection. And what Lady Cecily would do when she discovered the loss.

Chapter Fourteen

Five trunks and many hours later, Cecily was disheveled, tired, and famished, not to mention dispirited. It was dull, monotonous work sorting through Jonathon's papers, without even the prospect of sparring with the duke to keep her entertained.

Not that she'd wanted him to assist her. Not that she entirely trusted him to do the job properly, either. Men were notoriously bad at looking for things. They so often missed what was right beneath their noses.

And then, too, there was the danger that if he found that letter she'd written to Jon enclosing her first installment of Sir Ninian's adventures, he'd read it. That would be the surest way for him to smash her betrothal to smithereens.

Cecily couldn't get her earlier conversation with Rand out of her head. He'd seemed so vitally interested in her schemes. The urgency in his voice, the compelling light in those striking eyes of his . . . He'd elicited far more information from her than she'd ever meant to tell. She'd never known such a connection with anyone, not even with Montford, whose mind always seemed the most attuned to her own.

That feeling had been . . . extraordinary. Then suddenly, it was as if a candle had snuffed inside Rand. He'd withdrawn again. He'd even made her feel a trifle foolish for chattering on so long.

Had she imagined his earlier interest? She didn't think so. What had she said to make him become so guarded?

Ah, but what was the sense in worrying at that problem like a dog with a bone? Once she found that letter, she would not need to see Rand again.

The idea ought not to provoke such a feeling of loss inside her. How long had she known the dratted man? Hardly any time at all.

And she must stop calling him Rand, even if it was only in the privacy of her own mind.

Resolutely, Cecily forced her thoughts back to the matter at hand.

She hadn't discovered any of her correspondence to Jonathon in the trunks, but she had found letters from various other relations, friends, and even lovers. She grimaced. At least, she assumed they were love letters, judging by their lingering scent. The last thing she wanted to do was read one of those.

A cursory inspection told her that all the other trunks contained correspondence to do with business matters. Jonathon had been organized, after a fashion. He had at least stored personal papers together, separately from his other documents.

So then why weren't her letters there with the personal papers? Had someone removed them? Had Jon? Perhaps he'd kept them elsewhere. Perhaps they were still in the house, liable to be discovered by Bertram or Lavinia or one of the servants at any time.

She had no choice but to keep sifting through the rest of the trunks in the hope that her letters were caught up with other documents.

First, however, she must show her face downstairs. It was past noon and Lady Arden would wonder where her charge was.

"Might I have a word with you, Ashburn?" Norland bustled into the library, where Rand was engaged with his housekeeper, who had some last-minute questions about the menu for this evening.

"Thank you, Mrs. Juteney." Rand dismissed her with a smile and rose. "Why don't we take a turn in the gallery, Norland? Dismal day, or I'd suggest a walk outside."

"What? Eh? Oh, yes, of course."

"I'm told you've been sequestered in your bedchamber all day," Ashburn remarked as they paced beneath the enigmatic stares of his forebears' portraits.

Norland nodded. "When I heard Grimshaw was attending, there was no time to waste, you know. Must have everything just so when I lay out my plans to him."

"I understand," Rand said. "I trust you have everything you require?"

"Yes, yes, thank you. Kind of you to send up a sandwich. When I work, I forget everything else."

"Including your betrothed," murmured Rand.

Norland shot a quick glance at Rand and looked away. He gave an uncomfortable staccato laugh, rather like the bray of a donkey. "As to that, Lady Cecily and I understand one another well enough. She doesn't wish me to live in her pocket. Indeed, nothing would displease her more, I daresay."

"And what do *you* wish, Norland?" Rand cocked an eyebrow. "I thought you went on quite happily as a bachelor. I confess this betrothal took me by surprise."

Norland's harried expression deepened. "Well. Yes. I mean, I must own I was a little, ahem, surprised myself."

"Oh?" What an intriguing confession.

"Long-standing arrangement between the families, of course," said Norland. "But after my first wife died, God rest her, I quite thought . . . Well, that is to say, I did not realize Lady Cecily's parents still held to the original, er, understanding between the families. I'd been married and fathered two sons since then."

"Ah," said Rand. The implication was clear. Norland had been trapped into honoring an arrangement that no one, least of all the groom himself, thought would ever be enforced. Arranged marriages were not so common now as they once had been. Only the highest sticklers insisted on them in this modern, romantic age.

"Daresay life will go on the same as it ever did once we're married." Norland rubbed his cheek with the back of one finger. "We are quite agreed upon that."

Rand clasped his hands behind his back as they walked. "Really? It's been my observation that everything in a man's life changes when he weds. Though of course, I've no personal experience of the matter." He paused. "Lady Cecily get on all right with your mama, does she?"

"Ah." Norland glanced over his shoulder, as if afraid his terrifying parent might pop out from behind a couch at any moment. "Forceful female, my mother. Says she'll school Lady Cecily to her liking if it kills them both."

"Did she just?" Rand wished quite fervently that Cecily were present to hear this. "And do you think she'll be successful in that endeavor?"

Norland rubbed his nose. "Can't see it myself, but there's no telling with women, is there? My mother has never been brought to a stand yet. She's a formidable lady."

"As is your betrothed."

"Ye-es." There was marked uncertainty in Norland's tone.

Cecily might not know it, but to avoid being harnessed to the dowager's yoke through her son, she must engage in battle with the dowager. She would have to win the war for mastery over Norland if she wanted the freedom to pursue her own interests.

Rand doubted Cecily would have the patience or the stomach for that particular fight.

"I shouldn't think they'll see much of one another at any rate," said Norland hopefully. "I'll set Cecily up in a snug little house in Town. She doesn't wish to interfere with my mother's running of the estate and the household, so they're unlikely to, er, disagree on very much."

"I see."

Rand did see the attraction of such an arrangement from Cecily's point of view—at least in theory.

But in practice? What a God-awful mess! He'd seen what came of this kind of marriage before. Separation was never as cut-and-dried as Cecily might like it to be. She might believe herself autonomous, but by sheer virtue of being the wife of a man who was ruled by his mama, she'd find her freedom curtailed at every turn.

Rand clapped Norland on the back in sympathy. "You will lead a dog's life, my friend."

Norland puffed out his jowls. "Really, Ashburn! Why do you say that?"

"Two strong personalities—your mama wanting one thing, Lady Cecily wanting the opposite. And you, my dear fellow, *you* caught in the middle. Good Lord, you'll never get any peace."

Rand went on to paint a dismal portrait of life married to Lady Cecily Westruther, giving Norland example after example of instances where Cecily and the dowager would be bound to lock horns.

"Where will you find time for your work with all of that going on?" said Rand mournfully. "Genius such as yours requires tranquillity, freedom from such trivialities. Your wife ought to be a helpmeet, not an unwelcome distraction."

Noting that his companion had fallen into troubled silence, Rand let him contemplate the bleakness of his future.

Rand was considering his next tactic when he heard the crunch of carriage wheels and the clop of horses' hooves on the drive.

He crossed to the window. "Ah! It looks like more guests are here. Will you excuse me? I must go down to greet them."

His companion's frown lifted magically, as if with Rand's exit, Norland's troubles would depart also.

Rand suspected that despite the groundwork he'd laid during their conversation, he had a lot more to do in order to shore up his position. Norland was only too ready to bury his head in the sand and trust that everything would work out for the best. He would not be allowed to do so, however. Not while under Rand's roof, at any rate.

Rand paused to add, "I expect the rest of my guests to arrive this afternoon. Dinner will be at seven."

"Eh?" Norland started, as if he'd already forgotten Rand was there. Vaguely, he said, "Oh, I shan't dine tonight. There's too much to do before tomorrow."

"You will dine with us, Norland," corrected Rand pleasantly. "Lady Cecily is in a strange house with people she doesn't know. You will pay her the compliment of attending and seeing to her comfort."

A certain amount of absentmindedness ought to be tolerated in someone of Norland's genius, but that did not excuse bad manners. Cecily would not be humiliated by her fiancé in this house, in front of Rand's family and friends. Not if Rand had anything to say in the matter.

Norland huffed with impatience. "But if I'm to be prepared for tomorrow, I must—"

"I insist, Norland," Rand said in a gentle tone that brooked no argument.

With a nod and a slight smile to his guest, he left the room.

Chapter Fifteen

Within five minutes of entering the drawing room for tea, Cecily had taken the measure of the other houseguests.

Freddy was nervous—no surprises there. He kept attempting to buttonhole Rand, but his cousin slipped away like an elegant and particularly elusive eel. Cecily was sorry to observe the downcast look on Freddy's face. Clearly, the younger man was not forgiven his transgression with that rampant female in Ashburn's library.

Freddy's mama, Lady Matthew Kendall, was a harridan of the first order. Cecily had seen women like her before and was not fooled by her effusive protestations of affection for her nephew.

From Rand's lack of warmth in return, Cecily deduced that he was not fooled, either. Indeed, his jaw hardened whenever she addressed him, as if it was an effort for him to respond with civility.

Mr. Garvey, Rand's friend, was relaxed and witty and agreeable. Cecily found Miss Garvey to be equally good company, though the young lady was clearly smitten with Rand.

Miss Garvey did not do anything so vulgar as to make sheep's eyes at her host; she merely blushed whenever he addressed a remark to her.

Cecily could hardly blame Miss Garvey for that. Rand appeared more handsome than usual that afternoon. She only hoped she herself did not betray the thrill that shot through her every time his brilliant gaze rested on her.

It rested on her frequently. She found herself wondering whether he felt, as she did, that it had been a long time since last they spoke.

They did not have an opportunity to exchange more than a few words until dinner, when Cecily was seated at Rand's right.

It was a small party, and generally a congenial one, since their host had placed his aunt at the other end of the table from himself. That served to pay her the charming compliment of nominating her as hostess while ensuring that she was too far away for her nephew to be obliged to converse with the woman.

Excellent strategy, thought Cecily. She could not have done better herself. Although she was sorry to see Rand had also placed poor Freddy out of range of easy conversation, too. Why that should bother her, she didn't know. It was none of her business, was it? Still, she ought to see what she could do for the young man. She thought Rand's continued coldness overly harsh.

Everyone appeared charmed by their company, save one exception: Cecily's betrothed looked as if a thundercloud hovered immediately above his head.

"What did you do to get Norland down here?" Cecily asked Rand under cover of the general conversation. "He looks as sulky as a bear."

He lifted his brows. "I? Nothing. I merely requested his presence, that is all."

Cecily rolled her eyes. "A request from you is tantamount to a royal decree. To him, at least."

His lips relaxed and those tiger eyes gleamed. "I wouldn't put it quite like that. Nor will I apologize for reminding your betrothed of his manners. He shows a distressing lack of courtesy toward you. It . . . irks me."

"Well, if I don't mind it, I don't see why you should."

She did mind it, of course; she was not made of stone. Rand's presence seemed to make her embarrassment more acute. But she would mind a husband who meddled in what didn't concern him far more than a man who didn't concern himself with her at all.

He sipped his wine. "I should have thought the answer to that question perfectly obvious."

Refusing to be drawn into that conversation, Cecily sipped her burgundy. She comforted herself with the fact that she would be obliged to deal with this kind of thing for only a few more days. Less, if she found that letter.

"Do you know," Rand added in a low voice, "I cannot decide whether it is when you scowl like that or when you are animated, speaking of your passions, that I most want to kiss you."

She choked a little on her wine.

"I think it must be when you scowl," he mused

softly. "Because I am seriously considering consigning my guests to the Devil and hauling you upstairs to make love to you at this very moment."

The wine burned her windpipe. She put her napkin to her lips and coughed. She managed, "I think Norland would have something to say about that."

"Do you really?" Rand contemplated this. "I wonder if he'd notice."

Rand's guests were delighted with the proposed expedition to Cambridge. A picnic by the Cam and perhaps a punt on the river would be just the thing to make the most of the spring weather. Lady Arden graciously agreed to chaperone them; unexpectedly, Rand's aunt decided to come along as well.

What do you want now? thought Rand. His aunt was at her most affable when she desired something from him. Hadn't he learned that the hard way?

The ladies hurried off to complete the necessary preparations. Oliver Garvey lounged on a comfortable chair by Rand's desk and drawled, "Coming on to rain again this afternoon, I should think."

"If it does, we can take refreshment in a tea shop," said Rand calmly.

"Quite right." Garvey paused. "Not one to pry, dear boy . . ."

"Heaven forbid," Rand muttered. He inclined his head. "Why is it that I hear an imminent 'but'?"

"*However,*" said Garvey, "just thought I'd drop a word in your shell-like."

"My shell-like is all agog," said Rand. He knew what was coming but saw no way to avert it.

Garvey rubbed his elegant nose. "Devilish tricky thing to tell you your business, but remiss of me not to. Fond of you, Ashburn, which is why—"

"Oh, out with it, man! It's not as if I don't know what you're going to say."

Relief relaxed Garvey's features. "Well, I daresay you don't like it, but I'll tell you to your head, Ashburn. I would not venture into that territory if I were you."

"And what territory might that be?" Rand rose and walked around his desk. He leaned against it and folded his arms, waiting.

"Not going to do any good to loom over me like that," said Garvey. "I ain't afraid of you." He threw up his hands. "Montford's territory, of course! Good God, man, the girl's to be married in a week!"

"Which is why," said Rand deliberately, "I must act now."

Garvey's jaw dropped. "My dear fellow. You want to *marry* her?"

"I am *going* to marry her," said Rand grimly.

Recovering his usual nonchalance, Garvey inspected his fingernails. "Uh, dear boy, does the lady know that?"

Rand did not answer, just stared blandly at Garvey.

"Right. Of course. None of my business. But Lord Almighty, Ashburn, be careful what you are about. Montford is not a man to cross. And those cousins of Lady Cecily's . . ." He shuddered. "Steyne in particular. Now, *there's* an ugly customer. Did you hear about that business with Elliott?"

Rand held up a hand. "Calm yourself, Oliver. I

am not shaking in my boots over any Westruthers, ugly customers or otherwise. But to set your mind at ease—and this is for your ears only—it so happens that in this instance, I already have Montford's support."

"Well, that's a first," said Garvey after a stunned silence.

"Probably a last, too," said Rand. "Shouldn't you see to your cattle?"

Garvey glanced at the clock and rose. "Yes, I suppose I should." His blue eyes sparkled. "This little jaunt into Cambridge part of your plan?"

Rand shrugged. "How should it be?"

"I don't know, but I know you, Ashburn."

"I can't imagine what you mean by that." Rand smiled as Garvey got to his feet.

"I hope you know what you're about," said his friend, drawing on his gloves. "I don't want to be a second at any duels."

Rand snorted. "Can you imagine Norland fighting a duel?"

"Dear boy, that's what I keep telling you. It's not Norland I'm worried about."

Cecily was like a cat on hot bricks, anticipating Rand's next move. She dreaded being alone with him; if it weren't for Tibby, she would have cried off from the proposed excursion.

It rather astonished her to learn that the entire party was to go. She'd expected Rand would try to get her on her own.

In fact, far from monopolizing her, Rand offered a place in his curricle to Miss Garvey. Cecily could either drive with Mr. Garvey or beg a seat in the barouche.

Mr. Garvey it was. Rand's friend was amusing company, but Cecily was obliged to stare at the backs of the Duke of Ashburn and Miss Garvey the entire way. It made her rather sour to see their heads bent together as they appeared to share an amusing conversation. Miss Garvey had a truly infectious, jolly laugh. Cecily wondered what Rand was saying to her to make her laugh so very often.

So when they'd disembarked and refreshed themselves at a tea shop and Ashburn finally suggested that he and Cecily ought to call on Miss Tibbs, she all but snapped at him.

"Yes, let us go now, shall we? I must hope the basket of food I brought is not spoiled."

His eyes glinted with mirth, as if he knew the true reason she was so cross. "Indeed. Let us make all haste to Miss Tibbs's cottage."

As they bowled along in Rand's curricle, Cecily avoided looking at her companion. Yet she felt his presence in every cell of her body.

At any other time, she would have taken intense interest in her surroundings. The awe-inspiring architecture of the university colleges, the bustle of students in their billowing gowns. The lazy glide of punts on the Cam.

As a girl she'd longed to be part of all this. She'd envied her brother being so at home here among the intellectual elite, while she would always remain an outsider due to her sex.

The day she had finally accepted her dream would never be, that some things were impossible even for the sister of an earl, was one of the saddest—and the angriest—days of her life.

"Tell me about this Miss Tibbs." Rand's deep voice broke her thoughts as he guided his horses around another bend. "She was your governess for many years, was she not? A woman of determined character and great moral courage, I presume?"

She gave a gurgle of laughter. "How did you guess? Good Lord, how we tormented the rest of the governesses who were sent to us. Tibby was the only one who could stick beyond a week or so."

"You are fond of her," he said.

"Oh, yes. She is one of the family." She wrinkled her brow. "That is, she does not always see eye to eye with my guardian, but that is only to be expected. She's a dyed-in-the-wool bluestocking, you know, and has very progressive ideas about women's rights."

"I see. Does she dislike men in general, then?"

"Oh, no! But she greatly dislikes the institution of marriage. She approves of Norland, though." She considered that. "I believe he's the only man of whom she does wholeheartedly approve. I can't think why, for he is in general completely dismissive of the female intellect. He thinks it's an oxymoron."

"He seems to judge Miss Tibbs a woman of superior sense," said Rand.

"Did he say that to you?" When he nodded, she said thoughtfully, "I expect that is because she listens to *his* lectures with interest."

He glanced at her. "You think her interest feigned?"

"No, I am quite certain it is not. Which makes it

all the more curious," said Cecily. "However, one can never predict human nature, can one?"

She looked about her, suddenly conscious that they had been driving for nearly a quarter of an hour now. "Do you know the area well? I have never been to this cottage before."

"Norland told me the way," said Rand.

They drove on for a few miles, taking numerous twists and turns. How on earth did Rand keep all that in his head? Cecily was sure she couldn't have done so. But then, her sense of direction had never been her strong suit.

When they finally came to Wisteria Lane, Cecily was puzzled. Norland had said he was just passing and called on Tibby, hadn't he? How odd. This cottage did not seem to be on the way to anywhere.

While Rand saw to his horses, Cecily let herself in at the cottage gate and walked up the path.

The garden was neatly kept, the path clear of leaves and weeds, the flower beds a riot of spring color.

The cottage also seemed strangely silent.

Rather surprised that no one had come out to greet her, Cecily knocked on the door.

She had not written to Tibby to apprise her of the visit, concerned that if she knew Cecily was to call, Tibby would fret about how to entertain her.

All Cecily wished to do was to ascertain if Tibby needed anything and leave her a basket Rand had been kind enough to order prepared.

She hadn't thought that out very well, had she?

Still, no one came to the door.

Could they possibly be from home? But Norland had said Tibby's sister was too ill to be left.

Perhaps both sisters were resting. Nighttime was often the worst for invalids, so their nurses tended to snatch sleep when they could.

"Everything all right?" Rand spoke from behind her.

She started. "Oh! Well, actually, I'm not sure. There was no answer at the door, so perhaps we have come at a bad time." She bit her lip. "I ought to have sent a note."

"Shall I knock again?" asked Rand.

"No, don't do that," said Cecily "I have a feeling they might be resting. Best not to disturb them."

Rand glanced up at the windows on the upper floor.

He nodded. "We'll leave the basket." He set it down on the front step, where it would be shaded by the overhanging roofline.

As they turned to go, a light patter of footsteps approached the door. It opened, and Tibby's face peered out.

"Cecily!" she exclaimed.

Cecily embraced her companion fondly and then held her at arm's length, surveying her slight form keenly.

Miss Tibbs was precise as a pin as always, but there was a weariness about her eyes, as if she had not slept properly since she'd left Montford House.

"My dear Tibby!" said Cecily. "Norland told me you looked sadly pulled and he was right."

"His Grace said that?" Tibby looked aghast. "Pray, Cecily, believe me it is no such thing. But do come in. I don't know what I'm about to keep you standing on the doorstep."

Tibby caught sight of the duke then, and faltered.

"Oh. This is the Duke of Ashburn, but don't mind him." Cecily felt all at once that she ought not to have brought Rand. His presence would scarcely set Tibby at ease.

Tactfully, she refused her old governess's invitation to enter. "We came only to bring you this basket, and to ask if you need anything else."

Tibby glanced down at the basket. "Oh! Oh, how kind."

But again, it seemed Cecily had not judged the situation well, because her companion looked most discomfited.

"Has there been any improvement in your sister's health, Tibby?"

Tibby's mouth trembled. "She is very poorly, I'm afraid."

"You cannot leave her. I understand," Cecily said. She glanced at Rand. "We must be going."

Rand started forward with the basket, but Tibby said, "Your Grace, really, no, I insist! I can manage it." She took the basket from him.

Rand looked an inquiry at Cecily. She gave a slight shake of her head. The basket wasn't terribly heavy, and perhaps Tibby did not wish them to venture farther into the cottage.

"Thank you so much for your kindness, my dear," said Tibby. "Your Grace, thank you for bringing Lady Cecily to see me. I regret the circumstances which . . ."

She faltered and Cecily cut off the embarrassed speech, leaning forward to give her companion a quick kiss on the cheek. "Write to me care of His Grace if you need anything else, won't you? I shall be at Anglesby another day or two."

Tibby gave a rather strained smile. "Yes, my dear. Of course I will."

"I am nearing the end of my search among Jonathon's things," said Cecily as they set off again. "I've told Lady Arden I wish to leave tomorrow."

That came as no surprise to Rand. Ever since he'd kissed her in the attic, he'd sensed her urgency to complete the task she'd come for and be gone.

He made no protest against her departure. Tempting as it was to prolong their time together at Anglesby, he needed to return to Town to put his plans into action also.

The time had come to lay some of his cards on the table.

"If you do not mind, we won't rejoin the others just yet." Rand drove them to a quiet stretch of the Cam, where weeping willows trailed their long green fronds in the water.

They found an appropriate spot for him to throw down the blanket he'd brought. Cecily put out her hand to allow him to help her sit down. Then she angled her parasol to shade her face from the sun.

The parasol was a lacy affair, and when she held it a certain way, tiny pinpricks of sunlight danced over the creaminess of her skin. She looked fresh as a daisy and completely untouchable, all in white, with her legs tucked demurely to the side.

She was such an elegant little creature. So lively and full of wit. She would be a duchess for the ages, remembered through generations for her vivacity and charm, for her intelligence and her amazing capacity to give.

But he was air-dreaming of a future that might never be if he didn't put a stop to her marriage to Norland. He'd hoped this letter she searched for would provide some inkling as to why she was so reluctant to admit her feelings for Rand, but had to concede he was stymied.

He drew the small bundle of letters from the inner pocket of his coat.

"I believe these are what you were looking for."

Her eyes widened. She almost snatched them from him. "How did you—? Oh! I could embrace you! Thank you!"

With an effort, he resisted the temptation to take her up on that offer, immediately.

Clearly unconscious of teasing him with the notion of her soft body pressed to his, Cecily untied the black riband that bound the letters together. Feverishly, she sorted through them, her breathing growing more rapid, more distressed as she went through the pile.

She looked at him sharply. "Is this all? Was there nothing else?"

So he was right. The letter she wanted was not among the ones he'd found. "That is all. I discovered the bundle in one of the trunks. I have been searching in spare moments, too."

The sudden suspicious light in those lively dark eyes was all too justified; he knew that. Completely unreasonable of him to wish it weren't there. To need her to trust him, even though he knew himself to be unworthy of that trust . . .

"You have it, don't you?" She said the words quietly. "Will you use it? Can you truly be so desperate to end my betrothal that you'd humiliate a good man—?"

"Good God! What is this?" he said, straightening. "I give you my word I do not have any other correspondence of yours. This was all that I found." He held up a hand as if to take an oath. "Upon my honor, Cecily."

She stared into his eyes, and the ire slowly died from her expression. Puzzlement took its place. "But the letter I want, it should be here. There is nowhere else it would be."

Rand shrugged. "Perhaps he did not keep it."

"No, no, I know he kept it." She held up the small stack of letters. "I even saw him put it in here."

"Maybe he took it out. Perhaps he destroyed it before he died," said Rand. "There are any number of possible explanations."

Slowly, Cecily said, "Or Lavinia could have found it."

"Lavinia?" Rand straightened. "You mean Lady Davenport?"

"She was the one who sold you those papers, was she not?"

He frowned. "Yes. I suppose she could have taken it. But why should she? And how would she have had time?"

And what else might the countess have taken?

Christ! The implications didn't bear thinking about. Of course, it was unlikely the countess would know what she'd stumbled across, but still . . .

"First we must finish going through those trunks," said Cecily. "If that fails, I will find a way to search Lavinia's things. I know her secret hiding place. If she has anything to conceal, it will be there."

He would need to be there, too. "Her London residence?"

Cecily's eyes narrowed. "I believe so. I believe that if she has my letter and wants to use it against me, she will use it any day now. I wonder what price she might demand in exchange."

"I suppose I need hardly tell you my services are at your command."

She glanced at him. "Thank you, but it would be easier for me to conduct a search on one of my visits there."

He smoothed a hand over the blanket beside him. "And are you going to tell me what is in that letter? What can you have written as a child that would be so damaging to you now?"

She looked away from him, staring out over the peace of the water. Then she looked back. "I was young and stupid and something of a rebel. My parents had chosen this man to marry me, a man years and years older than I. Well, I was spoiled and silly and I wrote a little book. A satire lampooning the Duke of Norland. I called him Sir Ninian Finian the hapless knight and invented a series of madcap adventures for him. He got into all sorts of hot water, from which the precocious Henrietta Peddlethorpe rescued him."

She sighed. "It was wrong of me. But no one would ever recognize Norland in that fictional character, except . . ."

"Except that you wrote about it in that letter to Jonathon," Rand finished.

"He'd seen the likeness and reproached me," said Cecily. "I wrote that letter justifying my ridicule, point by point." She blinked rapidly. In a brittle voice, she said, "Do you know, I don't think I like my younger self at all. However, I did alter the way Sir Ninian looked in later episodes. And of course, after a time the character became his own person and not a caricature."

"But if someone gets their hands on that letter, they could make it public."

"Yes." She swallowed. "It would ruin me and make a laughingstock of him. I couldn't bear it."

He hesitated. "You were a child, Cecily."

She flung out a hand. "Do you think that will matter to the gossips? Of course it won't!"

"And you thought that I would use this letter against you if I found it." The notion that she'd thought him so base fired his anger.

She threw him a guarded look. "Well, I didn't know, you see—"

"Are you ready to go now?" he said abruptly. "The others will wonder what's keeping us."

"Why yes, I—" She broke off. "Good God, Rand, are you angry with me?"

A muscle ticced in his jaw. "Angry? Why should I be?"

"Oh, not the least reason in the world," she retorted. "Yet you are. I can tell. *You* might think you are the iceberg of the ton but your eyes give you away every time."

He stared at her. She bit her lip, as if sorry to have said so much.

"Tell me this,' he said abruptly. "You wrote that scathing summary of your betrothed's character many years ago," he said. "But has your opinion of Norland altered since then?"

She took a deep breath. "I was a silly, headstrong little girl, puffed up in her own conceit. I bitterly regret writing that letter."

"That is not an answer."

She remained silent.

Harshly, he said, "Did you truly think that *I* would go to the scandal-sheets with that story?" Try as he might, he couldn't erase the wounded outrage from his tone.

"No, I thought you would hold it over my head as blackmail," said Cecily, looking him straight in the eye.

Her words slid beneath his ribs like a stiletto. The pain of it nearly robbed him of speech. "Charming notion you have of me!"

"Well, you've shown yourself to be utterly ruthless when you want something," said Cecily, her gaze averted now. She shrugged. "How should I know where you would draw the line?"

He reached out and captured her pointed chin in his fingertips, turned her head so she faced him. "You know," he said softly. "You know me better than you want to admit."

For a breathless moment, her eyes seemed to darken with emotion. He wanted to pull her to him and love her with all the intense heat that burned inside him, incinerate her objections, claim her for his own. He wanted to explore every inch of her—body, heart, mind, soul. He wanted so very badly to *know* her, in every sense of the word.

With a small gasp, Cecily jerked her head away, as if he'd burned her in truth and not only in his imagination.

She planted the point of her parasol in the ground and jumped to her feet. "This is absurd and wrong and . . . and we ought to join the others before they wonder where we are."

Chapter Sixteen

Rand maintained a smooth, unruffled demeanor for the rest of the day, but he seethed inside.

Cecily had told him she intended to leave his house tomorrow. She must lose no time in locating that missing piece of correspondence, she said. If she didn't find it in one of those trunks tonight, she must search Lady Davenport's house.

As it happened, he had an imminent appointment in town himself. If what the Duke of Montford had written to him was true, he needed to cut short the house party almost as soon as it had begun. Which was excessively bad form. However, he didn't care if he offended his relations. He must simply trust that Garvey and his sister would understand.

Norland walked among the clouds at the moment, having secured an in principle agreement from Grimshaw to fund his next scientific project. Not even veiled threats from Rand could move Cecily's betrothed downstairs for dinner after the meeting with Grimshaw.

Rand decided it didn't matter.

His world had narrowed to one person. The rest of them could go to hell.

He had made the cataclysmic discovery today that Lady Cecily Westruther had the power to wound him. Which was laughable, really, considering how thick-skinned he'd been in his pursuit of her until now. Nothing she had said or done had deterred him from chasing her once he'd set his mind to it.

Nothing she had said or done since had convinced him she didn't want him, too.

He'd as good as told her he'd go to any lengths to win her. He planned to take extreme measures; she'd discover as much when she returned to London.

So when she accused him of keeping that letter so as to blackmail her, why had he all of a sudden become thin-skinned? Why had that barb stung?

He wanted her and resented her power over him in equal measure. If Garvey were privy to all this mess of thoughts and emotions, he'd counsel Rand to let her go. After he stopped rolling about the floor laughing, that was.

But he couldn't release her. It wasn't within his power to do so. Without even meaning to do it, *she'd* captivated *him*.

He couldn't let another man have her. Couldn't allow her to deny what was between them any longer.

He'd make one last attempt to persuade her tonight, before she left.

One last chance to settle this amicably, before he declared war.

* * *

When dinner was over and she had spent a decent amount of time in the drawing room afterwards, Cecily claimed fatigue and retired for the evening.

Instead of going to her bedchamber, she went straight up to the attics with a renewed sense of urgency but without an awful lot of hope. Tonight should see the completion of her search, for good or ill.

Disregarding the toll kneeling on the attic floor took on her fine muslin gown, she threw open one more trunk and attacked its contents.

With only the candle Ashburn had given her to light the room, Cecily's eyes soon grew tired. All the late nights and early mornings were catching up with her.

Her vision blurred and she had to keep blinking it clear, but she pressed on, sorting through the great morass of papers. It was past midnight when she'd finished the last trunk.

As she went slowly down the stairs, she felt defeated. If that incriminating letter had been anywhere, surely it would have been in that trunk she'd found with all the other personal correspondence. Slim chance of finding it among the rest.

On the landing, she saw the glow of another candle moving up toward her and heard a firm tread on the stair.

Rand, of course. He rounded the staircase and looked up. "Ah," he said softly. "I hoped I'd find you up here."

He came swiftly up the staircase and stopped on the landing, where she stood next to a deeply recessed window.

The sky must have cleared, for moonlight streamed over them, making candlelight scarcely necessary.

"Any luck?" He set down his candle on the windowsill.

"Only a dusty gown and a paper cut for my troubles." In an offhand gesture, she indicated the index finger that still smarted from the place where a piece of foolscap had sliced it.

He captured her hand and tilted it to the light so as to inspect the damage.

Her stupid heart bounded into her throat. One touch brought her body tingling to life. This was madness!

"Ah." He located the tiny cut. His gaze flicked to hers and his stern mouth quirked up at one corner. "Shall I kiss it better?"

Before she could refuse him, he brought her fingertip to his lips and pressed a kiss to the small cut.

Heat flashed over her. She gasped and would have drawn her hand free, but he took her fingertip a small way into his mouth and gently sucked.

The warm, moist pressure of it lasted but a moment, but in that moment, her insides turned warm and moist, too.

Briefly, she closed her eyes, and her body swayed a little toward him. He removed the candle from her grasp and set it down.

"Are you still angry with me about today?" he asked in a low, gravelly voice.

"No," she said. "Though I thought it was rather you who was angry with me."

"What a pity," he replied, ignoring that last sally. "I like it when you're angry. You have the most speaking eyes, Lady Cecily Westruther. They tell me all kinds of things you would not wish me to know."

"How indiscreet of them," Cecily said. She made her tone skeptical, but she could not help wondering if what he said was true.

"Do you want to know what they are saying to me now, Cecily?"

Yes. "No."

"They are saying 'take me.' "

She tried for a scornful laugh but it came out a little shakily. "*Take* me?"

"Do you deny it?"

"Of course I deny it." How could she possibly do otherwise?

Ashburn was in a strange mood tonight, she thought a little desperately as he moved toward her. She retreated a pace, an involuntary response, but he followed. One more step and her back was to the wall. Mere inches separated their bodies.

Candlelight warmed his features, burnished his eyes to gold. There was both a wildness and a firm sense of purpose to him tonight. Something deeply feminine within her responded to it, wanted to feel that wildness, capture it for her own.

His low voice seemed to speak from inside her. "Shall I obey those eyes of yours, Cecily? Shall I make you forget everything but the feel of my touch? Shall I do things to you that will bring a blush to your cheeks whenever you think of them? Give you a taste of how it could be between us?"

Cecily's mouth had gone dry. Her heart pounded so hard, the sound of it seemed to crowd her brain. She brought her hands up in a halfhearted, defensive gesture. He caught her wrists, pinned them to the wall on either side of her head.

She felt exposed, panicked, helpless to escape him, and the combination set her ablaze. Dimly, she knew it was a fiction that he held her completely in his power. She might have called a stop to this restraint at any moment. But it was a fiction she wanted—needed—to preserve.

His tone grew softly menacing. "*Shall* I?"

Another flare of heat. She swallowed hard but said nothing. Let him read the answer in those chatty eyes of hers.

"Have it your way," he ground out. "I am tired of waiting for you to come to your senses. If this is how you want it, so be it."

With his hands clamping her wrists, Rand kissed her with such force that her head pressed back into the cool, hard wall. He ravished her mouth with deep strokes of his tongue, unleashing upon her all his frustration and pent-up desire. She was trapped, overwhelmed, overcome. And she'd never felt more alive in her life.

His mouth was everywhere, at her throat, at her breast, his teeth gently biting her nipples through layers of gown and corset. Shock at such boldness held her silent at first, but she soon abandoned any thought of resistance. He did not release her wrists until she sagged, boneless and mindless, against the wall.

Her arms dropped to her sides. They both knew she would not take advantage of her freedom and try to leave. The time for running had slipped into the past like a dream. Now was all that mattered.

Now, with his mouth on her, sliding, nibbling, licking. Now, with his hands, those large, dexterous hands caressing, touching, building her pleasure, stoking her need.

The intensity of feeling was something she'd never experienced before. The tall, shadowy form who ravished her thus was Rand, Duke of Ashburn, she reminded herself, and she shivered at the mere thought.

Her eyelids had long since lowered in languorous enjoyment of the moment, a string of delicious sensations that shocked her and delighted her in equal measure.

As Rand used one hand to gather the material of her skirts, her eyes flew open.

" 'Sh," he said against her mouth.

Cool air flowed around her ankles, then her stockinged legs. She felt the heat of his hand on her bare thigh, just above her garter.

The place between her legs ached and throbbed as he stroked upward, tantalizingly close, but not nearly close enough. His breathing was harsh and hot in her ear. "Tell me you want this and I'll give you everything you desire."

A frown creased her brows. She didn't know precisely what he meant. She didn't know *what* she wanted, but of course he knew better than she did. Which was vaguely galling, but desire and need won over caution and pride.

"I want this," she murmured, clutching at his shoulders. "Show me."

Without hesitation, his hand found the place between her legs. She'd grown embarrassingly wet there but the sharp gasp he made when his finger-tips found her moist folds of flesh told her he didn't mind that at all.

The terrifying, awestruck excitement of it was almost unbearable. He was touching her there! So gently, with such attention and care. She trembled at the shocking sweetness it. The intimacy, the knowing.

He bent his head to touch his forehead to hers. His breath, warm and soft and faintly laced with wine flowed against her parted lips.

His eyes were closed, she realized, his expression intent as he learned the contours of that secret place.

And then he touched something exquisitely sensitive that made her breath catch in surprise. He circled slowly, stroked, rubbed, until the very soles of her feet tingled with a strange, intense heat.

And then the warmth gathered in that place where he touched her and all of her seemed to draw tight, bunching, winding tighter until her quickened breathing turned to sobbing, ragged cry. He took her mouth and plunged one finger inside her, swallowing her cries as she exploded into shimmering brilliance, like a firework in his arms.

He crushed her to him, kissing her as if he might drink in all the pleasure he'd given her. Her body shaped itself to his in the most intimate manner; she felt the hot hardness of his member pressing against her. Dimly, she understood what she might never have comprehended otherwise, the craving for that part of a man. The need to be filled by it, by him.

Because even well-pleasured as she was, she made the shocking realization that she was far from sated. The aching need to return the pleasure he'd given her surprised her almost as much.

All of these jumbled emotions came to her through a barely conscious haze. He made no attempt to take advantage of this rare moment of pliancy, but he kept her senses befuddled with kisses.

His lips drifted over her cheek. "You are special, Cecily. So very special," he murmured into her ear. "I won't rest until you're mine."

Suddenly, and far too late, the awful truth of what she'd done came home to her. She tensed in his arms.

He was so attuned to her, he reacted at once. "Don't," he said fiercely, pulling away, taking her by the shoulders as if to shake her. "Just *don't*, Cecily."

And he was right. What a fool and a hypocrite she would be to start bleating about her betrayal of Norland now, when she'd been the one to take and take that exquisite torture and offer nothing in return.

So she made no recriminations, silently hating herself and her weakness.

She had to make herself say it. "This doesn't change anything." She could not betray Norland like this! It would never, ever happen again.

"No, it doesn't," he agreed, his expression harsh. "I still want you. I want you to be my duchess. More, I think, than anything I've wanted before. And you are too stubborn, too *frightened* to see what's best for everyone concerned."

His voice rasped. "Damn it, Cecily, admit you want me too. Is that so hard?"

She squeezed her eyes shut and let her head fall

back against the wall. Yes, it was hard. Impossible, she thought wearily, as her body turned cold and her pulse slowed and her mind slowly but surely sharpened back into focus.

Impossible. Wrong. And she was a fool, a traitor and a coward but she'd wanted him so much . . .

Once again, Rand took her silence as an answer. He sucked in a breath. "You'd throw it all away, wouldn't you, so that you can be untouchable, so you can be safe."

Her lips were numb. She had to force the words through them. "I will never break my betrothal."

He stared at her for a long time. "Very well, then," he said. "You leave me no choice. No more diplomacy, no more games. This, dearest Cecily, is war."

Rand's words rang in Cecily's ears all the way home from Cambridgeshire. When he kissed her, touched her, when the world fell away, she was more than tempted to agree to anything he demanded of her.

But that was folly of the worst kind. Quite apart from the scandal and the insult to Norland and his family, if she broke her betrothal and married Rand, she would soon become precisely the sort of female she'd vowed never to be. Dependent on him not only for material things, but for her happiness as well. She'd vowed long ago never to let her happiness rest on any one person. Especially not a *husband*.

Rand would never let her live her own life in her own home with a large enough income at her disposal to do as she pleased. She would not be permitted to bat an eyelid without consulting him first. He was that kind of man: powerful, arrogant, altogether too accustomed to getting his own way.

No, she must try to put him out of her mind and concentrate on finding a way to search Lavinia's room for that confounded note. If she had no luck there, then she must take her chances and pray that the letter in which she had lampooned her future husband never came to light.

She did not like the second option. Living with the harsh, ridiculing words of her younger self hanging over her head like a Sword of Damocles would not be pleasant. The letter had not been in Rand's attics. There was only one place left to look.

Back in London, Cecily bided her time, then called on her cousin Lavinia when she knew the countess would be from home.

Reeves informed her as much, so she said, "Never mind, I shall try again another day. Perhaps I might pop down to the kitchens and say hello to Mrs. Palmer—"

She'd been stripping off her gloves as one who was sure of her welcome, but when she looked up, she realized the butler looked troubled.

"I'm sorry, my lady," he said, his mouth trembling a little. "My orders are not to admit you when the countess is from home."

The poor man was clearly distressed and embarrassed at breaking this news to her, so she didn't argue. "Oh, that's quite all right, dear Reeves. I would not wish to get you into trouble."

"If I might be so bold as to request you not to attempt to gain entry through any of the other staff either, my lady," said Reeves. He made a helpless gesture. "We have all of us been threatened with instant dismissal if one of us so much as lets you past the hall."

He looked so mortified that Cecily reached out to give his hand a quick pat. "Pray, do not concern yourself, Reeves. I'll go at once. Do give Her Ladyship my regards. I'll call again tomorrow."

"Drat and blast!" muttered Cecily as she collected her maid and hurried back to Montford House. What was she going to do now?

Housebreaking had become quite a habit with her, Cecily reflected as she made her way to her cousin's mansion that night.

This time, it was a house she knew well and there was no difficulty entering it. She knew Lavinia and Bertram were at a ball in Richmond and would not return until dawn. If a servant caught her, she'd merely explain she wanted to play a practical joke on her cousins.

All in all, it was the easiest bit of housebreaking she'd ever done.

Except for one thing. The Duke of Ashburn had insisted on coming with her.

How he'd known of her plans she'd no idea. Had he been watching her? When he'd appeared from the shadows, she'd been almost willing to believe in what the rest of the beau monde said about his omniscience.

"Have you ever broken into a house before?" she whispered as they watched from the mews at the back of the house until all the lights went out.

"Do you know, I don't believe I have," he replied, as if surprised at himself. "I am looking forward to broadening my experience."

She rolled her eyes. "It would be safer if you kept watch. I can be in and out in no time."

"And miss all he fun?" he said, an amused note in his voice. "Not likely."

Scowling, Cecily moved off. "This way."

Gaining entry to the house was not terribly difficult. Most of the servants had been given the evening off, due to their employers' absence. It was a simple thing to use the key she'd never returned and let herself and Rand into the house through a back door.

She felt the heat of Rand behind her, heard the sound of his breathing as he followed her up the back stairs to a narrow servants' passage.

She found the door she wanted and eased it open.

The moonlight leached all color out of Lavinia's boudoir, making it appear more subtle, less garish than in the daylight hours.

"Stay there," she whispered to Rand. "We don't want to wake Pug."

Swiftly, she crept over to the chaise longue where the small dog lay curled up, snoring.

Having assured herself that the pug didn't stir, Cecily moved beyond the boudoir and into Lavinia's dressing room. Without pause, she found the shelf where Lavinia kept her marquetry wooden box full of secrets.

"Key?" breathed a masculine voice in her ear.

She jumped, emitting a soft shriek. "Confound it, do you never do what you're told?" she demanded in an exasperated whisper.

"Rarely," he murmured back. "As I was saying . . ."

"No," Cecily whispered. She didn't want to waste

time looking for the key. She took the box and, stepping around Rand, went back into the boudoir, where there was a little more light.

Extracting two pins from her pocket, she set to work.

It seemed to take forever to pick the lock. She was even more frustrated by her lack of dexterity because it was Rand's presence that caused it. Or, at least, it was her *reaction* to his presence, a reflection that was even more humiliating than the clumsiness itself.

She wanted so desperately to appear competent in his eyes that she was all fingers and thumbs. Which was ludicrous. Honestly, why should she care what he thought of her?

She tried again, concentrating this time, and heard the telltale click. "There."

Quickly, she opened the lid of the box.

Tempted as she was to pore over Lavinia's illicit treasures, Cecily kept herself on track. She sorted through the few papers that lay inside but did not find her letter. Then she took out the false bottom and laid it aside.

She gasped. A familiar necklace gleamed subtly against the velvet interior.

"My pearls!" She stared at the necklace in growing anger. Lavinia hadn't lost them at all. That wretch! Oh, she should have known Lavinia was leading her a merry dance. She'd been such a fool!

"The letter?" breathed Rand. He quickly sifted through the other contents of the box. Mostly, it contained jewels and love letters from men who were not, of course, Lavinia's husband.

She replaced the false bottom. "It's not there."

Cecily took the pearls and kissed them before putting them in her pocket. Then she replaced the lid on the box and returned it to its hiding place.

Rand said, "She will know you have picked that lock."

Cecily nodded. "Yes, she will also know that I took the pearls, since I shall wear them. But she will scarcely demand that I return what she stole from me."

The effrontery of Lavinia, to claim she'd lost the pearls in play and all the time, there they were in her box of treasures! How could Lavinia have thought she'd get away with it? The necklace was renowned for its beauty; Lavinia couldn't risk wearing it in public. Cecily would have been bound to hear of it.

Had Lavinia intended to sell the pearls? Or was it enough to deprive Cecily of them?

"Are you satisfied?" Again, he spoke close to her, into her ear. "We shouldn't linger."

With a slight shiver of awareness, she nodded. She was as satisfied as she could be that Lavinia didn't have her letter.

"Yes, let's go."

She didn't know what did it. Neither of them made a sound, but Pug was snoring one moment; the next he'd sprung to his feet and started yapping his wizened little head off.

Cecily dived for the dog and clamped a hand over his muzzle, but it was too late. Footsteps sounded close by.

Without a word, Rand grabbed Cecily's hand and dragged her through the servants' door.

They clattered down the steps and dashed through

the empty kitchens and out the back door. They didn't stop running until they were in sight of Montford House.

Cecily and Rand were both breathless and laughing when they finally halted. Cecily bent over and put her hands on her knees, dragging in painful lungsful of air.

"That was most diverting," said Rand. "Let's not do it again."

She laughed up a him. "Craven," she taunted, quite forgetting that she hadn't wanted him along on this venture at all.

Something made him go very still as she lifted her face to his. Then he reached out, took her head in his hands, and kissed her, full and hard on the lips.

Her pulse switched from a canter to a gallop, thundering in her ears. She felt more alive than she had in months. The exhilaration of it swept through her, setting every nerve ending aflame.

It was the danger, she thought vaguely. A reaction to the thrill of nearly getting caught . . .

Then she lost the capacity to think altogether.

But his kiss was all too brief. Ashburn lifted his head and looked down into her eyes. His features were coldly beautiful in the moonlight but his eyes were hot and brilliant.

"Damn you, Lady Cecily Westruther," he muttered. "Why did I have to fall in love with you?"

Suddenly, air seemed in short supply. Cecily struggled to fill her lungs. "But—but I . . ." Words wouldn't come.

He gave a sardonic crack of laughter. "No, no, don't say a thing. Your expression is so eloquent, you needn't trouble yourself to explain your feelings. Those speaking eyes of yours betray you, my dear."

He framed her face with his hands and his voice turned low and urgent. "I can't let you marry him." His thumbs stroked back her hair. "Not while your heart beats so fast against my chest when I hold you, not while your lips cling so sweetly to mine when we kiss. Not while there might be hope for us."

She wanted—ought—to tell him there was no hope, none at all. That he offered her a life she did not want, had never sought.

But . . . He *loved* her? She couldn't seem to speak the necessary words of rejection that would break their connection forever.

Rand loved her. The words, so stunning in their profound simplicity, seemed to have shattered her mind, scattered the pieces to the winds.

Before she could collect them, form some coherent response, Ashburn's face hardened to granite. "I cannot let him have you, Cecily. I simply can't."

Rand, the Duke of Ashburn, *loved* her? Feeling wretched, Cecily did not even bother to undress but climbed into bed with her footman's costume on.

She shivered uncontrollably beneath the covers. How had it come to this? How had she let Rand gain so much purchase over her emotions? He couldn't love her. Men like the Duke of Ashburn didn't know what love was.

He desired her. He wanted her to be his duchess. He was possessive, autocratic, insufferably sure of himself.

No, that declaration was a desperate last attempt to make her throw Norland over.

But she didn't truly believe that. Ashburn was not the sort of man who played such games. She respected him too much to believe him capable of such a despicable piece of deception.

He loved her. Or at least, he genuinely believed that he loved her. The notion was a huge weight in her chest, a sick roil in her stomach.

Of course, she was drawn to him, no question of it. He was exciting and dangerous, attractive and, she suspected, highly skilled in the art of making love. He was intelligent and quick-witted and above all, he *listened*. The Duke of Ashburn was a difficult man to resist.

She had not done a good job of resisting his physical overtures. But if she'd the slightest notion his heart was involved in the business, she would have tried harder. It had been convenient, self-serving, and foolish to believe he had no heart to lose.

And now he said he loved her. Did that change everything? Or nothing at all?

Lying in her bed, wakeful and restless and horribly confused, Cecily wished most heartily that she'd never met the Duke of Ashburn. The life she'd mapped out for herself so long ago, the longed-for independence, would slip away if she threw Norland over and married Rand.

And what about her feelings? If she loved Rand, wouldn't she leap at his proposal, count the world and all of her former ambitions well-lost? If she loved him, wouldn't she allow Montford to find a way for her to break her betrothal to Norland without creating a scandal?

Yes, she'd been making excuses. She'd never intended to give Rand a chance.

The seconds crawled by until each minute seemed to stretch for hours.

Love.

Other girls fell in love with reckless abandon. They bandied that word about at the smallest provocation, flung their hearts after men who scarcely noticed them or remembered their names. The poets made falling in love look so easy.

But it wasn't easy for her. Rand was right. To love someone—really love them—took an enormous amount of courage.

She wasn't at all sure she had the fortitude to love Rand the way a man like him deserved to be loved. Wholeheartedly, without reservation.

Cecily had reservations. All too many of them.

But she was nothing if not tenacious. She'd always prided herself on her daring when it came to physical things, practical things. Could she take the risk of shining a light on her emotions? And if she discovered that what she felt for the Duke of Ashburn was love, what then?

Could she ever find enough courage to be his wife?

Getting horribly drunk after one had one's heart trampled to pieces was a worn-out cliché and damnably ineffectual besides. Ashburn stared down into his brandy glass and resisted the sudden urge to hurl it against the wall.

Besotted. That's what he was. In every sense of the word.

Hadn't he learned the hard way that one cannot buy or barter for love? He'd been so determined *not* to love Cecily, hadn't he? So sure that he could possess her and take her to wife without ever succumbing to tender emotions himself. His childhood had been a grim lesson in giving his love too freely. He'd thought himself hardened indeed until Cecily came along.

From the beginning, he'd known she was special. He'd pursued her madly, ignoring the signs that his heart was far too deeply engaged. Between them there was sympathy, a meeting of minds, shared dreams, ambitions, even a level of trust. And a world of desire and passion he ached to explore.

Cecily teetered on the edge of love; he was sure of it. Why couldn't she let herself fall?

Rand took Montford's letter from his pocket and smoothed it out. He stared at the elegant, precise handwriting.

If he had any sense of self-preservation, he'd cut his losses and walk away. She was so clearly convinced she'd be happier with Norland. Who was he to stand in her way?

But the mere thought of her saddled with that insensitive oaf for a husband made Rand's blood race, thick and hot through his veins. His very soul rejected the notion of her marrying anyone but him.

He couldn't let her go. Couldn't let her make such a colossal mistake. She would think him high-handed and dictatorial, no better than the Duke of Montford. But by God, he *loved* her. He might not be able to command her love in return, but at least he could prevent her throwing any chance they might have away.

The Duke of Ashburn strode into the extraordinary meeting of the Ministry of Marriage as if he were the commander of this group of powerful aristocrats and not its prodigal son.

His big shoulders were shrouded in a drab greatcoat with a plethora of capes. A high-crowned beaver hat sat low on his head, its brim shadowing glittering eyes, a straight blade of a nose, and rapier-sharp cheekbones.

His well-formed mouth lifted a little at one corner, as though he was ever so slightly amused at the effect his sudden appearance had created. In his left hand, he gripped a long menace of a whip.

Ignoring the murmurs of surprise and disapproval that passed around the long dining room, the duke laid the whip on the long mahogany dining table and removed his hat. A casual flick of the wrist sent the hat spinning through the air, to land in a startled footman's quick hands.

Ashburn took his seat at the head of the table, a place ordinarily reserved for the chairman of the meeting. He stripped off his gloves and tossed them down next to his whip, then picked up the meeting's agenda.

The Duke of Montford watched this ostentatious entrance with mingled irritation and amusement. Ashburn had never set foot in one of these meetings, despite having the right as head of his noble house. Clearly, he meant his first visit to be a memorable one.

"Good God, sir! What is the meaning of this?" exclaimed Lady Warrington.

One sleek brow quirked up but Ashburn didn't raise his gaze from the page. "My dear lady, I am here for the same purpose as you are." He waved a nonchalant hand. "Do carry on."

Having assimilated the agenda's contents, Ashburn let it fall from his long, elegant fingers. Then he leaned back in his chair, dug his hands in his pockets, and looked bored. With his hooded lids drooping over those startling golden brown eyes, Ashburn reminded Montford of a well-fed lion contemplating a nap in the sun.

Montford said, "I am sure we are honored by your presence, Your Grace. Might one ask why so *sudden* an interest in the proceedings?" He knew, of course, but it would not do to appear complicit in Ashburn's scheme.

With a mocking look, Ashburn said, "Do you think I mean to usurp your authority, Montford? Far from it."

"*I?*" Montford said blandly. "I have no more authority here than the next person."

"Ah," said Ashburn with a low laugh. "My mistake."

He cocked his head, then looked around at the rest of the ladies and gentlemen gathered around the table. Softly, he said, "But what do we wait for?"

The answer stood behind him, looking confused and more than a little put out.

Lord Delmere, the chairman of the meeting, had

arrived in Ashburn's wake. He hovered indecisively behind the seat Ashburn had appropriated, a frown multiplying the wrinkles on his high forehead. Clearly, Delmere wanted to order the duke to move but didn't dare.

"There is a place vacant beside me, Lord Delmere," said Lady Arden, smiling. "Do sit down and let us begin."

The meeting proceeded more efficiently than usual, with comments and arguments kept to a minimum. Thankfully, the most cantankerous of their number was absent today: Lord deVere had been called out of Town on important business. Montford was relieved that his old rival had stayed away. Aside from Lady Arden, deVere was the most likely member of the ministry to smell a rat at Ashburn's sudden appearance.

The anticipation built; everyone waited for the Duke of Ashburn to reveal the reason for his presence. Were they curious? Apprehensive? Or eager to enjoy a little blood sport?

Knowing his cohorts, Montford suspected the last.

But Ashburn kept his own counsel throughout, merely casting his vote along with everyone else when necessary. The rest of the time, he sat in an elegant, insolent slouch, his chin sunk into the snow white folds of his cravat. Silently, he contemplated some undefined spot on the table before him, his thick black eyelashes shadowing those liquid amber eyes.

But when the chairman inquired if there were other business, Ashburn roused from his abstraction.

"Lady Cecily Westruther's marriage to the Duke of Norland," he said in his deep, drawling baritone. He looked up. "Has a date been set?"

"The wedding is less than a week away," Montford answered evenly.

Ashburn sent a quick glance around the table. "I hereby exercise my right of veto to stop the match from proceeding."

A gasp flew through the room; then a buzzing murmur broke out. Montford did his best to look shocked and angered, as if he hadn't conspired with Ashburn to achieve this very result.

Each member of the Ministry of Marriage had one chance to veto an arranged alliance. Once exercised, the power of veto could never be used again by that family.

While it was true that this power existed, no one had possessed the gall to invoke it since the ministry was formed.

"Good God, Your Grace!" exclaimed Lady Arden. Despite her allegiance to Ashburn, this was too bold even for her. "Surely it is too late in the day for this. You ought to have raised your objections in the proper course of discussion, not waited until the eleventh hour."

Ashburn shrugged. "I have the right. I'm exercising it."

Pandemonium broke out then, all of it directed at Ashburn. Their slings and arrows glanced off the armor of his imperturbable calm. He even smiled—a faint, upward curl of the lips—when the noise rose to a din.

Lord Delmere banged his gavel for silence, bleating, "This is indeed most irregular! And, might I add, most ungentlemanly of you, Ashburn. Ungentlemanly in the extreme. Why, I—"

Ashburn turned his head to look at Delmere, who blanched and let his voice fade to nothing.

Everyone knew that for all his youth, Ashburn was not a man to be crossed.

Montford supposed he ought to make a show of opposing Ashburn's gambit. "Might I suggest we adjourn the matter until we've all had the opportunity to consider the implications?"

"No, that won't do." Ashburn regarded Montford with a slight smile. "You want to stall the process until it's too late. I'm exercising the right of veto against Lady Cecily's marriage and I'm doing it *here* and I'm doing it *now*."

Lady Arden's eyes widened. "Are you in love with the chit yourself, dear boy? Is that what this is about?"

His eyes lit with amusement and a little challenge. "In love? *I?*"

"Then why?" demanded Lady Warrington. "What objection can you possibly have to the match?"

Instead of answering her, Ashburn gestured to the secretary, who had been scratching away, madly trying to keep up with the comments that flew around the room.

"Enter it in the minutes, will you, Mr. Wicks?" Ashburn scanned his audience, seemingly unconcerned at the furor he'd created. "If there's nothing else to discuss, shall we adjourn?"

When no word or sign came from Rand for the next few days, Cecily concluded that he had abandoned the thought of winning her.

That was for the best, of course. She ought to count herself lucky to have escaped him so easily. If he truly meant to wage war on her marriage, she had little doubt he'd find a way to annihilate it.

The hollow feeling inside her had more to do with a series of sleepless nights than any sense of loss or . . . or longing. Or anything like that.

She spent the morning shopping with her maid, but without Rosamund or Jane, spending her pin money felt like an abominably flat way to pass the time. Even a new bonnet could not entirely lift her spirits.

She needed to get on with those schemes of hers, but she felt as if she hung in an odd state of suspension. Planning anything when she was about to be married seemed like tempting Fate in some strange way.

She no sooner set her foot in Montford House after her shopping expedition than the duke bade her attend him in his library. "Would you spare me a few moments, Cecily?" Montford said.

"Yes, of course," she said, unpinning her hat and handing it to a footman.

It never rains but it pours, she thought, and turned on her heel to follow her guardian to his domain.

"Sit down, Cecily." His Grace indicated a chair on the other side of his desk. Cecily searched her memory, but she could not think what she might have done. Certainly nothing Montford might have discovered, at all events. Nothing worthy of the duke's famous Speech.

Now that she observed him, Montford's patrician features appeared grave. Grimmer than usual, she thought, as if he had some terrible news to impart.

"Oh, Good God, Tibby's sister!" Cecily said, sitting abruptly. "Has she taken a turn for the worse?"

"Not that I have heard," said Montford. "However, I fear Miss Tibbs will not be at liberty to return to London for some time."

"That is a shame, of course. But I scarcely expected her to do so," said Cecily. "I think her sister must be gravely ill, don't you?"

"I fear so. This has nothing to do with Miss Tibbs."

A worse prospect occurred to her. A clutch of fear. "Not Jane. The—the baby?" Her voice cracked as she said the last word. She had tried not to let her concern for Jane show, but everyone knew of the high mortality rate of women in childbirth. She gripped the edge of the desk. "For pity's sake, Your Grace, tell me!"

"Calm yourself, Cecily. It is nothing like that. Jane is in perfect health."

Relief swept over her. She drew a long, unsteady breath. "But then what is it, Your Grace? If it is something unpleasant, do not keep me in suspense."

"It has nothing to do with Tibby or any of your cousins, Cecily." He paused. "It has to do with you."

She didn't like the sound of that. From the time he'd taken charge of her, Cecily had prided herself on being a handful. Yet, she'd be the first to admit that the consequences of disobedience could be mighty unpleasant if Montford chose.

This time, he surprised her by saying, "Your situation troubles me, Cecily."

"Does it?" So she wasn't in for a dressing-down after all. "In what way?"

His brows knit. "That is part of what troubles me. There is no logical reason for my concern. Norland is highborn, titled, wealthy, genteel, amiable. He would not beat you or abuse you; if he had *affaires,* he would be discreet. We negotiated the most favorable marriage settlements possible on your behalf."

"What more could any lady ask?" Cecily agreed with an inexplicably sinking feeling. She wished to get this interview over with. It was exceedingly awkward to discuss what sort of husband Norland might be.

"And yet . . ." Montford used a fingertip to push his papers into line. "And yet for you, Cecily, that is not nearly enough."

She flushed with embarrassment, pride, but mostly denial of this unprecedented statement. "But, Your Grace—"

He held up a hand to silence her. "I have urged you before to reconsider, have I not? Then, there was no other worthier candidate for your hand. *Now,* however . . ."

"Ashburn," whispered Cecily. "He has spoken to you, hasn't he?"

"He would make you an excellent husband, Cecily," said Montford.

"Why?" she demanded, panic rising in her throat. "He is no better born or wealthier or—or in any way superior to Norland!" In fact he was one hundred times more dangerous to her happiness than Norland could ever be.

"And yet, the difference between the two men is quite vast, wouldn't you agree?" said Montford.

She did not make the obvious answer to that. Instead, she said, "I am persuaded that I'll be happy with the Duke of Norland. I have made the right choice and I shall stick to it. You—you should be glad of that, Your Grace. Imagine the talk if I cried off now."

"Jane and Rosamund seem content in their marriages," Montford said in a musing tone. "I confess, I am surprised."

"Their cases are different from mine," Cecily argued. "Surely you do not mean to forbid my marriage to Norland at this late stage!"

He shrugged. "It would be improper for me as your guardian to prevent your marrying a man who is demonstrably eligible. But mark my words, Cecily. If it were in my power, that is what I would do."

As she digested this, he steepled his fingers together. "However. It is incumbent on me to inform you that an impediment to your marriage to Norland has arisen."

"An—an impediment?" She swallowed. The letter. They'd found it. She was finished. Utterly ruined. Oh, but poor, poor Norland!

Stomach churning, she managed not to blurt out her wretchedness. "W-what sort of impediment?"

Montford's dark eyes seemed to penetrate her thoughts. She braced herself for an inquisition.

He said, "Did you know that the Duke of Ashburn had a seat on the Ministry of Marriage?"

The dissonance between her expectations and

Montford's question made Cecily blink. Her mind struggled to change tack. "No, I didn't. Well, I suppose if I'd thought about it, I might have guessed he would. He is the head of the house of Kendall, just as you are the head of the Westruthers. But—but what has that to say to anything?"

"A great deal, as it happens." Montford leaned forward. "There is a rather draconian power in the rules of the ministry that says each noble house may veto one marriage sanctioned by the ministry. Once exercised, that family may never use the power again."

A *veto*? In a low, trembling voice, she said, "Ashburn has vetoed my marriage to Norland?"

She sensed that beneath Montford's bland façade, he watched her keenly. "Apparently. Yes."

Hurt, betrayal, and a good dose of fear swirled like a whirlpool inside her. She shot to her feet. "But this is outrageous! I—"

He held his hands, palm outwards to silence her. "Histrionics will not help you in this instance, my dear. I suggest that instead of railing against Fate, you put that rather fine mind of yours to good use. Once you have thought it over, you will see that the wisest course is to accept this outcome with good grace."

"No, no, I won't accept this. Good God! Did neither of you even think to consult *me*? To ask what I wanted?"

Of course they had not! Who ever consulted a mere female about her future?

"If it's any consolation, we did not consult Norland either," offered the duke.

Cecily ignored that piece of frivolity. This was

exactly the sort of high-handed behavior she'd wished most fervently to escape by means of her marriage to the docile Norland. She'd been right all along about Ashburn. How could she tolerate such a man having dominion over her?

Biting her lip, she began to pace, desperate to think of a solution. "Is there a right of appeal against this veto? Surely there must be." She whirled on the duke and held out her hand. "Show me those rules, if you please."

The duke pursed his lips. "I'm afraid I can't. The rules of the Ministry of Marriage are confidential. Your betrothal to the Duke of Norland is at an end. Accept the decision as final, Cecily. You will only make a fool of yourself if you don't."

He gathered up the papers that lay before him on his desk and transferred his attention to them, signaling the interview was at an end. For the space of a minute, Cecily battled the urge to throw herself on the floor and kick and scream like a child throwing a tantrum.

But of course that would only confirm his obvious belief that she could not govern her own affairs or know her own mind or judge what was best for her.

There was no point arguing with Montford; once he'd acted, he never reneged.

Cecily swept from the library, seething.

Ugh! The insufferable smugness of those men, coolly deciding her and Norland's fate! Montford and Ashburn were two of a kind. She'd known that from the beginning.

So this was what Ashburn had meant when he'd declared war on her back at Anglesby. How stupid of her to believe he must have forgotten that stern resolve.

Well, she would not meekly wave the white flag in surrender. He ought to know her better than that.

Chapter Seventeen

Rand watched Cecily pacing his book room like a small tigress, lethally beautiful in her fury. Her elegant hands were clenched into fists, her skin flushed a rosy pink. Fire smoldered in those dark eyes. She was so different from the other bloodless aristocratic girls he'd known, she might have hailed from another species.

He loved her like this, loved to see all that passion rise up in her, even if it was the angry kind rather than the amorous.

At this point, he'd take any sort of passion he could get.

He couldn't resist adding fuel to the flames. "My lady, this visit is most improper. You should have sent for me and I could have called on you at Montford House."

She all but bared her teeth and snarled. "I needed to speak with you alone. Besides, it would become known throughout London if you called on me. We would be a byword in no time at all." She flung up her hands. "What am I saying? We are a byword already, thanks to you!"

"But all I'd have to do is make your presence here known to compromise you," he said calmly. "That is a greater risk than a little gossip, I should think."

Not to mention the very real danger in which her virtue now stood. Cecily was no longer betrothed to Norland, so she could no longer use him as an excuse to deny her passion for Rand.

She glared at him. "You would not be so base as to trumpet my disgrace to the world."

So she trusted him that far, then. He placed a hand over his left breast. "It warms my heart to hear you say so."

She snorted. "Look, I've thought about this and it can't be right that you have the power of veto over my marriage. The Ministry of Marriage had nothing to do with arranging my betrothal to Norland. How can they now dissolve it?"

He paused. This was precisely the argument he'd raised with Montford, after all, when they'd discussed the scheme.

Smoothly, he said, "Ah, yes, but Montford *is* bound by the ministry rules. He has the power to forbid the match under the terms of his guardianship."

"It's a clear abuse of his power, then!" she retorted. "Surely he cannot allow a third party to dictate his actions."

The intelligence he so admired in her could be deuced inconvenient at times. Well, perhaps she was right, but he wasn't about to agree with her. Instead, he regarded her with a gleam of amusement. "Do you plan to take Montford to court over it?"

She simmered with temper. "Of course not! How

should I? Besides, the most infuriating part of it is that he *is* doing what he thinks is best for me! Utterly misguided and patronizing though it might be."

Briefly, she met Rand's eyes, and the air sizzled between them. She turned away. In a muffled voice, she said, "But he's wrong."

Rand took a deep breath. "Cecily, why are you here?"

She swung to face him. "To demand that you withdraw that confounded veto, of course!"

His jaw tightened. "I believe I told you back at Anglesby that this was war, my dear. I cannot let you marry him. I need time to make you see—"

"Do you know, you had almost won before you pulled this trick?" Her eyes glittered, still with anger, and perhaps also with tears. "I'd all but convinced myself you were right; that love would conquer all." She closed her eyes, as if in exquisite pain. "And then you used your power to coerce me. To force me to do as you wished."

He was thunderstruck. "I acted to stop you taking a step that would ruin all of our lives!"

She went on as if she hadn't heard him. "Why would I be better off with a man who does not scruple to ride roughshod over me when it suits him than with a man who allows me to act as I see fit?"

He stared at her, incredulous. "You would prefer a man who left you to your own devices out of indifference to a man who would love you, cherish you, respect your intelligence, share your dreams? Why do you have to do it all on your own, Cecily?"

"But you do not respect my intelligence, Rand," she said, ignoring the question. "You aim to prevent me marrying the man of my choice. The irony is that by doing so, you have proved I was right to choose him in the first place."

She stopped pacing and looked at him. "For such a clever man, you can be very foolish, you know."

Deliberately, he said, "And for a woman who knows her own mind so well, Cecily, you have very little acquaintance with your heart."

"Love makes women weak and slavish," said Cecily, pacing again. "But not me. Did you think once Norland was out of the way, I'd fall into your arms?"

Had he thought that? No, but he'd hoped. Even at this moment, when he could shake her for being so pigheaded and stubborn, his arms literally ached to hold her.

She pressed fingertips to her temple, as if her head hurt. "Men like you and Montford are accustomed to manipulating everyone to get what you want. Often with the most altruistic motives, I'll grant you that." She drew a breath. "Perhaps it is because neither of you has allowed yourself to truly love another human being that you view every other person in your life as a pawn or an adversary to be maneuvered or vanquished. But if you love someone, you should care about what they want, too, Rand. You shouldn't use your advantage to *make* them fall in with your plans."

For a long time, he couldn't speak. The turmoil inside him was too great. "So this is your opinion of me," he said in a low voice. "I commit one desperate act to stop you doing something that was irreversible, something that would have destroyed the happiness of all three of us, and you think that means I would ride roughshod over you once we were wed?"

He threw out a hand. "I would hope that once married we would discuss things, argue them out and reach a decision together. I have no desire to dictate to you. Why should I, when I so admire your determination and independence? Those qualities are what made me fall in love with you."

In a strained voice, she said, "I am sure you mean what you say, Rand. But if something else arises that you judge to be an equally desperate case, you would act the same way again. If I married you, you would always be able to pull rank and command me, as my husband. I would grow to hate you for it, I think. And if I didn't, if I submitted, well, then I would no longer be myself."

Had she plunged a knife into his chest, he could have borne it better. "That all seems very logical, Cecily, but I don't think it's the entire truth of the matter. You are afraid to trust me with your heart."

Her lips twisted. "You are right. I *am* a coward. Before this, I almost thought I'd found the courage, the blind faith to ignore my more rational objections. But now . . . Well, I ought to be grateful, I suppose, that this happened before it was too late." Her gaze met his, and for the first time, he glimpsed pain in those velvet eyes.

"Good-bye, Rand."

He did not even attempt to stop her when she left.

Cecily rather expected the news that came two days later. Rand had withdrawn his veto, allowing the world to think he'd merely played some ruthless sort of power game with Montford by issuing the veto in the first place.

Cecily's wedding to Norland would go ahead.

Norland himself had been out of town on a research mission while all this went on. Montford had written to him, first when Rand issued the veto and later, when he withdrew the same, but they'd had no word from Norland in return. Perhaps both letters had missed him and he'd remained oblivious of the entire thing. She supposed that would be for the best.

Disgusted, Montford had washed his hands of both Ashburn and Cecily. He clearly thought Ashburn weak for giving in to Cecily's demands.

She wondered about that now. Had Rand granted her this boon because he saw his case was hopeless and decided to finish with the entire business? Or had he actually accepted the force of her arguments, weighed them, and decided she was in the right? Had he wished to show her she was wrong about him?

Whatever the case, hers was a hollow victory. Small comfort that she did the right thing, the honorable thing, in forging ahead with her marriage to Norland.

The day her wedding arrived, she felt numb. Which was fortunate, because she was not at liberty to indulge her own emotions. Out of pride, she made herself appear lively and happy to Jane and Rosamund. The effort wearied her to the point of exhaustion.

She did her best to take an interest in her gown and the bonnet she would wear and the flowers she would carry. Long ago, she'd insisted on a quiet wedding in the drawing room at Montford House with only immediate family present.

She rather wished she'd made a bigger fuss of the whole thing now. That would make her feel at least some nervous excitement about the ceremony. As it was, she struggled to impress upon herself the utter life-changing significance of this day.

Jane and Rosamund gathered in Cecily's bed-chamber, ostensibly to help her get ready. Jane could not do much more than throw comments and suggestions from her reclining position on the chaise longue. As had lately been her wont, she soon fell into a soft doze, her hands placed protectively over her pregnant belly.

Cecily scrutinized her closely. Was Jane's face a little paler than usual? She was so big with child, Cecily worried her cousin's time would come upon her at any moment.

It was an anxious business, childbirth. Jane was, as she'd said numerous times, as healthy as a horse. But that did not mean the birthing part would be plain sailing.

Terror gripped Cecily with a sudden swiftness. What if Jane did not survive the birth? What would Constantine do? What would they all do? She could not bear to lose Jane.

"Best not to think about it," Rosamund murmured in her ear. "And best for her if you don't stare at her as if she is not long for this world."

Cecily started and cut her gaze to meet Rosamund's. She bit her lip. "I can't help it," she whispered, fingering the lace edge to her dressing table.

"I know, darling, but do try," said Rosamund, smiling at her. "It is a natural part of life, after all, and the rewards are great."

Cecily clutched Rosamund's hand, squeezed it tightly. "Yes, I know."

But she also knew that when Rosamund's time came, as it inevitably would, Cecily would be out of her mind with fear for her. That was the terror of loving someone. But the rewards . . . The rewards *were* worth the risk. The pain and anxiety of childbirth meant a new small life to love.

She would not exchange a single one of her cousins for the pain and worry of loving them, of fearing for them, of one day losing them. Life was so precious. To be lived just once, with honor and kindness but with valor, too.

The motto of the Westruthers came back to her, as clearly as if she heard Montford speak those words in her ear: *To a valiant heart, nothing is impossible.*

"Now, dearest," Rosamund was saying, "shall we try this new way of doing your hair?"

Cecily shook her head. "No, I . . ." Shakily, she rose from her dressing-table and looked at the clock. "No, I think I need to go out. There's something I must do."

Rosamund stared at her. "*Now?* But, Cecily! What about—?"

She snatched up her gloves and bonnet. "Do not worry. I'll be back soon."

Cecily did not make it as far as the hall before a footman handed her a letter.

She almost put it in her reticule without looking

at it, but the handwriting caught her eye. It was Norland's.

Cecily ripped it open and read:

Dear Cecily,

When your guardian informed me of the Ministry of Marriage's decree against our union, I was, in short, astonished and appalled.

However, upon finding myself suddenly at liberty, my entire existence underwent the most surprising transformation. The scales fell from my eyes, as it were, and I realized that I had long harbored a tender emotion toward one who is known to you intimately.

I dare to hope this news will not distress you unduly. We have always been good friends, you and I, but now I believe there is one who lays claim to a higher place in your affections than I could ever win.

By the time you read this, I shall be on my way to Cambridge to beg Miss Tibbs to do me the honor of being my wife.

Your affectionate friend,
Norland

"Merciful Heavens!" Cecily stared blankly at the letter in her hand. The world seemed to have turned upside down. *"Tibby?"*

"My lady?" The footman still hovered at her elbow, awaiting her wishes.

She glanced at him, then back at the letter. Dear God! How could Norland be so stupid? She could not let this happen!

"Thomas," she said to the footman, "please have the carriage brought around and send for my maid. Tell Saunders to pack quickly for an overnight stay."

The news was so unexpected, she could scarcely comprehend it. And yet . . . and yet it had been there, all along, as plain as the nose on her stupid face.

Norland's attentions to Tibby during his weekly visit to Montford House. It was *Tibby* he'd come to see, not Cecily! Norland suggesting that Tibby live with them. A tactless, awful gesture, but he had acted out of love, even if he had not recognized it at the time.

And Tibby! Tibby's reaction when Cecily told her of Norland's proposition had been awfully strange, hadn't it? And almost immediately afterwards, Tibby's sister had taken ill. Had that been a mere coincidence, or had Tibby run away from an intolerable situation and lied about her sister's bad health?

Rather than stand by and watch the man she loved marry Cecily, Tibby had removed herself.

Oh, but Cecily had been so cursed offhand about her marriage, hadn't she? Good Lord, Tibby must have wanted to scratch her charge's eyes out for the casual way she'd behaved toward Norland. The way Cecily had outlined her intention to ignore Norland as much as possible once they were wed.

And all that time, Tibby had been forced to remain silent. What agony she must have suffered! For Cecily was willing to lay odds that Tibby knew her own heart far better than Norland had known his.

"Carriage is ready, my lady." Saunders, Cecily's maid, arrived, carrying a bandbox.

Cecily came to herself with a start. "Oh! Of course. Yes, there is no time to lose."

At that very moment, Rand was admitted by a footman into the hall. There was a letter in his hand; she didn't need to see the seal to know it was from Norland. And from the look on his face, she realized Rand had known.

He'd known about Tibby and Norland all along.

Chapter Eighteen

Clutching her own letter, Cecily stared at Rand with a shocked, bewildered look on her face. That expression cut him to the core.

Damn him for a fool! What had he thought she'd do? Cry freedom and leap into his arms? He ought to know it was never that simple with her.

He gestured to the paper in her hand. "You've heard, then."

She swallowed hard. "Yes. I've heard. And I'm going to put a stop to it."

She swept past him and marched out the door and down the steps to the awaiting carriage.

After a stunned moment, he went after her and arrived on the pavement to hear her give instructions to the startled coachman that he was to take her to Cambridge. Reasonably enough, the man demurred that he needed instructions from the Duke of Montford before he'd take Cecily so far afield.

To her maid, Rand said, "Wait here."

Rand glanced up at the coachman. "I'll talk some sense into her. Drive around town until I tell you to stop."

He followed her into the carriage, and after only a few seconds' dithering, the footmen put up the steps and closed the door. He saw that Cecily fumed and fretted at his interference, but he would not let her do this.

"How dare you override my orders?" she flashed at him.

"Montford's coachman wasn't going to drive you to Cambridgeshire, for Heaven's sake! Have a little sense, Cecily."

"But I must go after Norland," she said impatiently. "You don't understand!"

Her urgency made his stomach churn. He gripped her hand. "It's over, Cecily. Can't you see that? For God's sake, let him go!"

She surprised him by returning the clasp of his fingers and looking at him in the strangest way. "Do not worry about me, Rand. Believe me, your concern is unnecessary."

There was the oddest note in Cecily's voice, a sort of tightness, as if the words were half-strangled as they came out. He couldn't seem to gauge her mood, even when she sat back on the banquette opposite him and he could see her face.

"I cannot believe you are chasing Norland all over the countryside," he said. "Good God, woman, where is your pride?"

"I am not chasing him," she said with dignity. "Well, I mean I am not chasing him for the purpose you are thinking. Good gracious, why on earth should I wish to marry him now?"

The matter-of-fact statement made him lightheaded. He pinched the bridge of his nose. "Then why were you going to Cambridge?"

Her pretty mouth firmed. "I must catch up to Norland before he proposes to Tibby, that's why."

"But you just said—" He spoke through gritted teeth. "If you do not wish me to throttle you on the spot, you troublesome chit, tell me in plain words what it is that you think you are doing."

"I am going to give them my blessing, of course," she said.

Rand felt the relief of it like a series of hot and cold showers over his body. He sat back against the squabs and simply looked at her. "Couldn't you write them a note?"

"No, no, don't you see? I must go myself. I must be there to tell Tibby to her face that I do not mind if she marries Norland. In fact, I shall never forgive her if she doesn't. Do you think she will accept him otherwise?"

Slowly, he said, "I see."

She shook her head, dark ringlets bobbing. Her lips trembled a little with emotion. "I am to blame for so much suffering! Tibby ran away to Cambridge to escape an intolerable situation." Cecily sniffed and hunted in her reticule for a handkerchief. "She loves him, Rand. I am sure of it! The things I said about him! I cringe when I think of how I took Norland for granted when all the time she must have been eating her heart out over him. No wonder she was so strange when we went to call at the cottage."

"So you want to hare off to Cambridgeshire to assure your companion that you don't mind being jilted in favor of her?"

She opened her eyes wide. "Of course. She is the dearest and best of creatures and she will make him the most perfect wife imaginable."

"Just like that." Now he shook his head—in disbelief. As the carriage bowled along, not toward Cambridge but in the direction of Hyde Park, he looked away from her.

Rand told himself he should applaud such generosity of spirit. Much as he wanted to come to terms with this sudden reversal, he could not.

He wished he could escape the feeling of resentment the suddenness of her change of heart brought up in him. Why was she so ready to give up Norland to make her old governess happy, when she'd so steadfastly refused to give him up for Rand?

Was this the same young woman who had turned her back on Rand in order to throw herself into a loveless marriage?

She spoke softly into the stillness between them. "Rand?"

"Yes."

"Do you know where I was going when that letter came to me?"

He shrugged, his jaw hardening. "I haven't a clue."

"I was on my way to see you. I was going to call the wedding off."

He froze, scarcely daring to hope she told the truth.

She made a funny face and looked away. "You might not believe me, but it's true. You said I was afraid, and you were right. I realized . . ." She hesitated, licking her lips. "I was getting ready for the wedding this afternoon and Jane was there. Do you know my cousin, Lady Roxdale?"

He blinked a little at this seeming non sequitur.

"She was big with child, you see. . . ." Cecily's

mouth twisted a little. "She will have her baby any day now. And I've been terrified. What if something happens to her? It is not uncommon for women to die in childbirth. What if she leaves me, too? How on earth would I bear it?"

She paled, as if realizing what she'd said. Of course, she knew his own mother had died in childbirth. "I'm sorry! I—"

"Don't be," he reassured her. "You are right to be concerned, of course. I'm sure everyone who loves her feels the same."

Her voice was hollow. "But I asked myself, Would I trade the years of knowing and loving my cousin Jane for the safety of never losing her? Of course not."

She met his eyes. "The answer seemed so obvious, so simple when I asked myself that question about you."

He'd been holding his breath all through her long explanation. Now he couldn't breathe if his life depended on it.

With a rustle of skirts, she moved to kneel before him in the confined space between the two seats. She took his hand in her small one and turned her face upward. Those brilliant dark eyes gazed into his, unshadowed by flippancy or denial.

And that was when he knew.

"I love you, Rand," she said in a broken whisper. "I've finally found the courage to love you." She bit her lip. "I don't know if you even want me now, but if you will have me, I am yours."

He took a deep, shaky breath. "Cecily, my beautiful, infuriating, clever idiot," he said, and pulled her into his arms. "Come here."

* * *

There was a different flavor to this kiss, thought Cecily dimly. It was equally desperate and as full of passion as their others, but the taint of betrayal and fearful apprehension was gone.

She was giddy with the freedom of it. Terrified, too, but it was an exhilarating, swoony sort of terror. The thrill of finally giving in to her desire made Cecily feel unexpectedly powerful. Invincible. As if there was no trial of the heart she couldn't face.

Somehow, she was half beneath Rand on the banquette seat in the carriage, offering her throat to his devouring kisses, running her hands over his big shoulders, cradling his jaw as she kissed him back.

Rand gasped for air and muttered something in her ear about damned confined spaces, yet despite the awkwardness of it all, he managed to set her body on fire with his touch.

He'd turned her into a throbbing mass of melted woman. She thought she might go mad if he didn't put an end to this great chasm of need inside her.

"Shouldn't do this," he said, taking her mouth again. "Not in a carriage. Not for your first time."

She kissed him back, smoothing a hand over his short hair. "I don't mind," she panted.

Oh, please, let us do this in the carriage! She wanted to scream it, but that would shock the coachman even more than he was already. Rand had pulled down the blinds at some stage to shield them from prying eyes.

"No." He drew back. "It's not enough. I want to see you, taste you, touch you. *All* of you, not just the bits I can reach while we're in this damned shoe box."

She looked at him, at the amazing eyes now darkened to brandy, the short hair ordinarily so neatly brushed now looking rakish and disarranged. The flush on his lean cheeks.

His cravat had disappeared somewhere along the line, and his shirt lay open to reveal a tantalizing glimpse of manly chest. She'd done all that to him, she thought with no small measure of smugness. She could not wait to see what other havoc she might wreak on his appearance.

Having denied herself this pleasure for so long, it seemed a crime to abstain another second. "Please?"

She wound her arms around his neck and kissed him. Soft, clinging, coaxing kisses.

"Please, Rand," she whispered, smiling against his lips. "Take me. I don't want to wait."

Rand wished he might capture this moment on canvas. Lady Cecily Westruther begging for him to take her in a fast-moving carriage as they circled London for the umpteenth time.

But the very masculine satisfaction he took in that notion was swamped by another very masculine feeling, one of acute and urgent discomfort in his nether regions that was not likely to be assuaged any time soon.

If she weren't a maiden, he would have been sorely tempted to give in to her blandishments, but she was, so he couldn't coax her to straddle his lap and ride him to oblivion as he dearly wished to do.

Groaning with frustration and regret, he drew back from Cecily and captured her roguishly inquisitive hands in his.

"We must stop this."

Her fingers returned the clasp of his hands, but those pretty red lips pouted. "Why?"

His words came out in a growl. "Because there isn't the space or the privacy in here for me to do everything I want to do to you."

She gave a delicious little shiver. He felt it down to the soles of his feet.

"That sounds decadent."

The images running through his mind made decadence seem tame by comparison. "You have *no* idea."

She blushed charmingly and he reminded himself once more that she was untried and virginal. God, it was going to be hell on a man to take it slowly when he did finally get her to a bed.

"So after all that, will you take me to Cambridge?" She hadn't lost sight of her purpose, it seemed.

"I'll take you to Cambridge," he said on a resigned sigh. "But we are getting married first."

Chapter Nineteen

"You cannot simply substitute a groom," said Jane, with an amused gleam in her eye. "Won't Norland's name be on the special license?"

"You forget, dear Jane, the power of the Duke of Montford," said Cecily.

"And the determination of Cecily's groom," added Rosamund with a chuckle. "The way Ashburn looked at you, Cecily, I thought he might devour you on the spot!"

Cecily blushed at her cousin's choice of words. "He is impatient. I must confess, so am I."

"And yet, mere hours ago, you were about to marry another man," said Jane, a trifle dryly.

Rosamund tilted her head and tapped her chin as if in deep cogitation. "Who was it now? Who told me that *she* was the only one of us who would meekly do her duty and not make any fuss over her marriage?"

"Do you know, I can't recall," said Jane, her gray eyes guilelessly wide. "I own it does sound terribly *familiar. . . .*"

"Stop it, both of you!" Cecily laughed and scowled at once.

"But, dearest Cecily, you *must* allow us to say we told you so," said Rosamund, holding up a hand. "Just once and then we will say no more."

"Only once?" said Cecily. "I believe you've said it approximately twenty-six times since I told you the news."

"She so hates to be wrong," Rosamund said to Jane on a confidential note.

"She does, doesn't she?" agreed Jane. "And the maddening thing is that she so often *is* right. Our Cecily is a clever little puss, but then love addles even the geniuses among us."

"Only look at Norland," said Rosamund.

"Or the besotted way Ashburn looks at you," added Jane.

Cecily could not assault a pregnant woman, but she cheerfully picked up a cushion and threw it at Rosamund, missing her by a mile. "If I weren't so disgustingly happy, I would point out to the two of you that we are *all* of us fools when it comes to love."

"Well, I'd rather be a happy fool than a clever cynic any day," said Rosamund.

"Do you know something, Rosamund?" said Cecily, clasping her mother's pink pearls around her neck. "So would I."

So it was without much further ado that Lady Cecily Westruther became the Duchess of Ashburn in a small, private ceremony.

Cecily had found time to dispatch a letter that

might well reach Miss Tibbs before Norland did, explaining the happy circumstance of Cecily's marriage and assuring Tibby she would never be forgiven if she did not accept Norland's hand in marriage.

For only think, dear Tibby, Cecily wrote, *if Norland should create such a scandal all for nothing. You owe it to him to accept, not least because you are one of the few women I know who could manage Norland's mama. After all, if you could manage Westruthers, you can manage anyone!*

Her own wedding was as brief as it could be. Ashburn lost no time in whisking Cecily home to Ashburn House once the register was signed.

"This has been the longest afternoon of my life," he said, carrying her upstairs, to the collective astonishment of his servants.

Cecily laughed up at him, a little breathless at this high-handed way of conveying her to their destination. She felt a dizzying and surprisingly pleasurable sense of helplessness as they headed down the hall.

Rand kicked open the door to his bedchamber, strode to the bed and tossed her onto it. Her body sank into the mattress, her head cradled in soft pillows. She watched him close the door, marveling that she now possessed such a magnificent husband. He had upended her carefully laid plans and shaken them loose and she found that despite all her earlier resistance, she didn't mind a bit. She was impatient for her life with Rand to begin, excited at the possibilities.

He moved toward the bed and stood there, looking down at her.

Cecily spread her hands, palm down over the slippery satin coverlet and smiled up at him.

What she saw in his face made her smile fade. Her heart gave a sharp pound and leaped into her throat. She wanted this, so very much. She knew she had nothing to fear, but apprehension roiled in her stomach.

"Are you going to ravish me now?" she asked. Her tone was teasing, but she felt anything but flippant inside.

"Oh, yes," he said softly, his gaze traveling slowly over her, as if mapping the territory he was about to explore.

His gaze stripped her bare. Any response she might have made fizzled and died on her tongue. She bit her lip, almost sick with nerves. This was it. He would come to her now. No more running, no more excuses.

Golden heat flared in his eyes. Impatience seemed to pour from him as he proceeded to remove his clothes. His movements had lost their elegant fluidity; he yanked and tugged at his accouterments with no regard for the impeccable cut of his coat or the ruination of his linens.

It was still broad daylight outside. The days lengthened as summer drew nearer. Cecily's family had been both scandalized and delighted when Ashburn had refused all offers of entertainment and refreshment in order to get his bride to himself.

Now, she enjoyed watching his masculine form clearly revealed as he shucked his clothing. His chest was broad and defined by hard muscle; his stomach flat, hips lean. Sunlight poured through the long windows to gild him, a stern angel glimmering with latent power.

Cecily lay back on the coverlet in a cloud of white silk, with her mother's pink pearls around her neck. She tried very hard to quell the hard flutter of butterflies that insisted on throwing themselves about in her stomach.

His hands went to the buttons of his trousers and paused. Cecily swallowed hard. For some reason, the sight of his thumbs slipping between the waist band of his trousers and that smooth male skin below his navel made breathing rather difficult.

She wanted to look away but her gaze was riveted. She knew what would happen next. She wanted him, wanted this.

Yet, to be so inexperienced and untutored made her feel off-balance. She was wholly dependent on Rand's instruction in the bedchamber. Oh, she'd picked up bits and pieces of theory over the years and of course Rosamund and Jane had made sure she was informed on the essentials. She knew what the mighty bulge in those elegant trousers portended. Yet, when it came down to it she felt as ignorant and unsure as any other well-bred virgin.

Rand tilted his head, perceptive as ever. "Are you afraid?" His voice was soft, his look one of tender amusement, laced with desire.

"Not precisely." She was still eyeing the way his fingers had paused at the fall of his trousers.

What did she have to fear? Only the unknown, she supposed. She trusted Rand to be gentle, clever, understanding.

He undid one button. She blurted out the truth. "I am really rather terrified of getting it wrong. What if I disappoint you?"

He stopped undressing and instead, approached the side of the bed. "Impossible. You never need to worry about that."

He stretched out a hand to stroke her with his fingertips. He began at her lips—just a touch of the pads of three fingers, like a parent hushing a child. The brush of his slightly roughened skin against her mouth sent hot chills through her. Her lips parted as a surge of need rose inside.

Then his fingers skimmed over her chin, down her throat, fingering the hard, lustrous pearls that doubled around her neck once like a choker, another time dipping down to her waist.

"The famous pink pearls," he murmured. Raising the necklace to his lips, he kissed it and she felt that kiss as if the pearls were an intimate part of her.

Then his fingers resumed their leisurely trail. They wound a path between her breasts, close to where her heart thumped an erratic rhythm. Down over the blonde lace at her bodice, to her stomach, with a short pause to investigate the location of her navel beneath the layers of silk.

Tiny thrills scudded through her as he moved down, farther still. A panicky, urgent feeling swept over her as his clever fingers found that magical place between her legs and touched it through the pristine whiteness of her gown.

Pleasure jolted through her, sharp and immediate. As he touched her, she felt restless, aching with a need that seemed to build and expand. She wanted to move, to rip all the pins from her expertly coiffed hair, to kick off her kid slippers and rid herself of her gown, her underthings, every barrier between the pressure and the texture of his fingers and her body.

But she kept still because she sensed he wanted her that way. She'd closed her eyes at some stage, but curiosity got the better of her. She opened them, to see that Rand's gaze focused on the actions of his fingers with that intensity that was peculiar to him.

Then he met her eyes and gave her what she needed, touching her, rubbing and pressing until the pressure was too much. She cried out, convulsing beneath his hands.

With a fierce look of satisfaction, Rand pulled her to the edge of the bed and kneeled down. Vaguely, she thought he was going to remove her shoes. Before she knew it, he'd bunched her skirts to her waist and his mouth was on her, hot between her legs and he was prolonging those blissful spasms with wicked caresses of his lips and tongue.

If she hadn't been so mindless already she might have found the words to protest. Instead, she was helpless to stop him. And when a new series of quakes thrilled through her body she lost the will to deny him.

She closed her eyes again, touched a fluttering hand to the back of his head. "Rand, please . . ." she whispered.

He took her over the edge once more, and again, until she was as boneless as a rag-doll, drunk on sensual bliss. Yet, she was far from satisfied. A need for him deep inside her throbbed in her blood. She wanted him with a desperate, feverish longing.

His weight made the mattress dip beside her as he moved over the bed to kiss her. She wound her arms around his neck and kissed him with enthusiasm and joy.

Slowly, he undressed her, touching her body, skimming skilful fingertips over her skin. Her desire for him all but consumed her. She heard herself murmur incoherent pleas, her hands grasping for his shoulders.

But when she was naked he stood back, holding the long rope of pearls in his hands. He watched her as he threaded them through his fingers. She noticed his breathing was ragged at the edges. "Cherries and cream and chocolate," he said hoarsely, reaching out to touch the dark red tip of her breast.

He gazed at her as he dribbled the strand of pearls over her skin, circled the coolness of them around her breasts, trailed them over the tight flesh of her nipples, then wound them in figure eight to frame her breasts.

He bent to suckle. First one breast, then the other, licking and laving with the flat of his tongue, flicking with the tip, sending arrows of pleasure zinging through her body to quiver in her loins.

She bucked with the force of it; the pearls fell away and now it was his hands circling her breasts, cupping them, squeezing lightly, stroking. Pearls trailed over her midriff, pooled in her navel, spilled over the soft mound of her belly. She felt the cool hardness of them slipping between her legs.

She arched again, gasping as the hard, smooth gems lightly brushed that tender knot of flesh

Rand had tormented into exquisite sensitivity. A thousand nerve-endings seemed to spark to life once more.

She sucked in a breath, placed a hand over his. It took her a moment to gather the courage to ask. "Come inside me, Rand. Love me."

He bent and kissed her deeply, their hands interlaced at her breast. "Oh, God, Cecily. What you do to me."

Straightening, he dropped the pearls onto the bedside table, removed the rest of his clothes. Without giving her much time to do more than cast an incredulous look at the size and rigidity of his member, he climbed onto the bed and stretched out beside her.

Jane and Rosamund had educated her well and of course, she knew the theory of romantic coupling. They had warned her, with a few snorts and giggles that she might be shocked at first at the man's size; that this one time, it would hurt. But could anything have prepared her for *him*?

He shifted his hip. She felt his extraordinary appendage against her thigh and blushed.

There was banked fire in his eyes, but understanding too. "Touch me, Cecily," he said in a roughened, deep voice. "I'd like it very much if you did."

Lowering her gaze, she put out a tentative hand and pressed her palm to his chest. He felt hard and warm, yet soft, too and the hair there was like a mass of fine wire. With her fingertips, she traced the contours of muscle and bone, marveling at all that hard male beauty. Her hand trailed over his shoulders and down one arm, then back to his chest.

The hitch in his breathing told her she gave him pleasure with this tentative exploration. When she brushed a questing fingertip over his nipple, the large rod of flesh between Rand's legs twitched.

"Oh!" She snatched her hand away.

He laughed silently, caught her hand and replaced it.

Having investigated the flat, brownish discs on his chest, her hand skimmed his flat stomach. Rand gave a soft moan; his hand encircled her wrist, gently drew it down.

"Touch me, Cecily. Please." There was a strained longing in his voice. He'd never needed anything from her before, she realized. She wanted to give him everything she had, everything she was. Her cheeks flamed; her heart thudded with apprehension, but she couldn't deny him. Didn't want to.

Lightly, she feathered her fingertips over his penis, making him gasp.

She nearly exclaimed in wonder at the strangeness of it. The skin there was so soft, so magically soft, a contrast to the hard length of muscle beneath. She stroked, as much for her own pleasure as to elicit another strangled moan of pleasure from Rand.

The head of his penis was all interesting ridges and contours, smooth and a little moist. She followed the length of him down to the softness of testicles nestled beneath. Fascinating and strange, this male apparatus. Curiously thrilling to hear his gasp, feel his body tense as she took those sacs lightly in her hand.

She watched Rand's face as she explored him. He'd closed his eyes and wore an expression that spoke of pleasure mixed with an agony of restraint. On occasion, his teeth gritted, as if in effort.

The short, spiky black lashes that fanned beneath Rand's eyelids made him seem curiously vulnerable. Her heart, hitherto such a well-regulated organ, turned over in her chest, filled with love.

She bent to kiss him and whisper, "Take me, Rand. Love me now. Please."

His eyes opened and locked on hers. Without breaking that compelling gaze, he rolled his hips so that he braced himself on his elbows on top of her, his legs between hers, his member, thoroughly known to her now, nudging insistently against her tender folds of flesh.

The depth of emotion in his gaze as he pushed a short way into her reassured her more than all of his patient preparation of her body.

She blinked at how hard and large he felt, pressing, pushing, attempting to slide into her and, "Oh, God!" He stretched her almost unbearably, until the burn of it turned to sharp pain.

He was trembling, panting, his face a hard mask of concentration. She grasped his upper arms and felt the tension in them. This was hard for him in some way, too.

"It's all right," she whispered, to reassure herself as much as him.

"I want so much to make it better than all right," he gritted out, kissing her temple, then her lips, flexing his hips in another thrust. "But I very much fear . . . this time . . ."

He took command of her mouth and all of those swoony, melting feelings returned in full force. She relaxed into the kiss, into him, felt his member thrust even deeper than before.

The pain wouldn't last beyond tonight. She knew that, so she tried to ignore the sting as he stroked inside her, abrading the spot where her flesh had torn. She loved the sense of closeness, in spite of the discomfort. It was the most extraordinary feeling, a deeper connection than the merely physical. She ran her hands over his shoulders, down his back.

He moved faster, deeper, until echoes of sensation played glissandos up her spine. She moved with him, against him, trying to get the rhythm of it, unsure of what, exactly, she ought to do, but eager to participate.

He muttered something that sounded like an apology, threw his head back and shuddered in her arms.

Afterwards, they lay in the waning sunshine together, naked, slicked with sweat. Cecily stared up at the canopy above her and smiled at nothing in particular.

"It will be better next time," he said, on a note of reassurance.

She laughed at that, though she knew what he meant. "How could it be better?"

He turned his head on the pillow to look at her. Those golden eyes of his narrowed with amusement. "I shall take great delight in showing you. Tomorrow, when you are rested," he murmured.

He drew her into the protective circle of his arm and they both drifted to sleep.

* * *

Rand woke in the middle of the night with the miracle of Cecily beside him and an aching hardness in his loins. He wanted her again.

No, that would be barbarous. He would simply look at her and marvel that she was his at last.

Having her in his bed, finally possessing her, loving her, was unlike any feeling he'd ever known. He'd pursued her with such single-minded determination that he'd given little thought to more mundane considerations.

Ought he to allocate a bedchamber to her? He supposed he must. Yet, he wanted her to sleep every night in his bed. As a husband, he had the right to command it. And yet, knowing Cecily, nothing would be as simple as that.

Something else that was not at all simple: How the hell was he going to tell her what he ought to have told her from the start?

Well, if not from the beginning, at least before she'd agreed to marry him.

But there'd been no time for second thoughts or hesitation once she'd accepted him. The thought of Jonathon hadn't crossed his mind, not once, since he'd received that ridiculous letter from Norland. Even if it had, he was not good enough at self-deception to believe it would have made a difference. He couldn't risk telling her the truth in case he lost her, yet again.

He watched her there, with a delicate hand pressed to the pillow supporting her cheek, dark lashes fanning against her creamy skin, those delicious red lips parted slightly, the glossy, dusky curls tumbling all over. He wanted to give her the moon and the stars, everything she wanted, more than she'd ever dreamed.

And he decided then and there that he would not tell her about Jonathon. Not until he could give Cecily her brother back, too.

Chapter Twenty

It was some days before Cecily turned her mind to the world beyond Ashburn House's front door.

Her betrothal to Norland and subsequent marriage to Ashburn had created an awful lot of speculative whispers among the ton. Not that a Westruther cared for that, of course. And no one would dare do more than whisper. Ashburn would not take kindly to slurs cast on his duchess and everyone knew he was not a man to cross.

So Cecily did what any Westruther would do when faced with public curiosity and censure. She threw a party.

A ball, to be exact. The most anticipated ball in the history of balls.

"I have set it about that I've invited Norland and his new bride," said Cecily gaily as she dragged Rand around the florist's. "They will all come to see the sparks fly. Won't they be disappointed when we turn out to be completely amicable and ridiculously in love with our chosen spouses?"

Rand raised an eyebrow. *"Ridiculously?"*

She stood on tiptoe to kiss his aristocratic nose. "Utterly, madly, reprehensibly, *irrevocably* in love."

"Exactly how much is this costing me?" said Rand, sounding supremely indifferent.

"I shall provide you with a faithful account," Cecily promised.

He waved a hand. "No, please don't. I don't think my heart can stand the shock."

The ball was a huge crush, which meant it was an enormous success. Cecily had never managed to get to Cambridge, but she was gratified to hear her meddling had done the trick: Tibby made no demur on the grounds of loyalty when Norland claimed her hand.

"You ought to have warned me off him ages ago," said Cecily now. "If I'd had the least idea, my dearest Tibby, I would never have held buckle and thong to our engagement. I deserve to be horsewhipped for such insensitivity."

"How can you say so, dearest Cecily?" said Tibby, dabbing at her eyes with the corner of a pristine handkerchief. "Indeed, my only consolation is that you have found happiness, too."

She looked over at Rand. "So handsome and distinguished!"

Yes, thought Cecily, no other man present could match her husband in looks and sheer force of character. He cast them all into the shade.

He certainly made his cousin Freddy look nervous and ill at ease, as if his cravat were too tight and his coat did not fit him properly across the shoulders.

"Tibby, will you excuse me? I need to rescue that poor boy."

She arrived in time to hear Rand say, "Ah, Freddy! There you are. I knew you'd be among the first to wish me happy."

The comment was scathingly ironic, given that Freddy might have harbored expectations of stepping into Rand's shoes someday. Unreasonable though it might have been to suppose Rand would remain single, or if he did marry, his wife would not bear a son, it was still a possibility that a young man might hope for in his more selfish and optimistic moments.

Clearly, Rand had not yet forgiven Freddy for the incident in the library on the night of the masquerade. Cecily had tried to explain that to Rand but she sensed his hostility ran deeper than the events of that night might warrant. She could not count herself successful in mending that bridge, but she had not given up trying.

Cecily smiled warmly at her husband's cousin. "Delightful to see you again, Freddy. I trust you are dancing this evening? I see that Miss Trescott has just arrived. Perhaps you would care to ask her to dance?"

Freddy immediately hightailed it off to form part of the latest beauty's court, leaving Cecily with Rand. "Shall we take a short turn on the terrace? I wish to speak with you."

He bowed and offered her his arm and escorted her outside.

"It would not kill you to be kinder to the boy," she murmured as they strolled beneath colored lanterns bobbing in the breeze.

He glanced down at her. "You are settling into your new role as wife rather well, aren't you, my dear? But yes, I suppose you are right. If he were from another family, his follies wouldn't bother me half as much. It is my prejudice that so often magnifies his faults."

"Prejudice?" She considered that. "I know Freddy's mama is . . . well, perhaps not the most congenial of ladies. . . ." She broke off, unwilling to be critical of Rand's family.

He stopped at the balustrade and braced his hands upon it, looking out at the rolling vista that undulated down to the river.

"Why do you dislike your family so much?" she asked. "You always seem so alone."

He sighed. "It is a long and tedious story, but I will try to give you the short version. When my parents died, I was a babe, as you know. So of course, my paternal relatives stepped in, in loco parentis."

"I see," said Cecily. "Did you go to live with them?"

"No, I was brought up all alone at Anglesby. Well, as alone as a child can be with an army of servants, and several nurses and nannies to see to his needs."

"Poor little boy," said Cecily softly.

"Oh, nonsense!" said Rand sardonically. "I daresay I must have been the luckiest infant alive. No expense was spared to entertain me."

With a wry smile, he shrugged. "I had adults vying for my favor from far too young an age. What I needed was love, of course. I was so hungry for it that I imagined it into being where it never was. I suffered disappointment after disappointment. My relations treated me like a pawn to be played with, not a child who needed affection."

He paused a moment. "If I seem isolated, it is because I never was able to trust anyone's motives after that. I have Garvey and perhaps a handful of friends and a wide circle of acquaintances. But I have not trusted anyone with my heart again. Not until you."

Cecily stared up at him. Now she knew where that pain and loneliness she'd sensed inside him came from. She stared into his eyes and willed him to understand. Her love would never be conditional on what he could do for her or his material possessions, his power and prestige.

But she did not need to tell him. He understood all that. And that was why he trusted her with his heart.

Their lovemaking that night seemed to have an added poignancy. After a long struggle, both of them had finally released their fears and doubts. Their connection went deeper, each caress touched their hearts, each sigh came from their souls. Rand did things to her that she would never have dreamed she'd allow, much less enjoy.

And with that newfound trust came confidence. Cecily turned wanton, reckless, powerful in her sensuality, a challenge and a spur to him in bed as she was in every other arena. They drove each other to new heights of passion, soaring above the world, until they found bliss together as one.

As dawn reached across the sky and the chill nipped at their toes, Rand barely retained the strength to pull the covers over them.

Cecily snuggled close, all soft, pleasured sighs and drowsy feminine warmth. She seemed disinclined to talk, and indeed, words would be inadequate to express the emotions they'd just shared. He was content to let that perfect communion of their bodies speak for them both.

As his eyelids grew heavy, Rand realized he could not remember ever feeling so sated and at peace before. Smiling to himself, he played with the unruly corkscrews of Cecily's hair until her deep, steady breathing told him she had fallen asleep. Then he followed her into slumber.

Some hours later, Rand opened his eyes with a vague sense that something in the room's atmosphere had shifted.

A movement from the corner of the bedchamber made him sit up abruptly. He glanced at Cecily to see if he'd woken her, but she slumbered on.

It took a while for his eyes to focus on the figure in the corner of the room. Sunlight streamed through the window behind him, making it harder to recognize detail.

"Jonathon?" Rand breathed. "Is that you?"

Though he knew the truth, had known it all along, Rand was as shocked to see his old colleague as if he'd seen a ghost.

"Jesus!" He was in bed with the man's sister! Did Jonathon know it was Cecily lying there beside him? There'd be hell to pay if she woke.

Moving as quickly and quietly as possible, Rand snatched up breeches and a dressing gown and put them on.

With another quick glance at Cecily's sleeping form, he motioned to Jonathon to follow him into his dressing room.

"We have to be quick," he said softly. "My valet will come in at any moment."

He took stock of Cecily's brother, a man who was supposed to have died some years ago in a laboratory fire. He was gaunt and pale, but with the same dark hair and large brown eyes that Cecily possessed.

"You don't look too bad for a corpse," said Rand.

"Much obliged," replied Jonathon, his face relaxing a little.

The subtle gleam of humor left his eyes, and his mouth turned grim. "I had word someone was looking for me, Ashburn. No one has looked for me for a very long time."

"Do you know who?"

Jonathon shrugged. "No names. You know how that goes."

"Whom do you suspect?" said Rand. "Who knows about you besides me?"

"If you've told no one, that leaves Cousin Bertram," said Jonathon. "And he has every reason to want me to stay in hiding."

And every reason to want Jonathon truly dead, Rand thought.

"You haven't told anyone, have you, Ashburn?" murmured Jonathon with a hint of menace. "I heard you married my sister. I suppose you felt you had to tell her, did you?"

When Rand didn't answer, Jonathon hissed between his teeth. "Ah, hell, Ashburn! No woman could keep a secret like that."

His body rigid with fury, Rand said, "When I think of the hell I'm going to get when she finds out, I resent that remark, Davenport."

A shaken voice spoke from behind him. "J-Jonathon? Jon?"

Rand was just in time to catch Cecily as she collapsed in the dressing room doorway.

Revived and fortified with brandy and a cup of strong, sugary tea, Cecily sat huddled under a blanket, watching her brother with a disorienting feeling, as if it were all part dream, part déjà vu.

She had laughed and cried and hugged Jon until he laughingly begged her to let him catch his breath. She could not stop touching him, framing his beloved face with her hands. She could not stop looking at him and trying to imagine what it must have been like for him all these years.

Her anger and resentment she reserved for Rand.

They'd explained it all to her: the need for Jonathon's disappearance, the lie about his death. She'd barely listened or been able to grasp the details. He was *alive*. Flesh-and-blood Jonathon. He was *here* with her. She wanted to keep hugging him, to keep at least one hand on him at all times to make sure he was real.

It seemed that Jonathon had invented a volatile explosive that could have revolutionized military warfare if only some practical way could be found to stabilize it.

Horrified that a purely academic exercise had handed him the power to destroy so many lives at once, Jonathon had found himself caught in a tug-of-war between the government and darker forces who wanted that formula. Both sides wanted to use the explosive to kill on a massive scale. Jonathon couldn't live with the idea that he might have invented such a deadly weapon.

Then he'd had the idea of disappearing and taking the knowledge with him. But he needed some contact with the world he'd left behind. He needed one person to know and to help him destroy all evidence of his work. That person had been Rand.

Rand had known. All this time, Rand had *known* that Jonathon was alive and he hadn't told her. The deep, immense anger Cecily felt toward her husband could not find expression now. Not when there were vitally important things to attend to.

Such as bringing her brother back from the dead.

"But if you resurface now, how will that help us?" said Rand. "Even after all these years, won't they be after you again?"

"Ah. Well, you see, that is where our friends at the Promethean Club come in," said Jonathon. "In fact, it was your idea, Ashburn. You tried to persuade me to do this years ago."

Rand ran his hand through his hair. "It will be career suicide."

Jonathon gave a bitter laugh. "What career do I have now?"

"What are you going to do?" asked Cecily.

"The plan I proposed was to discredit Jonathon's research," said Rand. "It was only ever a rumor that got out of hand in the first place. We will have experts say that the research is faulty, that the formula simply doesn't work."

Jonathon looked at the ceiling, stony-faced. Cecily knew how difficult it must be for him to have his work dissected and torn to pieces like that, but if it would bring him home . . .

She said, "When can we start this process?"

Ashburn nodded. "I'll take care of it today."

He eyed Jonathon, carefully avoided Cecily's regard. "The two of you should take some time to talk, but don't let anyone see you, Jonathon. We are not out of the woods yet."

Cecily thought she must have terrified her brother with her incoherence and her need to touch him, as if he would disappear again if she didn't keep him physically anchored to the spot in some way.

She was not at all herself, and he had changed in ways she could only guess at during his long exile. "But I kept your letter by me, always," he said. "You know the one about Sir Ninian Finian?"

Misty-eyed, Cecily nodded. So that was why she could not find it among all those letters. If only she'd known.

If only they'd trusted her.

Oh, she supposed she could understand why Jonathon had not wanted to burden an eleven-year-old with his secret. But later . . . *Why* hadn't Rand told her?

Jonathon said, "I can scarce believe it. *You* married to Ashburn!"

"Yes." She tried to smile. "Yes, it does seem rather difficult to believe, doesn't it?"

He looked a little grim. "I'm not sure how I feel about that."

She was no longer at all certain herself, but she

said lightly, "Well, I couldn't very well ask your permission, could I?"

"What happened to old Norland, then?" said Jonathon.

"He is not old," she said, from habit, then put her fingertips to her temples. "Norland fell in love with my governess, Miss Tibbs. You don't know her," she assured Jonathon as his brow puckered. "But truly, dear brother, it all turned out for the best."

Had it? Had it really? Her heart ached at Rand's betrayal.

When Jonathon took his leave, he placed his hands on her shoulders and pressed his lips to her forehead the way he'd done so many years ago.

"Courage, little one. With luck and Ashburn's good management, we'll push through."

She could not bear to let him go, but the servants were stirring, getting ready for the day. They couldn't hide him in the house indefinitely.

Cecily flung her arms around her brother's gaunt frame, surreptitiously dashing hot tears away before he could see them. "Yes, you must go. I cannot tell you how much I long for your return to us. I hope we will not have too long to wait."

She hugged him hard and kissed both his cheeks, then hugged him again.

He patted her shoulder. "All will be well, little one. You'll see."

Rand stood in the doorway, waiting to escort her brother out. Cecily knew he watched her, waiting for a sign that he was forgiven. She couldn't give it. She simply couldn't bring herself to forgive him for his lie.

Rand left on his mission without a private word to her. He hadn't even attempted to justify his actions. She didn't know whether that was to his credit or not. She couldn't think of any excuse he might give that would satisfy her in any case.

He'd lied to her. He'd allowed her to go on believing Jonathon was dead. If he truly loved her, how could he have let her go on like that? A bewildering sense of loss weighed on her chest, pressed on her heart, despite her joy at having her brother back.

Rand still had not returned hours later, when Winters announced a caller.

This ought to be interesting.

Cecily checked her reflection and went down to see Lavinia.

"I suppose you've heard," said Lavinia without preamble. "The news of it will get out soon enough."

"The news of what, pray?" said Cecily. Good God, she'd borne quite enough startling revelations for one day.

"Your brother! Back from the dead," said Lavinia. "He had the effrontery to let himself into our house last night and warn Bertram of his imminent return."

Effrontery? Foolhardiness, more like it. Why on earth would Jonathon do such a thing? No one was supposed to know about this yet. But she knew why. His sense of honor dictated that he must do the right thing by his cousin, regardless of the possible danger to himself.

Lavinia glanced about her. "Might I possibly sit down? Or do you mean to keep me standing about?"

"I mean to keep you standing about," said Cecily. "You will not be here long enough to sit down, *dear* Cousin."

"Well! I thought you would have something kind to say to me, now that you know we shall be tossed from our home, dispossessed of everything but the clothes on our backs."

Cecily snorted. "I should feel sorry for you if I thought that would actually happen. Jonathon will give you a house and a pension, too, and you know it. Besides, I've no doubt you managed to feather your nest very nicely—" She broke off at a subtle wariness in Lavinia's expression.

She narrowed her eyes at Lavinia. "You knew, didn't you? All along, you sold everything you could, made every penny possible out of your tenure because you knew it wouldn't last. I hear Bertram won substantial sums from young greenhorns at the gaming tables, too."

Lavinia gave her a stony look. "I don't know what you're talking about."

"My pearls, for one thing," said Cecily. "That was a desperate gambit, wasn't it? Difficult to get a fair price for such a well-known piece."

Reddening, the former countess said, "You're insulting!"

"That was my intention, Lavinia," Cecily agreed. And believe me, I could go on all day. That is why I did not ask you to sit down, you see. I am sure you would not wish to remain here another minute!"

Cecily smiled sweetly. "Will you leave now or shall I have my butler escort you from the premises?"

With Lavinia gone amid a storm of furious indignation, Cecily sagged. The shock of seeing Jonathon again, the sheer joy of realizing he was alive after all these years, the pain of Rand's betrayal—all of this turbulent emotion left her spent.

Yet, she must decide how to deal with the situation in which she now found herself.

She couldn't do that here. She didn't think she could face Rand again, not without pouring out a load of recriminations, not without poisoning any hope they might have to put this awful betrayal behind them.

Rand returned to a quiet house. That was not such an unusual thing, but there was a quality to the quiet that he found disturbing. Or was that just his guilty conscience at play?

"Is the duchess at home, Winters?" Rand, handed the butler his hat and coat.

"Her Grace left you this, Your Grace." Winters handed him a letter affixed with a seal.

With a terrible clench in his stomach, Rand read. He scanned the missive quickly, noting only that she'd left and it was his fault and she didn't say where she had gone.

A violent sense of injustice ripped through him. He crushed the letter in his hand. Why had Jon come back now? If only he'd had the leisure to break the news gently, to then work toward Jon's safe return, Cecily might not have taken it this way.

Ah, but who was he fooling? Rand opened his fingers one by one and slowly smoothed out the single page again.

That one paragraph shouted at him as if it were printed in capitals and underlined three times:

Jonathon said he chose you to clean up after him because he knew you were a man who trusted no one. He chose well, Rand, didn't he? You did not even trust me.
Especially not me.

That wasn't true. He did trust her to keep Jonathon's secret. He simply hadn't had faith that she'd forgive him if he told her what he'd done. And he'd longed to fix things so that he could present her brother to her all redeemed and safe and reestablished in the world. He'd wanted everything tied up with a neat bow.

As it was, his plan was a gamble. If it didn't succeed, there would be no second chances. Rand would not convince anyone of Jonathon's death a second time. Unless he produced Jonathon's lifeless body, that was.

His first impulse was to chase after Cecily, to justify himself to her and beg her forgiveness. He was fairly certain he knew where she'd gone.

But she had suffered through much in the last week. She needed time to mull over all that had happened. And he needed to put his faith in her love for him. That was all he could do, he realized. There was no way he could persuade or maneuver or manipulate her into forgiving him, into loving him. She needed to arrive at that destination on her own.

In the meantime, he would do all in his power to make her brother a laughingstock as a scientist so he could take up his proper place in the world once more.

Sometimes in life, there were no good choices. Only the lesser of two evils.

Chapter Twenty-one

The first whiff of summer in the air at Harcourt made Cecily more than usually nostalgic for cricket on the lawn, lemonade and tea cakes, picnics and exploratory rambles, practical jokes. And above all, her cousins who had filled this place with their childish pranks and laughter.

She'd been here for weeks now, aimlessly wandering. She'd told herself she wanted to check on her collection of creative protégées in the village.

In truth, she'd come down here to brood over the wrongs of one Duke of Ashburn. And yet, her mind kept shying away from the subject. She didn't want to relive the awful hurt of discovering he'd kept such an enormous secret from her.

She most particularly didn't want to let herself blame Jon.

But the Duke of Montford commanded her presence at his annual ball and she must go to that, of course. No one refused an invitation to this event. It was the highlight of every season.

More important, she must come to a decision about how to live this married life.

No, she didn't want to blame Jon.

Yet, it had been Jonathon's decision not to inform her of what he meant to do when he'd staged his own death. It had been Jonathon who, in turn, had sworn Rand to secrecy.

Ought she to blame Rand for keeping his word? Her irrational self said, *Yes, of course!* If their positions had been reversed, *she* would have told *him*. Knowing how greatly she'd suffered from losing her brother, how *could* Rand have kept silent?

Perhaps he would have told her, eventually. Perhaps he was waiting for the right time.

But in not telling her and marrying her anyway, he'd taken away her choice. She would most probably have refused to marry him if she'd known him capable of such a great deceit.

She had come to the Duke of Montford's country seat to brood and to decide how this marriage of theirs would be. She needed time away from Rand to do that. When she was with him, it was so very easy to give in to whatever he wanted.

That was love for you. You had to be strong to give it and to receive it in return. Even stronger to remain true to yourself when that weaker part of you always longed to give and give everything you had to the other person.

She needed to regain her balance. How could she keep her self-respect when she loved Rand so much, she was prepared to forgive him anything?

Surely there were some things that were unforgivable, even in someone you loved? Only she didn't know where the limits of her own capacity to forgive might be.

* * *

She was out, they'd said, waving vaguely toward the lake and beyond. He'd searched for her until the twilight spread over the countryside like a velvet blanket.

He found her, finally, on a small footbridge that arched over a narrow stretch of brook. She had been idly breaking smaller twigs off a stick and throwing them down into the rushing water.

He paused before he got to the bridge itself, watching the way the breeze lifted and toyed with the little tendrils that curled at her temples. He remembered that first night they'd met, when he'd ached to reach out and twist that soft, dark loveliness around his finger.

Desire swept over him in a dizzying rush, but there was a sweet base note of tenderness that wound through that emotion. She looked very sweet and very dear standing up there like a child playing a game. And yet, he suspected her reception of him would be anything but sweet.

At the click of his boots on the wooden planks, she looked up, her face lightening as if she were glad to see him.

"Good evening, Ashburn," she said cordially.

Rand stopped short, feeling like he'd been kicked in the viscera. He almost expected her to hold out her hand for him to shake it.

He would have preferred her to ignore him or scratch his eyes out. Anything but this affable politeness. He realized he had probably made a mistake, leaving her alone for so long. But at least the business with Jon was wrapped up now.

"I hear my brother is making quite a splash in society," said Cecily.

Well, there went the element of surprise.

"Yes, I believe so," said Rand. "His tale of kidnap and memory loss is terribly romantic. The ladies find him pale and interesting."

"He'll take up writing poetry next," Cecily said.

"I shouldn't be at all surprised."

Silence lengthened between them.

"Will it answer, do you think? All of those academics discrediting Jon's ideas?"

"Oh, I think so," said Rand. "His credibility has been shot to pieces. He has been painted as a wealthy dilettante who dabbled in science and made grandiose claims that were entirely unsubstantiated. Even his mentors at Cambridge seek to distance themselves."

"Hypocrites!" said Cecily. She stared down into the water. "Poor Jon! It would be utterly galling to have all that said about you."

"I think, on balance, that he is not displeased. He has his old life back. I suppose he might even think of settling down now."

"And what of Bertram and Lavinia?" Cecily asked. "Will they keep quiet about Jonathon?"

"They aren't likely to tell anyone they knew he was alive while they occupied the estate and title. They have been assured a generous pension," Rand said. "On condition that Lavinia returns everything she misappropriated for her personal use from the estate."

"I doubt she can fulfill that condition," said Cecily. "I still wonder what she intended to do with my pearls."

He had the sudden, powerful memory of kissing

those pearls, of trailing them over soft, white skin. Of Cecily, lying pliant and rapturous beneath him.

"I was going to tell you about Jonathon as soon as he gave me leave to do so," he said.

"That may be so," she said. "I cannot blame you for keeping a confidence, can I?" Her lips trembled. She pressed them together; then on a gasp, she said, "But I *can* blame you for marrying me when I was ignorant of the truth."

He threw up a hand in frustration, knowing she was right and yet so desperate to get her back, he longed for her to say none of it mattered.

"Yes," he said, "I was a coward. It had taken me so long to win you, and then everything happened at once. You were so . . . resistant to the idea of marrying me for such a long time. Once you'd finally agreed, I didn't want to offer you the least excuse to cry off."

"You made the decision for me, in fact," said Cecily. "Once again, you gave me no choice."

"That was wrong. Please forgive me. But whatever I did, I did out of love for you. I hope that counts at least a little in my favor."

He put his hand on hers. "Cecily, I would like us to start all over again. I'll do whatever it takes. I'll court you as if none of this—Norland, the marriage, Jonathon—as if none of it had happened. Just you and me, Cecily. No more lies."

"That is quite unnecessary." She tossed the remainder of her stick into the brook and walked past him to descend to the other side of the bridge. "For better or for worse, we are husband and wife. I do not intend to make you jump through hoops like a trained dog, Ashburn. That would be demeaning for both of us."

All at once, he recognized this manner. It was the same one she'd used toward Norland. She had decided she would set him at a distance.

"No."

She stopped in the lee of a huge plane tree and turned her head to look at him sharply.

"*No!*" he said again. "You are not going to keep me at arm's length."

"Arm's length?" She raised her eyebrows in innocent inquiry, but those dark eyes snapped. She held out her hand, as if to refute this. "What nonsense. You haven't even tried to kiss me, you know."

And there it was again, that amused, slightly derisive tone. And he was damned if he'd stand for it.

He took the hand she held out and yanked her into his arms. "A kiss?" he growled. "I'll give you a kiss."

And he did. He gave her everything he had in that kiss. "I love you, Cecily." He groaned out the words. "I made a mistake. I'll undoubtedly make more and so will you. And we'll argue and fight and forgive each other because that's what two strong-willed people who love each other do. But don't ever leave me. Please."

In a breathless voice, Cecily said, "Who said anything about leaving you, Rand?"

Not good enough, he thought. And he swept her off her feet and tumbled her down to the grassy verge.

He settled between her legs, effectively trapping her by lying on her gown.

She pushed at his shoulders. "Not here. In a bed, where it's proper."

He gave her a wolfish grin. "No, sweet Cecily. There is not going to be anything proper about this."

She met his gaze and he saw the answering fire flare to life in those dark depths. Though he sensed she'd already surrendered, he pinned her wrists to the ground above her head while he kissed her, until her lips quivered and clung and her mouth opened to his kiss.

When he lifted his head, she gazed up at him, her eyes melting, lips plump with his kisses. The curling tendrils that always escaped her coiffure to frame her face stirred in the light breeze.

"I do love you, Rand," she said solemnly, clearly. "But if you ever try to ride roughshod over me again like that I will make you sorry."

"Make me sorry," he said, dragging his lips over her cheek, down her throat. "Just don't ever leave me."

"No," she whispered, clinging to him so tightly it was as if she squeezed his heart. "Never."

His chest seized with the relief of hearing her say it. "Oh, God, Cecily. I've never known such misery as these last few weeks."

Her body trembled beneath him, and when he pulled back to look into her face, he saw that her eyes shimmered with tears. "I was hurt and furious that you'd kept Jonathon's secret. But even when I tried my hardest, I could not stop loving you, longing for you. And now you are here, nothing else matters."

She framed his face with her hands. "This love is

more than either of us can control, Rand. But I'm not afraid of it anymore."

He knew what she said was true. With an inward sigh of relief and thankfulness, he plundered her mouth, kissed her throat, the swells of her breasts. Rolling on the cool cushion of grass, he brought her on top of him. She pushed up so that her thighs gripped his hips. He lay back in the sweet smelling grass and surrendered to her, enjoying her delighted assumption of command.

He looked up at that face, alight with determination and a hint of mischief and he thought he would never grow complacent loving this woman. He would never grow bored.

So he let her do what she wanted with him, groaned when she released him from his breeches and touched him, stroked his aching hard flesh. Felt the rush and the fire as she lowered herself over him, seated herself and clenched triumphantly around him, all wet heat and glorious pull and slide.

She looked down at him as she moved, and the tumble of dark curls fell over her face, caressing her breast. Her cheeks were flushed, her cherry lips parted.

Eyes glazed with passion met his gaze. "I love you, Rand," she breathed. "Come what may."

She gripped his hands, palm to palm, her fingers locked in between his, and he steadied her as she rode him the way he'd taught her all those weeks ago. When she threw her head back and reached for the moon and the stars in the velvet-soft darkness, he let go of any sense of control.

And trusted her to take him with her, too.

Epilogue

"This many Westruthers in one place at one time? The party ought to be declared a public nuisance," murmured the Duke of Ashburn in his duchess's ear.

"Nonsense," said Cecily, leaning her fragrant and deliciously feminine form against his chest. "You adore these big family gatherings and you know it."

She was right, of course. He smiled, because she knew him so well and because with her back to him like this, her glossy curls tickled his chin. They behaved scandalously in standing so close together, but no one at this intimate gathering seemed to mind. Indeed, Rosamund, Lady Tregarth, beamed upon them with approval.

A full reunion of the Westruther cousins, including the long lost Lord Davenport, had been delayed until the summer. This was principally due to the late arrival the Honorable Miss Margaret Black, daughter of Jane and Constantine, Lord and Lady Roxdale.

After Margaret's christening they all gathered at Lazenby to toast the baby's health and congratulate the proud parents. Despite Cecily's concerns, Jane had a relatively easy delivery and mother and infant continued to thrive. Luke, Constantine and Jane's adopted son, gingerly patted the infant's downy head and tried not to look as ridiculously pleased as he felt about his baby sister.

"Besides," said Cecily, with a sideways glance at her husband, "you are one of us now. Even Xavier tolerates you and that's saying something."

"But only yesterday, Lydgate threatened to punch my lights out," Rand complained.

"Oh, that just means he likes you," said Cecily. "He did punch Griffin once. Gave him a black eye, you know. And they are the best of friends."

"He did?" The man must have a great deal of courage to start a fight with the colossus that was Griffin, Earl of Tregarth. Not that he believed Viscount Lydgate a coward. He'd have written down the exquisitely dressed gentleman with the guinea gold hair for a fop if he hadn't seen him in action at Jackson's Boxing Saloon. "What for?"

Cecily shrugged. "He didn't think Griffin dressed appropriately when he came to pay his addresses to Rosamund." She grew pensive. "I believe Griffin crowned his iniquity by calling Lydgate a dandy."

"Well, that would do it," agreed Rand. He laughed. "What a family we have, my dearest Cecily."

We.

Cecily caught her breath. Despite her marriage being months old now, she still tingled all over whenever Rand coupled himself so closely with her.

Closing her eyes, she turned her head slightly, the better to inhale his scent. This was heaven itself.

There was nowhere she'd rather be than within the circle of Rand's arms, with all of her family near.

Her fears of losing her autonomy to Rand had been groundless. Secure in his own intelligence and ability, Rand delighted in seeing her fulfill her own dreams. She accepted his advice, but made her own decisions when it came to her projects. If she made mistakes, they would be hers alone.

Cecily watched as Jane carefully placed baby Margaret in Jonathon's arms, amid many protestations from Jonathon himself that he was a clumsy oaf, sure to drop her.

She could not imagine anyone less like an oaf. Her brother appeared elegant, pale and dissipated in his habitual black and white. The languid air suited his romantic dark looks exceedingly well. He had created a sensation among the ladies upon his return to London. Rumor had it he'd indulged in every sort of excess since.

Her heart twisted. The loss of his reputation in scientific circles had been hellish for Jonathon. In his shoes, she would feel the same. She understood the need to be reckless when one's life seemed to have lost purpose and meaning.

She worried about him, nevertheless. He wouldn't listen to her, of course. She was a mere sister and a much younger one, at that. At Cecily's entreaty, her cousin Beckenham had tried to persuade Jonathon to moderate his behavior, but Beckenham's warning had gone unheeded.

She must simply hope her brother did not damage himself before he came to his senses—or anyone else, for that matter. The Duke of Montford watched over him and so did Rand. That was a small comfort. Their subtlety might succeed where Beckenham's straightforward reprimands failed.

She turned her head a little to look up at her husband. "Do you think Jonathon will ever be happy?"

He kissed her crown, running his hands up and down her arms to grasp her shoulders. "Give him time, my love. It is a big adjustment for him."

"Yes. But I cannot help the feeling that he is about to do something reckless." She shivered. "Even more reckless, I mean. Something irreversible."

"I'll keep an eye on him," said Rand.

"Yes," she said, comforted. "I know you will."

Rand turned her in his arms. Framing her face with his palms, he fell into those dark eyes. "Any regrets on your own account?"

He knew the answer, but he never tired of hearing it.

She shook her head. "I am more myself with you than with anyone else. You challenge me, excite me, you make me feel safe. You make me want to give you all of that in return. I am so very happy. I cannot believe I ever contemplated a life without you. How utterly dreary, how empty that would have been."

Emotion bloomed in his chest. Regardless of everyone present, he kissed her, deeply, thoroughly, ignoring the whistles and catcalls from his newfound family.

"I love you," he said against her lips.

"Oh, my dearest, darlingest duke," sighed Cecily, shining up at him. "I love you, too."